Mayhem at the Marina

a Lexy Hyatt Mystery by

Carlene Miller

New Victoria Publishers
Norwich, Vermont

Published by New Victoria Publishers Inc., PO Box 27 Norwich, Vt. 05055, a Feminist Literary and Cultural Organization founded in 1976.

Printed and Bound in Canada
1 2 3 4 1999 2000 2001 2002

Library of Congress Cataloging-in-Publication Data

Miller, Carlene, 1935-
Mayhem at the marina : a Lexy Hyatt mystery / by Carlene Miller.
p. cm.
ISBN 1-892281-05-8
I. Title.
PS3563.I3763M39 1999
813' .54--dc21 99-25699
CIP

Thanks to Becky S. for the material that helped launch Lexy on this adventure, to KCJay for her enthusiastic support, and to Nanki for allowing me to borrow some of his behavior for Tiger.

One

"That's one satisfied smile." I traced the lines of Wren's face, highlighted by the soft glow of the bedside lamp—the golden eyebrows, the thin nose, the jaw line that curved just enough to soften the strong face. Then I touched my fingers to the moist lips of the firm, straight mouth.

"I'm one satisfied woman." She caught my hand in hers and nibbled the fingers. "Oh, I do like the taste of me on your hand."

To mask my groan of renewed desire, I propped myself on an elbow and stroked her wheat-blonde hair into the sweep and flow I loved to smooth my cheek against. Nearly four months and I was still uncomfortable with the power and suddenness of my responses to the quietly dominating Wren Carlyle.

Wren stroked my chin with the back of her fingers, the rounded nails sending a tingle all the way to my toes. "Happy last day of June, Lexy. Happy first day of vacation."

I laughed and kissed her fervently. We had packed a rented van the evening before for today's long drive to north Georgia from where we were going to start a three-week camping trek into the Blue Ridge Mountains. Much as I enjoyed my job as a *Ledger* reporter, I was excited over the opportunity to be truly alone with Wren. We were still in the early stages of structuring our relationship.

When we first planned the trip, she had laughed. "It'll be a good chance to test living together." Even though I was turned away from her, she had caught a whiff of my panic and touched my shoulder, saying, "Don't worry, Lexy. I don't mean to tease. I know you need thinking time. Just want to get you started on it. I want you in this house for real."

Now I deepened my kiss as she twined a leg about me and drew our bodies flush. I released her mouth slowly and her contralto voice whispered, "What happened to our night of solid sleep?"

I answered, "I woke up needy and helped myself to what was available."

"Aren't you the smug one." Wren nipped at my breasts, and I yelped as her teeth scraped my hardened nipples. Then her hand was between my legs, a finger teasing in the wetness. Her other arm went across the top of my chest and she held my upper body unmoving against the bed. She hummed her satisfaction at the straining of my lower body, the quivering of my legs. "Let's see how smug you can remain."

She teased unmercifully until I begged through gritted teeth for her to enter me. She watched my face as I struggled to control my reactions, to mute my cries of pleasure. She breathed deeply, her lips compressed in a taut, confident smile. She made no sound when I clamped on her hand in the throes of orgasm, but as I settled back and my thighs relaxed, she cradled me and crooned, "Sweet Lexy. Sweet, sweet Lexy. No smugness now."

"I'm not sweet." I knew my attempt at defiance was a failure.

Her retort was halted by the jangle of the bedside telephone.

As she scrambled upright and seized the receiver in the middle of the second ring, I looked at the clock. Not yet five-thirty! I saw the tension in her shoulders and heard the strain in her voice, but her terse comments gave me no information. To escape the feeling of eavesdropping, I rummaged in the covers for the old softball T-shirt I slept in and slipped off to the bathroom.

I estimated five minutes before returning.

Wren was sitting cross-legged, her arms tight under her breasts, her head down. Concerned, I sat on the edge of the bed and touched a knee. She lifted her head and her eyes, dark green in the dim light, searched my face. She said, "I have to ask for your understanding, Lexy."

"Not something you have to ask for, Wren." I glanced at the phone. "What's going on?"

She reached for my hand. "I told you that there had been someone special to me once—Nancy Marshall. I met her when I was fresh out of art school and working for a small design firm in Atlanta. She worked in an art supply department of a store I shopped at often. I thought everything was perfect 'til I blinked my eyes one day and discovered I was living with a stranger prone to excesses. Alcohol primarily. But other things, too. Smoking, some cocaine, expensive purchases beyond our means. I fought for her but I lost. When I realized I couldn't save her, I chose to save myself."

Her eyes were shadowed with pain. I moved closer and put my fingers in her hair. "The only choice an intelligent person could make. You know that series I did for the paper on all the self-help groups and their conclusions about the harm in co-dependency and enabling for both parties."

"I know. But when you walk away from someone in trouble, even when it's trouble of their own making and trouble you can't save them from, you carry away a niggling doubt about your own adequacies."

I gripped her shoulders firmly. "You'll never make me believe my Wren can doubt herself, or is in any way inadequate." I clasped her to me and smoothed my hands up and down her bare back. I could feel her warm breath through my shirt. "Was that her on the phone, Wren?"

"Nancy? No. It was a nurse calling from her room in Pinecrest Hospital outside Atlanta. She said that Nancy was refusing her medication until I was called." Wren's fingers bit into the flesh of my arm. "She's dying, Lexy—emphysema, liver and kidney damage. She has only two, maybe three weeks left...and no one comes to see her." She pulled back from me and I could see the strong Wren I so admired reclaiming her form.

"I have to go! I can't let her die alone."

I nodded.

Two hours later I watched Wren send one last glance my way as she drove the van from the driveway into the street. I had removed my stuff and tossed it in the trunk of my car. We had walked through Wren's small house checking windows and doors, unplugging appliances, holding back the regret for our lost time together. Her final words echoed in my mind. "I'm not leaving you, Lexy. I'm stepping back into the past for a moment. I may not owe Nancy that but I want to give it to her...and to me for the peace I hope it will bring. Wait for me here in the present?"

Again I had nodded.

I walked to my car trying to concentrate on everything but the absence of Wren. Despite the early morning hour, the air was so heavy with humidity that I felt I needed to swim through it. I remembered a line from one of H.D.'s poems I used to use when I taught English about air so thick with heat it could blunt the points of pears. The bleached sky forewarned of afternoon thunderstorms.

My stomach growled, digesting a half bagel and black coffee. Wren was gone.

I slammed the car door, then felt guilty about it.

Once back in my apartment I stood in the middle of my combined living-workroom wondering what to do with the day. I threw my tall form into the desk chair and glared at the blank computer screen. Forgetting that it was unplugged, I flipped the on switch and was disconcerted by the lack of the grinding noise that had so unnerved me at first. I muttered sarcastically, "All right. I'm on vacation."

My eyes drifted to the snapshots tacked randomly on the wall above the desk. My parents, a decade younger than now, stood in front of the grape arbor they had constructed. Mt. Dora wasn't far away. I could go visit for a few days. No. I had taken Wren there for an Easter weekend and a general introduction which had gone well, but I didn't want to explain our change in vacation plans.

My long dead Uncle Kurt grinned from a snapshot so old I had laminated it for protection. I knew my grin and my thick auburn hair were a mirror reflection of his. But I knew it only from pictures. My mother's twin, Kurt was killed in Vietnam. In a moment of teenage defiance over some now forgotten family confrontation, I had sacrificed my long tresses to match the Elvis lift and swirl of the snapshots. I still wear it that way minus the ducktail.

"So, Uncle Kurt, what do we do?" I imagined the tilt of his head and cocky stance to be saying, "Carpe diem! Seize the day! Throw yourself into the freedom!"

I went to The Cat instead. Since the popular lesbian bar and restaurant was closed during the day, I was able to park in front. I knew the owner Marilyn Neff would be inside doing paperwork and receiving supplies so I pounded firmly on the front door five times. Soon I could tell I was being viewed through one of the cut glass triangles. Then the door opened wide.

"What the hell, Lexy! Thought you and Wren would be way up I-75 by now." Marilyn looked past me.

I skipped down the three steps and toward my favorite bar stool. "Just me, Admiral. Something came up that Wren has to tend to. Vacation plans are shelved for the time being."

She came around the bar and placed her solid form in front of me. An overhead light heightened the sheen of her short, grayish blonde hair and glinted off her many rings. She dipped her chin and raised her eyebrows.

She may have eased my coming-out when I left teaching for journalism, but I had helped her by solving the murder of her former lover whose body was found in the supply room of The Cat. Still, I knew better than to ignore or challenge that look.

I said meekly, "It's something from before she knew me. Something private. And it's something I can accept and understand. I'm disappointed about the vacation, but we're okay. I just feel a little lost right now."

I adopted a wheedling tone. "Thought you might have some of Hal's cinnamon rolls on hand...and that cappuccino machine perking, if that's what those machines do."

I watched her decide to let me off the hook about Wren's disappearance. She faked a frown and jerked a thumb toward the hallway. I followed her to her office, delighted at the smell of French vanilla coffee and the sight of those rolls in a plastic bag.

A moment later I slouched in a captain's chair mumbling through a mouthful, "How did Hal hit on this recipe?"

"By accident. He forgot the sugar and they didn't taste half bad. So now he mixes up the dough with what he claims is just a pinch of sugar, a dash of cinnamon, and a double shot of chopped nuts." Marilyn reached back from her chair and tapped the cappuccino machine. "I give him this for his birthday and ten days later he gives me a bread maker for mine. Do you suppose we knew all along we'd end up exchanging with one another?" Her face fell and I knew she was wondering if her brother, suffering from prostate cancer, would be here for his next birthday.

"He's been looking good, Marilyn."

"Yeah. But when I wake up to the smell of fresh bread, I know it's the pain that got him up. I worry that looking good is smooth water hiding a rip current below." To cover her embarrassment at being so open, she slapped the desk top. "So, Miss Byline, what are you going to do with all that time?"

I sighed. "Don't know. Maybe just go back to work. Set up another vacation in August."

"No good, Lexy. When you lose out on what you expected and wanted, going back to the old grind just makes it worse." Wheels were turning behind her pale blue eyes. She smacked the desk again. "Something different is the order of the day. I'm going to put you on a boat."

I jumped and nearly spilled my coffee. "Oh no." I waved toward the wall of shelves containing ship models. "This is as close as I care to be to any boats."

"Well, you are going to get closer. You call me Admiral often enough so be prepared to take orders." She huffed as I hissed loudly through my upper teeth. "Won't work, kid."

I changed my manner. "You know I'm not at home around water. I don't care if I am a few months shy of being a native Floridian. I'm a throwback to Midwestern ancestors, to forest people. The first female I ever bonded with was in Gene Stratton Porter's *Girl of the Limberlost*. That's a forest in Indiana."

"I don't care if it's a national park on Mars. It's time you bonded with a water woman. Her name is Willow. At least for the time being. Too flimsy a name for such a solid boat."

I took the diversion. "Maybe not. Willow trees meant a lot to ancient women. Sacred to the Muses. Sorceresses and witches made wands from their branches. Medicine women used the bark to brew pain-killing potions."

She considered that. "I got the boat as medicine for Hal. He's wanted to get out on the water, but I've been afraid to risk sailing. He'd want to do some of the work. On a power boat he could." She nodded emphatically. "I'll keep the name. Maybe Wren could design a fancy wand and paint it on the bow."

"She'd love to." I couldn't stop a general sag of my body as I thought of Wren speeding away from me. Marilyn, sorting through some papers on her desk, didn't appear to notice. I finished my cinnamon roll and drained my mug. Rising, I reached for her empty mug. "I'll rinse these."

"You'll sit back down."

"Marilyn..." I was very nearly whining.

"Down, Lexy." She didn't even look up.

I dropped into the chair, stretched out my long legs crossing them at the ankles, and glared. When finally she looked up into that glare, the corners of her mouth twitched toward a smile. She said, "I'll bet you haven't unpacked yet."

"No," I grunted. "Everything's in the trunk of my car." Too late I realized I was feeding her ammunition. I straightened and began tapping a heel rapidly on the floor. "I'm no sailor. I can't run a boat."

"No problems there. You're just going to live on it for a little while. Do some different things. Meet some different people. She's docked at Lake Arrow. Cabin sleeps two. Has a small galley and a full head. That's bathroom to you. Course she's not shipshape yet. Needs re-wiring, cleaning, some carpentry. You might be some help. Robbie set me up with a young woman who's some genius at fixing things."

"Robbie? I see."

"Don't give me that lecherous look. We've just gone sailing a few times. Ate some meals together. I may be near fifty but I'm not dead."

Robbie. Detective Roberta Exline. She and Glen Ziegler had investigated the death of Darla Pollard in the supply room. I had seen the chemistry between Marilyn and the detective but hadn't been certain anything had come of it. Now it appeared that something had. Or was in the process of doing so. I was pleased. I thought them a good match.

I made one more attempt to escape. "Marilyn, it's too hot to be on a boat. I'll suffocate."

Her look was scathing. "Lexy Hyatt. How can you be in your thirties and so out of it? You heard me say cabin. Ms. Fixit there probably has the air conditioning going by now. Have you lived your whole life with your nose in a book or against typewriter keys?"

I puffed up indignantly. "No. I've scraped this nose in the clay of many a softball field...and nuzzled a few women. Even got a laptop computer. Wren's helping me get more comfortable with it." Again I experienced the inner droop. Maybe Marilyn was right. Maybe I needed to throw myself into something different until Wren returned to the present and to me. I stood up and saluted. "Okay, Admiral. I'll go aboard."

Two

Shimmering heat rose from the pavement of the two-lane road meandering northeast across the Florida marshland. Any visible patches and threads of water were motionless. Egrets and great blue herons stood along banks or lifted their long legs ponderously in slow steps. Grackles and blackbirds perched on tall stalks, and pairs of cardinals darted single file across my path.

I had seen few vehicles since turning off the main highway. Part of me was enjoying the sense of isolation intensified by the stillness of the landscape and the surreal brightness. Part of me hungered for the presence of Wren. And that was a problem I had been wrestling with lately. No woman had ever drawn me so completely from myself into a world of two, but periodically I fled from it. It was something we had yet to talk about, which I had hoped might happen naturally in the neutral terrain of our vacation trek. I wanted a life with Wren Carlyle but the totality of such a commitment frightened me. She was right that I needed time to think about it. Maybe on Marilyn's boat...

Gradually the land on either side became firmer and evolved into the orderliness of truck farms. Storage and processing buildings relieved the flatness. Eventually I had to slow my speed to coast through a small community thick with pines and oaks, magnolias and palms, cherry laurels and camphor trees. Beyond the small town the road swung in a wide arc to the east then turned abruptly north to follow the shaft of Lake Arrow. I was stunned by the expanse of water. It was difficult to tell where the scarcely rippling blue of the lake began and the the clear sky ended.

Marilyn had thrown some facts at me as she walked me to my car. "It's a deep-water lake. The shaft part is over four miles wide and nearly twelve miles long. It widens into a rough arrowhead shape at the north end. That's where you'll find Cap MacKay's Marina and the *Willow.*" Her last words as I was pulling away from the curb were, "Hope Ms. Fixit lets you on board."

I had hit my brakes but she had already turned back toward The Cat and was giving me a backhand wave. I would have appreciated some information on Ms. Fixit. Knowing the Admiral, it was deliberate that I received none.

Wherever cabbage palms along the bank afforded spots of shade, someone was dangling a line into the lake—a lone man, pairs of women with children, teenagers. Small boats, their masts furled, floated further out. A few power boats, too distant for me to judge size, disturbed the glassy water.

To the west I saw the deceptively mild looking puffs of white clouds, heralds of the lumbering black bellies and towering grays that would darken the late afternoon.

The road angled away from the straight line of the lake to begin skirting the head of the arrow. In front of me masts of many sizes and heights were rising against the sky like a copse of bare trees. I turned onto a service road and saw that the boats were all balanced on cradle-like constructions. I caught a few of the names—*Anticipation, Sea Blossom, Dealer's Choice, Escape III*. I laughed out loud at *Teacher's Apple.*

I passed a gigantic building, a blight of rusting metal—probably a protected area for more boats. Next came a long blue rectangular building with white windows. Dark blue letters proclaimed it Treder's Sales and Service. The T was an upside down anchor. A smaller building, dingy white clapboard with fading red trim but clean windows, looked to be a diner. The sign was too faded to read. Several picnic tables huddled under a low sheet-metal roof at the end.

I paused in front of a squat, dull green building. A square sign on a post declared MacKay Marina. I pulled into the parking area and stared out at a bewildering array of boats all nosed into narrow piers which, in turn, jutted out into the cove like the teeth of a giant comb. I took a deep breath and puffed out my cheeks, expelling it slowly. Wasn't sure I was ready for such a foreign world.

When I got out of the car, the heat hit me with the impact of a physical blow. After the tinted windows, the brightness made me squint. I kept my eyes from the bright sky but I knew that somewhere above me an unseen moon was progressing toward the west. A former lover had told me once that my occasional bursts of uneven behavior had nothing to do with menstrual cycles but generally occurred when the moon was crossing a daytime sky. Now I didn't know if I wanted to blame my uneasiness on the separation from Wren and the realities of her life before me, Marilyn shoving me into unknown territory, or my gut-level awareness of how I'd miss the moon's reassuring night-time glow. I put my thoughts aside and pushed open the glass door into the marina office.

The walls were painted the same dull green as the exterior, the cement floor a battleship gray. A large desk filled the corner to my left. A man seated there had his back to me as he talked on the phone and watched out a side window. Standing where I was, I could see that he was watching a woman in a bikini tidying the deck of a small houseboat. Near another glass door exiting onto the docking area, an older man and a boy were arguing.

Several revolving racks to my right offered maps and pamphlets—marine, land, cities, tourist attractions and such. Another held booklets on fishing, birds, star navigation, sailing maneuvers, knots, and many how-to booklets relating to water activities. I busied myself looking them over until I could approach the man at the desk.

I chose one and tried to concentrate on the contents to avoid listening to the escalating argument of the two men outside—which proved impossible. I felt like I was hearing the dialogue of a play being rehearsed offstage.

Older man: All the lawyers in the world won't make any difference. That injunction's just bought you two a little time.

Boy: You're not going to win this one. You've been beating on us every way you can all your life. It stops now.

Older man: (harsh laughter) First an old man threatens me, now a runt. The next blockade I put up will be a cement wall. And it will stay!

I heard the door open and the sound of birds and people's voices squeezed through before it closed. I turned around in time to see the boy heading for the door I had entered. I discovered he wasn't a boy at all but rather a young man who happened to be short and slight in build. His long, sun-bleached blond hair was falling about his face as though he had been tugging at it in frustration. Veins in his neck bulged, straining against his skin. For the first time I understood the cliché about being mad enough to burst a blood vessel.

"You want something?" The hefty man at the desk had swiveled around and put down the phone. He tilted back and ran his hands across the paunch which pushed against the white T-shirt, a faded beer logo on the front. I couldn't help noticing the thick black hair sprouting on his hands and from the neck of the shirt. It was longer than the buzz cut topping his ruddy, fleshy face.

I said, "I'd appreciate it if you would point me down the right path out there. I'm looking for the *Willow*."

"Path?" His voice was thinner than I expected. "You don't sound like much of a sailor."

Even though his tone was close to sneering, I smiled and admitted I wasn't one at all. I followed his eyes to a large map of the marina on the wall. Small magnetic rectangles with lettering on their backs represented the location of each boat renting space.

He said, "Don't remember a *Willow*. What kind of boat?"

I didn't like earning another sneer. "I don't know. Not a sailboat. Owner is Marilyn Neff."

He flipped through a Rolodex. "No Neff listed here. No *Willow* out there." He hunched forward and looked at my boots. "Sure you're not looking for a campground?"

I pulled myself up taller and straighter. "Cap MacKay's Marina is what I want."

"Hell, there's the problem. His place is further up the road. Good thing you didn't ask when Steve was in here. He'd of sent you down lake the other direction." The phone rang and he turned automatically toward the window after picking up the receiver.

I left, happy to avoid expressing a 'thank you' I wouldn't mean. Back on the service road moving toward the point of the arrowhead, I very quickly came to Cap MacKay's Marina. The sign was painted with rich brown letters against a tan background and the 'C' wore a jaunty white cap. The building was gleaming white with deep coral trim. I pulled into the gravel parking area beyond which I could see five widely spaced piers extending into calm water. There were fewer boats than at the other MacKay's Marina. I was curious about the relationship.

The building's interior had broad windows and golden brown woodwork that seemed to reflect light rather than absorb it. There was a wall of drink and snack machines with card tables and chairs scattered in front of them. This time the figure at the desk, once again on the phone and back to me, was female. I could see short, iron-gray hair, broad shoulders, long legs clad in jeans stretched out and crossed at the ankles. The hand I could see toying with a paper clip was tan and wrinkled. I felt, a bit uncomfortably, as though I was seeing an older image of myself. She turned; the feeling continued as she flashed me a pleasant smile and held up a finger indicating just a minute. She tossed the paper clip and picked up a pen, the big kind good for fingers stiffening with arthritis, and quickly jotted on a pad while making single-word comments into the phone. Then she got up and I noted we were almost the same height.

"I'm Jill-of-all-trades around here. Real name's Margaret Gilstrap—Meg. What can I do for you?"

I was staring into eyes which were hazel but a third of each iris was also flecked with golden green.

She chuckled before I could comment. "I consider them my twin birthmarks. Don't know the medical explanation. Never tried to find out. I'm past seventy and have perfect eyesight. Figure I'll leave well enough alone." The accent was just a shade southern.

I would have put her ten years under that. "Forgive my staring. I'm looking for the *Willow,* Marilyn Neff's boat."

"Right. Come outside and I'll point her out." She walked with short steps but her lean body spoke of age-defying activities. She led me onto a concrete patio containing cement tables with shade umbrellas and curving benches. Four broad steps dropped down to light gray planking. She pointed. "Last finger. The one by itself. Know the child who's living on it and doing the repairs?"

"Child?"

She shrugged. "Like I said, I'm over seventy. If she's out of her teens, I'll eat a piece of tie-off rope. Quite self-sufficient. Does some work for us, too. Seen her and Dougie keeping company some." She seemed to catch herself. "I'm sounding like an old widow lady spying on the neighbors through lace curtains."

I laughed openly. "I've seen those old widow ladies when I visited up north as a kid. You don't look one bit like any I saw." I put out my hand. "I'm Lexy Hyatt. Thanks for your help." Her hand had known its share of physical labor and the grip was firm. I knew that I liked her.

I began walking toward the furthest of the five piers and Marilyn's boat.

A light breeze lessened the intensity of the sun overhead. Scanning the docile boats along the way, I wondered how they weathered the fierce and unpredictable local storms as I inspected how they were tied with strong ropes looped around pilings or clipped to metal rings.

The *Willow* was moored against the main pier so I didn't realize her size until I got close. I estimated her length at over thirty feet. Clusters of materials and tools lay on faded tarps stretched along her side on the gray planking. Similar clusters nearly obscured the deck area and seating ledges. There wasn't anywhere for me to stand or sit, let alone live. What could Marilyn be thinking?

A head of loose brown curls appeared between the cockpit seats, and a thin arm reached out to snatch a tool.

I called out "Hey."

The head tilted back revealing a sharp and intense face. I recognized the bump of a once broken bridge in the long, thin nose above compressed lips and a small but firm chin. The wide-set, dark eyes beneath straight brows challenged me to explain my presence.

"I'm Lexy Hyatt. Marilyn Neff sent me to..." I felt extremely awkward "...to live here awhile."

Her mouth dropped open. "I live here! I thought the Admiral trusted me to know what I'm doing!"

"The Admiral?" I covered my amusement.

"She told me to call her that instead of 'Miss Neff,' okay? And I don't need anyone looking over my shoulder, trying to manage things!"

Even though it had been only five years since I had dealt with contentious teenagers, I floundered. I said too defensively, "I'm the one being managed."

She came out of the opening onto the deck, picking her way carefully around the clutter. She was much shorter and thinner than I, tan and lean but obviously strong. I believed she could work anyone else into dust. She barked at me, "Meaning what?"

"I lost out on some vacation plans and was going back to work but Marilyn changed my mind for me. Said I might be of some use to the 'Ms. Fixit' genius in charge of repairing the old boat she'd bought."

Her features relaxed a little but she was still barking. "Don't call her old. She's not a junk. Outside was in pretty good shape. I've got the motor purring, improved the wiring, expanded the galley, a bunch of stuff." She wasn't boasting but I heard the pride. "Mostly on-deck stuff left to do." She looked me over critically. "You might be able to help me with some of that. Hand me things."

I could have shaken the little shit. I struggled to keep a cool tone. "Two people can really live down there?" I nodded to the door she had slid shut. I was having real qualms at the thought of close-quarters living with a testy teenager who was assuming control of the situation.

"Sure. Your head might brush the ceiling. But you don't really live on a boat this size unless you're out on the water. Docked, you sleep on it and live all around the marina." What Marilyn meant by my meeting other people, I supposed. She added grudgingly, "Guess you'd better come aboard and check it out."

I seized the stainless steel railing and prepared to vault over when she yelled, "No way, Long Legs! You ain't gonna pound those boots on my deck."

I gripped the rail tighter and spoke without inflection, "I said my name was Lexy. Yours?"

I caught a flash of anger behind her eyes before she looked away and muttered, "Charlie."

I propped myself against a piling. "I'll take off my boots, Charlie. Just don't say 'ain't' to me again." I had decided that a little challenging of my own might gain me some ground. I removed my boots and vaulted onto the small deck, grunting as one foot landed on a hammer. Then I padded after Charlie down narrow steps.

I took a deep breath of the air-conditioned coolness. Natural light spilled from small windows. Charlie touched a switch and the cabin brightened considerably. There was a V-shaped sleeping area and storage compartments.

She pointed toward a side area. "Got the galley ready to go. Refitted it for a microwave and small oven. Put in a new stove top and sink faucets. Fridge was okay. Just needed a real cleaning. It's not stocked with dishes or anything yet." She pointed to a door. "Head's there—toilet, sink, shower. Got some more to do on the shower. I mostly use the A-house, though."

"A-house?"

"Yeah. Meg calls it the Amenities House but everybody calls it the A-house. It's got toilets, showers, lockers, washers and dryers. You can pay a weekly or monthly fee for using it. I work mine off with odd jobs. Fixed a dryer and painted the trim."

"Where'd you learn how to do so much?"

"Don't know you good enough for that." It was said honestly, without belligerence. "Besides, you'd probably keep correcting my English instead of listening. You a teacher?"

"I used to be. It's not a skin you ever shed completely."

"Why'd you quit?"

"Don't know you well enough for that...yet."

She gave me the first smile I had seen. It brought real youth to her face.

Three

I sat beneath the shade umbrella at one of the tables outside the marina office, now unnecessary as the sun was blocked and the sky nearly covered by masses of clouds. The temperature had yet to drop significantly but the lake water was slate gray and rippled with ridges of white. A short while ago increasing rumbles of thunder had sent Charlie scurrying to put away tools and supplies. My offer to help was refused. I had accepted her reasoning that she knew where and how she wanted things and her suggestion that I get my things from the car before the storm hit. My large nylon carryall and a sleeping bag were at my feet. I was waiting for Meg who was helping a man put a bright blue canvas cover on his sailboat.

She approached with a smile. "Be with you in a minute, Lexy."

She lowered an umbrella and tugged it from the table. Immediately I did the same. We removed three each and I followed her to where she lifted a long lid under a window and dropped them in. She spoke a 'thank' you to my reflection in the glass and I was struck again by the feeling that, in her, I was seeing how I would age. It was an image I could live with. Suddenly I wondered if I would be doing my aging with Wren.

"Problem, Lexy?" Meg had turned toward me.

"No. Just a passing thought. Charlie sent me to check about a rent fee on the A-house."

"Got you taking orders, has she?" She led the way into the office.

I laughed ruefully. "She's nothing if not direct. I was sent without information on her and she didn't know I was coming. So..."

"So you're doing the testing dance around each other. And in mighty close quarters. I'd like to be a barnacle on the bottom. Not that there are any. Charlie really cleaned that boat when she was up on chains. Puts on goggles and dives under to check it out now." She unlocked a file cabinet and then tossed me a ring with two keys. "Large one's to the front door. Smaller one with the number is to your locker." She handed me a sheet of paper. "Here's the fee schedule. Need your signature."

I signed and paid for two weeks—partly because I didn't want to hear Marilyn's caustic remarks if I failed to hang in for that long and partly because something about Charlie intrigued me. I sensed something raw that needed healing. Marilyn would probably say I was still trying to pay off a debt I felt I owed for walking away from the classroom. Some truth there, I suppose.

I flinched as I saw a narrow streak of lightning appear to strike the lake and said in accompaniment to the boom of thunder, "Florida—lightning capital of the United States. Or is it of the world?"

"Don't worry. Some tough windstorms that are few and far between is all." Meg talked as she made entries into her computer. "Old Indian legend says the arrowhead is safer waters than the rest of the lake. Supposedly a piece of a star was put on a shaft and shot here from the sky by a mighty hunter as a gift to Mother Earth. Because it was so hot after its long flight, it melted the earth deep down and the hole filled with rain. Truth is, it's a unique lake. Deep water nearly to the shores. Then there's that deep-water channel leaving from near the point of the arrowhead and connecting with a deep running river. That wide-mouth channel is the reason you see a couple of really good-sized boats out there—the kind you normally see only on the Intra-Coastal Waterway or along the coast itself. They come down from Jacksonville, quite a few originally from points north and south of there. That fifty-footer is a floating palace."

It was easy to spot the boat she meant. It was at the end of the longer middle pier, painted ivory with a few narrow stripes of deep gold and brown. The gleam of stainless steel was everywhere and the side was dotted with eye-shaped windows. There was probably more living space down below than in my entire apartment.

"Oh, good." Meg was looking out the window again. "Here comes the second wind." At first I thought she was referring to the strengthening wind, but then realized she meant the sailboat aiming for its docking space. "They had to anchor and ride out yesterday's storm way down lake. Two women. Good sailors but not too much younger than me. Nice couple. And they are a couple. I loved my husband enough to know it when I see it in others."

I was so relaxed with her that she caught my surprise at her comment before I could mask my thoughts. She said, "Hope you're not the prejudiced kind, Lexy. This MacKay Marina is a kind of live-and-let-live place."

"And I'm that kind of person, Meg." I toyed with bluntly admitting that I was a lesbian but reconsidered when I thought of Charlie. No need to put the girl in an awkward position or create unnecessary barriers. And I was also busy considering what she meant by 'this.' So I asked, "What's with the two MacKay Marinas? Are they related?"

She sighed but I didn't think the irritation was directed at me. "Cap is Andrew MacKay. Stephen MacKay is his son. Dougie is his grandson. Steve inherited half the original marina from his mother. He and Cap couldn't run things together for reasons too complicated to go into now." More likely too personal to share with a stranger. "So Cap sold his half to Steve in return for a certain amount of money and the land for this one. Not much cooperation between them, I'm afraid."

"The young man get caught in between?"

Meg's eyes narrowed which brightened the yellow-green portions. "Not so much. He mostly stuck with Cap." Her expression relaxed. "Like me. My husband and I started keeping a boat at the original marina when Cap and his wife built it in the 1960s. We all got to be sailing and card-playing friends. Then about ten years ago Cap's Mary went. My Ben not too long after that. Our friendship helped Cap and me get through all that, and get on with living. He offered me a job—not because I needed money but to give me some activity and purpose. I followed him here." She grinned. "Enough boring biography. If you don't want to get wet, you'd better hotfoot it to the *Willow*."

When I got to the boat, Charlie was checking mooring lines and flipping some extra bumpers over the side to protect the *Willow* from scraping against the dock. The wind was fluttering her short curls. I clenched my jaw at another vertical bolt of lightning. "Anything I need to do?"

"Nope. Toss me your stuff." She glanced at my feet, now encased in old sneakers. "And come aboard."

The boat was bobbing now. I had to judge the movement before leaning out dangerously far to grip the railing. I vaulted over while looking into Charlie's smug face. Immediately I had to spread my feet to keep my balance. She tossed my bag and sleeping roll down below and motioned me to precede her. The boat lurched and I hit my hip hard against the doorway. I'd have a bruise there tomorrow.

Charlie showed me the compartments I could use and how the toilet worked. "You didn't need to bring the sleeping bag. There's sheets and all."

I explained, "I was supposed to go camping. The sleeping bag's to make me feel a little more at home. Will the boat move like this all night?"

"You're not going to get seasick on me, are you!" There was horror on her face, and I knew it was at the prospect of my barfing on her handiwork. "No. I'm just worried about staying on that bunk."

She made a face. "It's called a berth. You don't know anything about boats, do you?"

"Not much," I muttered self-consciously. Defensively I was about to rattle off a list of things I did know about when we both cocked our heads at the sound of a voice weakly penetrating from outside.

"Ahoy aboard the *Willow*."

In a flash Charlie was back on deck. I followed more slowly. Large drops of rain were beginning to hit. Roberta Exline stood on the deck. The wind had no effect on her compact, muscled frame but her dark brown hair was whipping about her face.

"Hey, Lexy. Heard you'd been shanghaied. Somebody take this." She held up a large plastic sack.

Charlie grabbed a line and pulled the boat closer to the dock. I gave her a sharp look, recognizing she hadn't done that for me. Only the hint of a smile indicated she noticed. "Long Legs'll take it," she said.

Robbie's eyes were mischievous as she handed me the sack and mouthed, "Long Legs?" Then she leaped on deck without touching the rail. This time I hit the other hip going through the hatch just ahead of the downpour.

The sack proved to contain a variety of deli sandwiches, raw vegetables, and small plastic bottles of fancy water. I didn't realize how hungry I was until my first bite of tuna on whole wheat.

Robbie said to Charlie, loudly due to the pounding rain, "Figured you could use something a step up from the diner or machines." Then to me, "Sorry about your vacation, Lexy. I've had enough yanked away from me to know how it feels. Had yesterday and today off. Couldn't believe I didn't get called in."

In thanking her for the food, Charlie called her Miss Exline. Robbie responded quickly, "Told you to stop that. If you're not comfortable with Robbie, make it Roberta. Wouldn't mind hearing that now and then." Charlie nodded with the first sign of shyness I had seen.

We were seated on the two sections of the bed, a table that Charlie had tugged from somewhere between us. Robbie looked the cabin over. "You've really done things since I was here last. The Admiral was bragging about how classy the varnished wood strips you added made it look. Says she's going to find the brasswork you want, too." Then she nodded her head toward me. "Think you have time to turn this reporter into a sailor?"

Charlie jerked up her head and the small chin seemed to sharpen. "Reporter! All I heard was ex-teacher."

I cut in. "We haven't had a chance to do much talking yet. Maybe this evening." To needle Charlie I added, "To help me keep this food down." Then primarily to Robbie, "How'd you two meet?"

A simultaneous lull in the rain heightened the uncomfortable silence that greeted my question.

Robbie said casually, "Just happened on each other."

Charlie's voice was gruff. "You don't have to cover for me. She's a reporter. She'd probably dig up the truth. Tell her straight out."

Robbie agreed, her manner carefully casual. She turned toward me, her brown eyes bright. "Charlie was spending some time at the Detention Center. Word got around that she was a whiz at fixing things. Took care of an old TV and broken workout equipment in the woman's rec room. Fixed some appliances, furniture, toilets. Even took care of a cell-block door that wouldn't lock. Kept opening and closing nonstop." She and Charlie grinned at each other over that. "She heard some of the correctional officers complaining about problems with their boats. Told them what to do. They'd have hauled them all in to her if they could have gotten away with it." She paused to munch on a carrot stick. "Anyway, some folks got involved in helping Charlie to get out early, but she had to have gainful employment and a place to live. That's how I got involved. Was telling Marilyn about it. She had just bought this boat. Came up with the idea for it to serve as both job and living quarters. A group of us sold it to the judge."

Charlie stared at me defiantly. I said, "Impressive—all the way around. And obviously a break for the *Willow*."

"Who gets to keep her name, I hear."

Charlie perked up. "For real! How come?"

After Robbie explained what I had told Marilyn about willow trees, Charlie looked at me with some respect. "It's bad luck to change a boat's name, but it didn't seem right for me to pitch a dumb fit about it. Guess the *Willow* and me owe you." Then to cover her softening, she said brusquely, "But that doesn't mean you can upchuck over everything tonight."

Robbie howled. "I think I'll take my leave on that."

But the wind rose again and the rain bombarded us. It was forty-five minutes before Robbie could leave. While Charlie accompanied her on deck, I stayed below, cleaned up and put the leftover food in the fridge. Charlie returned, busying herself about the cabin as I laid out my sleeping bag on my side of the V-shaped berth. Very aware of her speculative looks, I puzzled over what Robbie might have told her about me before leaving.

Finally she settled on her side and asked, "What's it like being a reporter?"

"Good, bad, indifferent, dull, exciting. Like most jobs, I imagine. I don't enjoy covering politics. Even when it's honest people trying to perform real service, I see them get all tangled up in the media and re-election games. I did a series on the terminally ill and how the medical profession dealt with their pain. The letters I received, especially from nurses, made me feel like maybe I had done something helpful. Then some things are real learning experiences—like when I lived a week in a fire station, and spent a weekend working midway games at a carnival." Charlie's eyes lit up at that. "Some of the hard-news coverage is rough—the car accidents, robberies, assault and rape...murder." I shuddered remembering a murder victim's sightless eyes. "But sometimes you get a real lift."

"Like how?"

"Well, I mean a real lift. I'm a hiker. Want my feet on the ground. Don't fly." I peered at her sideways. "Didn't used to go aboard boats."

She grinned. "Several weeks ago I was doing a fluff series on small airports and their offerings—skydiving, balloons, air shows. I found one that was mostly gliders. When I was a kid I loved those balsa-wood toy planes you put together. There was something nifty about making them soar and watching them glide to the ground. Anyway, somehow I got talked into going up in one. I still can't believe I did it."

"Bet they squeezed your balls." She laughed at my expression. "What was it like?"

I shook my head. "Even when I wrote about it, I couldn't capture it. You get towed up into the air by a regular plane. I was in a tiny seat behind the glider pilot. That first jerk really scared me. So did the drop when we were released. But then the floating...like nothing I had ever experienced. And the silence. Made me feel separate from everything but the glider itself. I didn't feel like I had just left the ground. I felt like I had left the planet."

"Have you gone up again?"

"No. Those sensations were too special. I don't want to lose them by doing it again."

Charlie reflected. "I kind of know what you mean. I went horseback riding just once. With a friend I made one summer. She knew horses and liked to ride. They were just stable nags for tourists and you were supposed to go with a guide and stay on trails. But they let her go out by herself because they knew how good she was. We went off trail and I was spending all my time trying to stay on and not be bounced to death. We mostly walked and trotted—which I thought was going to jar my teeth out of their sockets. Then all of a sudden she yelled for me to hang on tight and made her horse start running. Mine followed. I saw a log up ahead and knew what was going to happen. I grabbed the saddle horn with one hand, leaned down, and grabbed the mane with the other. And then we were flying!" There was a rapt expression on her face. "I know it was only a couple of seconds, but it was like you and the glider. We were one thing, that horse and me, and we were flying..."

We smiled at each other. I knew we had a long way to go—but Charlie and I were going to be all right.

Four

On some subterranean level I knew I was dreaming. I was in a small cage of curving steel bars bobbing in the water with no land in sight. Characteristic of a dream, I didn't question how I could be bobbing in the light chop rather than sinking. I was naked except for my hiking boots.

Suddenly Wren surfaced from below, her hair slicked back from her face, her green eyes dazzling. The rise and fall of the water permitted me glimpses of her full breasts, nipples hard and honey dark. Her smile was teasing as she stretched to float on her back, and my eyes went to her breasts, her flat abdomen, her hips.

The sky darkened and it began to rain. Wren swam to me and seized the bars, pulling us both below the water where everything was infused with an eerie glow. Wearing goggles, Charlie was opening colorful umbrellas, putting the shafts into plastic bottles and arranging them on the bottom. She never looked up at us. Wren reached through the bars drawing me toward her. We kissed and her hands played up and down my back and hips. Then her arms went around my waist pulling me tight against the bars. She smiled coquettishly at the sight of my breasts poking through the openings. She pantomimed kissing them just short of my erect nipples until I seized her shoulder and cupped the back of her head to force her to me. Then I made soundless cries as she sucked long and hard.

I was on my knees, my flesh imprinted with the bars in my effort to reach her. She eased away from me but her eyes promised. Turning her hands back to back, she grasped two bars and spread them apart effortlessly. I floated free of the cage and then we floated body to body. We turned and twisted as one. My arms became her arms. Her tongue became my tongue. When at last she parted her thighs enough for me to enter her, I thrust with two fingers and lifted her above me in the glowing water. Clamping a leg between mine, I rested my head against her hip and watched the movement of my hand, the arch of her pelvis.

She climaxed, one hand clutching my wet hair. When I felt her slacken, I left her slowly. She shot away and taunted me to follow. But when I reached her, she whirled me around and forced me back into the cage. The bars remained wide but I made no effort to leave. Wren's smile faded and she touched the bottom of the cage propelling me to the surface where it was dark and still raining. I sat back and stared at the opening. I called out her name, this time with sound, but it came back to me on the wind and I choked on the rain.

I awoke—and knew instantly where I was. I was hearing real wind and rain. The rocking motion was the *Willow*. I skimmed the dream before the images could fade but didn't try to interpret them.

That I missed Wren wasn't a dream. That I wanted a complete life with her wasn't a dream. But I was frightened at the thought of radical changes. But did I even know what changes would occur? How could I know I wouldn't like them? Was I afraid I couldn't measure up—that I would fail Wren as Nancy Marshall had?

I tossed and turned, fighting my thoughts, fighting for sleep. I lost both battles. Eventually the wind and rain and motion stopped. Then the faintest of gray appeared in the two small windows I could see. When it began a transformation to dusty rose, Charlie stirred and stretched. As she swung her feet to the floor, I sat up.

"You don't have to get up so early, Lexy. I'll be out of here in a minute. I work for Cap today."

"I've been awake a long time. I want to get up."

"Stomach?"

"Dreams."

When I came out of the head, Charlie was dressed and ready to leave. She said, "Left you half a ham-and-cheese for breakfast. If you want coffee, wander around the boats. Somebody'll offer you some."

I sat on the deck to nibble the sandwich and watch the sunrise. The rose gave way to pink, yellow, white. The sun appeared and the blue came with it. What was Wren waking up to see?

I stuffed the sandwich paper in the pocket of my shorts and went off in search of coffee, but saw no sign of life inside the office when I passed. I glanced down the long middle pier but kept walking. Many of those boats were large and ornate and had a snooty air.

I turned down the next pier which was bordered on both sides by sailboats of varying sizes. Some were partially covered with protective canvas, their sails wrapped as well—mostly in bright blue but I saw some green and maroon. Others were open and had an occupied look. A couple were already putting out onto the lake.

Near the end I spotted the boat Meg had been glad to see return before the storm. It was indeed named the *Second Wind,* white with touches of red. Stretched out on the bow was the largest, or at least the longest, cat I had ever seen—black except for four white feet.

"Well, Boots," I said, "Enjoying the morning?"

"Try Tiger."

I took a couple more steps and looked to the back of the boat. A woman with unruly hair as black as the cat stood there. She was a barrel shape atop toothpick legs dressed in loose shorts and shirt of some faded pastel.

"Tiger?" I questioned.

"Right. Donna's granddaughter gave him to us when he was a kitten. She'd read a book about a ship's cat and was determined we'd have one. That book cat was named Tiger for reasons obvious to everyone but little Kristen. She gave this one to us and she named him. So Tiger it is. He doesn't mind. Haven't seen you around. What boat you off of?"

"The *Willow,* but just visiting. I'm Lexy."

"Had your morning coffee, Lexy?"

"No. Would you be offering some?"

"You bet. And here it is. Come aboard. This is Donna and I'm Fran."

A second woman appeared holding a large thermal mug in each hand. She could have been posing for a senior-citizen advertisement for vitamins or some nutritious drink. Of medium size, except for a little sag to the skin she looked as trim and fit as she must have been in her youth. Her shorts were bright red, her blouse a crisp white. Neither was wrinkled. Her silver hair was perfectly coifed and framed an oval face made attractive by soft, high cheekbones and an inviting mouth. She smiled me a greeting, handing the mugs to Fran, then disappeared.

Carefully I stepped up on the bow and picked my way around the cat and the cockpit cover to the deck. Fran let me sit before handing me one of the steaming mugs. I saw that the black hair was a good dye job.

I replied in the negative to Donna's call concerning cream and sugar, and she re-appeared with a mug for herself. I had to sip carefully as a boat slowly chugged past on its way out, rocking the *Second Wind*. We made small talk about the beautiful morning, yesterday's storm, the marina.

Donna asked, "You vacationing, Lexy?"

"Yes and no. I was supposed to be hiking the Blue Ridge and camping with a friend, but she got called away on something personal. The Admiral, I mean Marilyn Neff who owns the *Willow*, sent me here for a consolation trip and to help Charlie."

"Admiral? Fits. Interesting woman," Fran said. "Saw her when she brought the girl and set things up with Cap and Meg."

"She's certainly a capable girl," Donna added. "We've seen her doing work all around here. In fact, young Doug suggested we have her check out our galley and see if it could be expanded. They seem to get along but she's quite the shy thing otherwise."

Fran disagreed. "Not shy—protective of herself." I looked questioningly into her shrewd, dark blue eyes. She continued, "When we still lived in Toledo, I volunteered some at a Youth Center. Saw my share of kids with that same kind of shell. I'd say your Admiral, and that other woman that shows up pretty regular, has put the kid in a good place to get her feet under her. That other woman—a cop like I heard?"

"Fran!" Donna compressed her lips.

Fran merely grinned and I noticed one of her front teeth was capped in gold. "Don't you pretend you're not as curious as I am."

I sidestepped her question. "There must be some kind of grapevine around here."

"You bet. Watching your neighbors and collecting dirt are big-time activities."

Donna spoke up, "Don't listen to her, Lexy. This is really a great community. And Fran is a great exaggerator."

They shared an intimate smile. When Fran turned back my way

again,the blue eyes were teasing. "I'll veer off on that question and try a different one. That Orlando bar I've heard your friend the Admiral runs—is it really a gay bar?"

"Fran Stover, whatever am I going to do with you?"

Fran cocked an eye at Donna, then raised her eyebrows to me, a blunt, knowing look in her eyes.

I answered after a little hesitation. "Ah...yes...actually it's a lesbian bar. There's a restaurant too. It's a nice place."

"Can you dance there?"

"Yes. Live band on weekends. Jukebox the rest of the time." I was slow in relaxing. Being open with people I didn't know well was sometimes difficult for me.

Donna surprised me by saying, "That might be nice."

Fran said warmly, "I think it would be very nice. We've never danced on a real dance floor. Or in front of other people." Then she seemed to toss off the mellowing as though it were an embarrassment and pointed toward me. "Now. Tell me..."

"Absolutely not!" Donna was adamant. "This polite young woman is not going to answer any more questions. Go get her another cup of coffee." Fran went. "I'm sorry, Lexy. Fran can be quite direct."

"No problem. I rather like it." After all, as a reporter I often had to come across with direct questions to strangers, and now felt as they must have when I came on strong.

We were laughing together when Fran returned with a thermos and refilled our mugs. The cat joined us and was testing out my lap. I began asking some questions of my own. "Do you live here all the time?"

Donna answered, "No, but a lot off and on. We have a house in Mossville, a little town not far from here."

"I came through it on my way here."

Fran said, "We started in a place between Orlando and Sanford. Kept the boat at Lake Monroe. Then found this place. Much more to our liking. Sure hope we get to stay." They both looked concerned.

Before I could decide whether or not to ask for an explanation, Donna began one. "There's been trouble about the road in front of Cap's part here. About a month ago his son started claiming that the road and land up to the county road wasn't included in the deed when he and Cap split a few years ago. That there was no right-of-way in and out of here. The road ends about a mile further. The rest of the land around the arrowhead is owned by the State. At first he and Cap just argued about it. Then a week ago last Friday Steve had a wooden barricade put up."

Fran took up the explanation. "For some people that meant having to put their boats in way down lake, leaving their cars or trucks unprotected. And those of us who keep our boats here still have to have somewhere to park. Also, Cap has an entry ramp a little north of here that locals can use for free. For some reason that always stuck in Steve's craw."

"What happened to the barricade?"

"Doug and Charlie took it down in the middle of the night. Not that anyone around here would admit that to the wrong people."

Knowing that Charlie was probably on probation, though I had yet to learn what she had done, I was certain Robbie didn't know about it. "And it has stayed down?"

Donna nodded. "Because Cap got a lawyer and he got an injunction. I suppose there's going to be a hearing or court appearance. I'm not sure what. I can't understand people like Steve. How can you treat your father like that? Cap is a good man."

I was remembering the argument I had heard a little of yesterday, apparently between Steve and his son. "Doesn't say much for blood being thicker than water."

Fran said harshly, "No. At least Doug doesn't have to care about that."

I was about to ask her what she meant when the cat gave a loud cry and leaped all the way to the top of the cockpit where he strutted back and forth.

"Has to be his pal Meg." Fran stood up. "Yep—"

Meg scrambled aboard with considerably more alacrity than I had, scooping up Tiger and greeting me. "See you found the good coffee, Lexy. Saw Charlie and Cap working on the Olivers' latest toy."

Donna said, "Another patch job no doubt. Those people are rough on boats."

"It's because they're always running aground to go screw in the shade." Fran was emptying the thermos into the large cap for Meg. "How do you think she got all those ant bites on her ass she was complaining about. Listen, Meg. What's the latest on the road?"

"Doesn't look good. The dimensions in the papers Cap signed all those years ago only covered a few feet beyond the dock. Everything went through an attorney the marina had used for years. Even though Cap and Steve were disagreeing on how to run things, it was supposed to be a friendly split so each could go in his own direction. It never dawned on Cap that there'd be any hanky-panky with the papers."

"It's not right," Donna said solemnly.

"No," Meg agreed. "The lawyer is trying to work something out about Cap having the right to expect good-faith procedures from his son. Don't know how far you can get with a claim like that. Cap thinks, at least he pretends to believe, that it will all get worked out. Dougie and I aren't so sure. We both know how cold Steve is. If not downright evil."

Despite the warmth of morning, I shivered at Meg's tone. Then she began to roughhouse the cat and his freight-train purr relieved the tension. A little more light conversation and we both took our leave. Meg pointed me toward the south end of the dock where I would find Charlie.

Charlie didn't smile when she saw me but neither did she glare. She and a deeply tanned man in paint-splattered shorts and sandals were inspecting the bottom of a two-seater jetboat, then turned it completely upside down.

When he straightened and stretched his back, I thought the man looked every bit the old pirate. His shaggy white hair was encircled by a navy blue bandanna. He had thick white eyebrows, a toothy grin, and a dimple. All he needed was a dagger between his teeth and a large ring in one ear. A bit of a stoop probably cost him two inches of height but his arms and shoulders were still muscled. Rivulets of sweat were making make their way through the matted white hair of his chest. There was an air of good humor about him.

"You must be Lexy. Marilyn Neff called me yesterday to say you'd be living on the *Willow* for awhile. How about sitting over there in the shade with me so I can pretend I'm being polite instead of furling my sails and sneaking a rest."

We went over to a shed where an overhang shaded a bench. He wiped his hand on his shorts before extending it to me. "Andrew

MacKay. Most folks call me Cap. That gal over there is something. Used to think nobody could beat my grandson at pulling more than their own weight, but that was before I saw Charlie in action. And she is a canny thing. I'd swear she can just touch something and know how to fix it." He drew a deep breath and let it out slowly. "Shame the world has turned itself over to machines and gadgetry—technology. Not too many places value her kind anymore."

"Marilyn does. And you seem to."

"Aye that. Don't mention it to the girl just yet but when I get out of an undertow that's snagged me, I may be able to offer her a job." He raised his voice. "Yell if you need me, Charlie." She nodded. He said, "She won't." He grimaced and tapped his chest. "Angina problems now and then. Not the kind of thing that kills you. Can't make Doug and Meg see that. And I think they've clued in Charlie."

He bent forward to look past me. I turned my head and saw Meg on the patio, pantomiming putting something in her mouth. Cap gave her a thumb-and-finger okay sign. He said, "See what I mean. She's making sure I took my medicine this morning. Can't fault her. We had three deaths in a row here about ten years ago. Makes you check the rigging more than usual." He slapped his knee. "Listen to me doing all the talking. Charlie says you're a reporter."

I told him about my job on the *Ledger*. In turn, he told me about the boats spread out before us, their people, the lake itself. I interrupted him often for an explanation of a nautical or marine term, hoping I could remember enough to impress Marilyn sometime.

"Done, Cap." Charlie had approached us. "Can you call the Olivers to pick it up? Tell them to keep it out of the water for at least five days. Maybe a week."

Cap gnashed his teeth. "Wish I could keep all those doodad water toys off the lake all the time. They're loud. Scare off birds and fish. The Olivers aren't too bad with theirs, but some others are right dangerous. I'll call them, Charlie. And I'll see to it they leave your money with Meg." He stood up and I did as well. "Going to be a big Fourth of July shindig here Friday, Lexy. Make sure you're in port."

He left and I asked Charlie, "Can I tag along on your next job and help?"

"It's grunt work, Long Legs. Filling all the machines in the office."

"That's fine by me."

She was right about grunt work. After she got the keys from Meg, she opened all the doors in the wall of dispensers. I followed her into a backroom where she toed the stacked crates of soft-drink cans. I hefted two at a time and started filling receptacles while she replenished the candy and snacks.

Meg called over from her desk. "Charlie, I got a distributor who'll put in two machines for containers of water and juices. You get any more good ideas like that, let me know. And I got some more of the little plastic coin tubes. On the shelf by the computer paper."

It took a while separating all the coins, counting and rolling them. Charlie made a careful record in a notebook for each machine. A number of people came in and out as we worked—passing through, exchanging pleasantries with Meg, asking questions, checking charts, getting drinks. Those who spoke to Charlie were awkwardly introduced to me. Some of the money went into a cashbox which Meg put in the bottom drawer of the file cabinet, the rest went into a large bank bag.

Before locking the machine doors into place, Charlie plucked two cans of Dr. Pepper and tossed me one. As she drank hers, she began wiping down each machine with a damp cloth. I walked over to Meg's desk and said, "My car is still right out there. Should I move it?"

She stood up and pointed out the side window. "If you want to be nearer the *Willow*, park across the road on the other side of that clump of small oaks." She waved toward the front window. "From Cap's trailer there to those oaks is going to be set up for our Fourth of July picnic Friday—barbecued ribs, hotdogs, hamburgers, all the fixings. Folks have contributed for a good spread."

"Where and what do I contribute?"

"Nothing." She chuckled. "If Charlie keeps you at scut work, you'll more than earn your part. Charlie, would you take this money bag over to Cap? He's going into town soon."

Charlie handed over the keys and picked up the heavy bag. With Meg returning the keys to the file cabinet and me continuing to gaze out the window, neither of us heard Steve MacKay enter. At Charlie's startled "Hey!" we both turned around. He had grabbed her by the arm and forced her back to the desk.

He said harshly, "Are you getting senile, Meg? Letting this little dyke bitch carry off money."

Meg slapped the desk so hard I knew it had to hurt. "You don't give orders here, Steve. And we don't take your criticism either. And let go of her."

He tightened his grip on Charlie's arm. He was taller than his father, his dark hair neatly trimmed, the planes of his face similar to Cap's, minus the dimple. There was no air of good humor about him, though.

Meg said, her voice quivering with anger, "What business do you think you have here?"

I saw his fingers dig tighter into Charlie's thin arm. I spoke low and sternly. "I think he should make it his business to let go of Charlie."

Charlie's eyes flew to me. His did as well, insolently raking me over from head to toe. He said, "Looks like you're letting a whole nest of queers burrow in, Meg—"

I responded, "Our money spends just fine." I took a step toward him. We were nearly of a height. His jaw jerked but he released his hold. I knew Charlie was staring at me but I kept my eyes on his. Meg had said he was cold. There was a blankness in his dull gray eyes that backed up her statement.

Meg said, her voice more under control, "Go on, Charlie." I nodded agreement and she went out the front door to cross over to Cap's trailer.

Steve MacKay glared at me but I stood my ground at the corner of the desk. He said to Meg, "I know there's too much rough water between us but that doesn't mean you can't act with good sense. You and Cap aren't up to running this place the way it should be. And Doug doesn't have the grit."

"You never bothered to know him when he was little. You don't know him now. We all are doing just fine. At least we were until you started flushing bilge over us."

His don't-blame-me tone grated. "I've offered Cap a reasonable deal for this place. I'd turn real profits, expand." He sneered at me. "Bring in a better class of people."

"What you mean are people who just know how to spend and use up. The kind who wouldn't care about the lake, or sharing and preserving, or just plain pleasant living. I can understand you not knowing Dougie, but how can you think Cap would ever drop flag."

His face darkened. "Then he can go down. The papers are solid legal. It's Cap's fault he didn't have the numbers checked out before he signed. He'll just use up time and money trying to fight me. My way he'd still get something. I'd give him some kind of piddling work to do if he wanted."

"And your son Dougie and your friend Meg?" Her words were laced with sarcasm.

"He's not my son and you're not my friend. Tell Cap." Steve MacKay stalked out, leaving a heavy silence behind.

The telephone broke the silence. Meg took a message for someone.

The moment she hung up it rang again. She said, "You're in luck, Marilyn. She's standing right here."

I took the receiver and Meg walked out the front door. Through the window I could see Cap crossing toward the office. He was well-groomed and neatly dressed—probably on a trip to the lawyer as well as the bank. Charlie was walking away from him at an angle I figured would take her to the *Willow*. I assumed he was joining Meg outside the door.

Marilyn told me that Wren had just called her after not catching me at home either late the night before or early in the morning. She had explained my whereabouts which supposedly Wren thought was just great. I jotted down the numbers where Wren could be reached on Meg's notepad. I gave only positive responses to the questions about Charlie and the boat. I didn't think the happenings at the marina were mine to spread around. I did think, however, that her sending me here was as much for Charlie as it was for me. I would need to corner her and Robbie soon.

Five

A narrow bench-like series of boards ran the length of the main pier. Charlie was seated on the one across from the *Willow*. Her hands gripped on both sides and her head hung down. I settled beside her.

She spoke without looking at me. "I didn't mean to make trouble for you and Meg."

"Hey," I didn't continue until she turned toward me. "You didn't do anything to apologize for. Steve MacKay's the person at fault here."

"But it's me he's mad at. He knows I helped Doug..." A guarded look dimmed the eyes she cut toward me.

I finished for her, "...take down the barricade. I heard about that."

Her eyes cleared. "He cornered Doug and me the next day. Called me a lot of names. Told Doug it made him look like a fag to be hanging with me. Said queers ought to be drowned like unwanted puppies and kittens. And now he's calling you that, too. And in front of Meg!" She frowned in pain. "I swear, Lexy, I haven't done anything to show I'm...I'm queer. I wouldn't do anything to embarrass Roberta and the Admiral. Honest!"

I shifted sideways drawing a leg up onto the bench. "Ah, Charlie. Being who you are is not something to be ashamed of. Some of the words we get tagged with don't help, I know. I prefer lesbian, or gay. But it won't embarrass the people who count—the good people. Robbie Exline and the Admiral are good people. So's Meg."

She relaxed a little." I don't know what I did to make Steve start on me about being qu...gay. I've hardly ever...I mean I haven't been...I don't...I mean..."

I risked a smile. "Are you trying to tell me that your gay experiences have been somewhat limited."

The smile she risked was delightfully sheepish. "There's only been one. And it was two years ago. The girl I went horseback riding with. It was just a vacation thing for her. But that's all right. I've got good memories. Guess that sounds dumb to you."

This time I risked touching her shoulder gently. "Count yourself lucky. Not everyone gets a good first time, one worth remembering forever."

Thoughtful wonder spread over her face and the last of the tension dissipated. I planned to see to it that Steve MacKay's vituperative words and attitude did not continue to do damage—though I owed him this breakthrough. More assured now, Charlie asked, "Do you have a girl?"

"I have a woman. And she has me. We were supposed to be camping together right now but something came up. I have a friend who would say that karma is at work here."

"What does that mean?"

"She'd say that it's my destiny to be separated from Wren for a while. That there are activities we need to do separately. Maybe there is something here at the marina I'm supposed to become involved in for my own development." I tilted my head. "Or someone I need to meet and interact with for the good of both of us. Maybe after my time here I'll know if it's time to set up housekeeping with Wren."

I could see Charlie absorbing a new concept, but her only comment was, "Wren is a funny name."

I explained how it was formed from the initials of her four grandparents' first names. Then I said, "What about yours? Charlie. Where does that come from?"

Tension flooded back and she went rigid. "It's just my name."

Before I could even start trying to figure what had suddenly gone wrong between us, a motorboat chugged up behind the *Willow*. The young man I had seen arguing with Steve MacKay, and whom I assumed to be his son Doug, was waving and calling out to Charlie to come tie them off. There was another young man with him whose shiny black hair and skin a smoother dark than a mere tan suggested Hispanic blood. He took Charlie's steadying hand and stepped up from the motorboat. Doug leaped effortlessly. His long blond hair was tied back with a black and red bandanna. Without anger contorting his features, he exhibited his grandfather's pleasure in people.

After Charlie's off-hand introduction, Doug welcomed me to the marina and was pleased by the compliments I paid Cap and Meg. I must have towered over him by a good seven inches. He was even a little shorter than Charlie, but where her features lacked the stamp of adulthood, his were set in a maturity that placed him somewhere in his twenties. He introduced us to the taller, darker young man whose shy smile dimpled his cheeks.

"This is Joseph—Joe Quinn. He works for Steve." Doug raised his eyebrows to Charlie. "But don't hold that against him. This is his day off. We've been cutting the high weeds along the shore back there." He waved toward the north-northeast. "Making it better for the people who'll fill in along there to watch the fireworks." For my benefit he pointed out into the lake. "They'll be set off from a barge out there. You'll have a great seat right here."

Charlie asked, "What about mosquitoes?"

"Cap's going to spray early Friday. But if we get a good breeze coming off the water, everything will be jake. You going to dive with me Saturday to scoop up all the junk left by the fireworks?"

"Sure." Charlie looked at me, her face carefully blank. "Would you like to go down with us, Long Legs, and help?"

I almost punched her arm before I remembered Steve MacKay's damaging grip. "You darn well know the answer to that, Ms. Fixit. Being on the water in a boat tied to the dock is as far as I'm willing to go for the time being."

Whatever I had done or said to irritate her moments ago was obviously forgotten or forgiven. She grinned and said to the fellows, "We've got a water baby here who hasn't earned any flippers yet."

They teased me a little more and spoke of the upcoming plans for the Independence Day celebration. Then Doug and Charlie drifted off far enough to talk privately.

Joe Quinn said kindly, "You don't have to be afraid of the lake, Ms. Hyatt. You can make friends with her, as long as you give her the respect she deserves. I live in a trailer park way on the other side. I've probably spent as much time on these waters as I have on land."

"Make it Lexy, Joe."

He opened his mouth, hesitated, then said, "I will. And I prefer

Joseph. And my last name isn't really Quinn. It is Quintana. I had been told I'd have it easier getting a job with a more American-sounding name. A job with Steve MacKay, I mean. Doug and his grandfather aren't like that."

When he spoke of MacKay, all congeniality fled his face, much like Charlie's just before he and Doug arrived. I said, "Why do you work for a man like MacKay?"

"I'm paid a good wage for a summer job. The marina isn't all that far from where I live. And sometimes he needs me because I speak Spanish. I get real good pay for that. He doesn't mind using a 'spic-spanic' when it suits him."

I caught the bitterness of the last remark and thought to myself that MacKay was probably too much a bigot to learn the language himself. Doug and Charlie finished their conversation and he motioned Joseph toward the motorboat, calling a 'good-bye' to me. Charlie tossed the line into the boat and waved them on their way.

She surprised me with a suggestion. "Want to go to the diner for lunch? I was supposed to paint the shed where you and Cap were sitting but he said not to." She frowned and stared out at the peaceful boats. "Cap makes a show of saying that everything is going to get straightened out. But when he puts off work that needs doing, it's like he's really saying why do something that might turn out to be for nothing." Her face set in earnestness. "Lexy, Cap's so much a part of this place I don't think he could live without it. He just can't lose it! And it would knock Doug down so hard he might never get up again. His dad's beat on him all his life." She reacted to my expression. "I don't mean real hitting. He tore him down on the inside. Doug was younger than I am now when he started living with Cap and helped get this place going. He talks to me a lot and I can tell that the good way he sees himself now is all tangled up with Cap and this marina." The timbre of her voice changed. "He's not like me. I never let myself get tangled up with where I was." She kind of shook herself. "Well, do you? Want to have lunch?"

"Yes, I do. I'm starving. But would you let me pick the place, assuming we're taking the afternoon off?" She gave me a wary look which I ignored. I continued, "I'd like to run into Orlando—to my apartment. I need to exchange some of my camping clothes for boating wear."

"You haven't done any boating."

I acknowledged that with a grunt. "I also need to make a long-distance call. And I want to bring back some supplies for the galley—coffee and such." Both hands went to her hips. "Oh, Charlie. I promise not to make a mess." I grunted again. "I can't believe I'm pleading with a bossy adolescent."

Wry amusement flashed across her face. "You're not used to being lowly crew, are you? Maybe it's that karma stuff working on you. I'll tell Meg we're going." She started to cross in front of me. "Smile pretty, Long Legs."

"What?"

"Smile pretty. You're being checked out."

I followed her line of sight to the large, fancy boat at the end of the middle pier. Sunlight was reflected in the twin circles of a pair of binoculars. It was uncomfortable knowing I had been drawn up close to a pair of eyes I could not see. The figure behind the binoculars was slender and bikini-clad. Strands of strawberry-blonde hair also reflected the sun. I drew myself more erect and narrowed my eyes, then shifted them decisively to Charlie.

She was watching me measuringly. "Cap calls her the Piranha Princess. Says she's the kind who could strip you of your flesh and make you enjoy it. Looks like I might have to babysit you in more ways than one."

My mouth dropped open as she began striding down the planking toward the office. I hurried after her resisting an impulse to glance toward the boat again. I wondered if the binoculars were following me.

In a reversal of roles, I put Charlie to work carrying in things from the trunk of my car to my apartment. The quick glance she gave me told me she understood full well. We had had a great lunch at an Italian favorite of mine—salad, pasta primavera, garlic rolls. Charlie had been ill at ease but enjoyed the food. I rather doubted that she had much restaurant experience. We had talked little and she had deflected most of my questions while asking none of her own.

"I'm going to tend to my clothes and shower, Charlie. You sort all that stuff and pick out what would be useful back on the boat. Do the same thing in the kitchen. If that cooler isn't enough, there's another one by the refrigerator. Make certain I have coffee."

"We're not setting up housekeeping. That's for you and Wren." There was a jab to her words that made me feel she had known when my thoughts had drifted back to the attractive figure behind the binoculars.

I showered and made my clothing exchange. Back in the living room I found Charlie squatting in front of a bookcase. I asked, "See anything you want to take with you?"

"I don't know. I haven't read an awful lot. Is there a book that's got stories in it like you told about the willow trees?" She was the uncertain little girl again.

I pulled a large book from the bottom shelf—Barbara G. Walker's *Woman's Encyclopedia of Myths and Secrets*. "Don't let the size bother you. It's arranged alphabetically so you can check a specific subject or just turn to any page." I selected another book—*Stoner McTavish* by Sarah Dreher. "I think you should meet Stoner. She's a land person but her life is still a voyage through uncharted waters. If you like this one, there are others that follow."

She added the books to the supplies she had placed by the door. The rest she had stacked neatly on my small kitchen table. I motioned her to follow me to the bedroom where I had laid out several shirts and shorts and jeans. I had noticed that she was wearing the same clothes as yesterday and they were thin from multiple washings.

I said, "Why don't you take a shower and then put on some of these?"

"I don't need handouts." Tough and touchy was back.

"I'm asking you to do me a favor." That confused her. I explained, "I have an aunt whom I dearly love. But she has her own way of seeing things. When I was a kid, she would give me what I thought of as silly little-girl junk. Even though I had been born a tomboy...and a bookworm. She wouldn't even do the books right. I'd ask for *The Black Stallion* and I'd get *Heidi.*" I had Charlie's attention. "When I got older—and bigger, taller, broad shouldered, cut off my curls—she switched to clothes. She didn't give me frilly things, but she bought them in the petite department." That prompted a snicker. "I've never been able to give them away to strangers. You'd make me feel good if you took them."

Without a word she made her selection and went to the bathroom.

I whispered into the silence. "You're as hard as a walnut to crack, Charlie, but I will get it done." I scooped up the rest of the clothes and took them to the front door along with two of my Eagles softball caps.

As soon as I heard the shower, I went to the telephone. I flipped through a stack of cards and came up with Robbie Exline's station number, but she was out in the field and I declined to leave a message. Next I called the number Marilyn had given me for the motel where Wren was staying. No luck there either. I stared at the second number, the one for Nancy Marshall's hospital room. I bit hard into my lower lip then muttered, "Come on, goose, she wouldn't have left you the number if she didn't want you to call."

Wren answered before a complete ring. Her throaty voice sent a pleasurable shiver through me. The second I identified myself, she said, "So, you haven't drowned yet. You should have heard Marilyn gloating about getting you on a boat."

I told her about the *Willow* and some about Cap, Meg, and the occupants of the *Second Wind*.

"Sounds like people I'd want to meet. What about your bunkmate?"

I laughed sharply. "Well, first off, she's taught me its berth not bunk. She's young, Wren. And complex. And in...in some pain." I hadn't fully realized that until I said it. I heard another voice in the background. "I don't mean to keep you from things, Wren."

"You're not. The nurse is checking Nancy's respirator and tubing. She's asleep. It's right that I'm here, Lexy. But it's knowing that you're there waiting for me that will get me through this. Talking about it will have to wait." My heart clutched at her words and I ached to reach through the phone and touch her. She added more lightly, "So don't go drown on me."

I, too, tried to keep it light. "No worry there. Besides, Charlie keeps me on a tight leash—or I should say, a short bow line."

We talked a while longer, neither of us wanting to release the other too soon. Just as Wren whispered a husky "I love you," Charlie entered the room. I smiled at her as I turned slightly to say my own "I love you" into the phone.

Embarrassed, Charlie sat down at my desk. When I hung up I said teasingly, "You look like you belong on a boat."

She had selected jade green shorts and a loose white V-neck with random streaks of yellow and light green.

She shifted uncomfortably on the chair and began perusing the pictures on the wall. "These people your family?"

I crossed over and stood beside her. Leaning to point, I identified my various family members.

Charlie said, "Your uncle and your mother don't look like twins." I explained about fraternal twins. She raised her eyes from the pictures to me. "You look like him."

"I know. It means a lot to me that I do. Means a lot to my mother, too."

I was astonished to see her eyes fill with tears. She struggled to choke off a sob. I knelt and covered her hands with mine. She tried to pull free in panic. I put my arms around her and urged, "Tell me what it is, Charlie. Let me help."

The words that followed seemed to be torn from her. "I don't know who I look like. I don't know who my family was. I don't even know what my name is!" Then she shoved me back on my heels and went to the door. Her voice was grim. "We need to be getting back."

I was resigned to getting information from her in fits and starts, but I resolved not to leave the marina until I had it all. Silently we loaded the car. Before I pulled away from the apartment building, I put Ani DiFranco in the tape deck. Careful glances told me when Charlie began to listen to the blunt, imaginative, sometimes jarring lyrics. At the tape's conclusion I started to eject it. Charlie said tentatively, "Would you play it again?"

I said, "Be glad to. She was a teenager when she wrote those. She's not much more than that now."

As we drove through Mossville, I asked Charlie if she had brought the cheese from my refrigerator. She had, so I pulled into an open-air market and purchased some fruit. Back in the car, I was pleased to see Charlie reading *Stoner McTavish*. After her brief outburst, I was doubly glad I had chosen it. Soon I parked where Meg had suggested, and Charlie and I worked as a relay team getting our new supplies to the *Willow*. I carried things to the back ledge of the pier, she took them from there to the boat. I noticed the care with which she handled the clothes

I had given her.

Though it was late afternoon, the few scraggly clouds did not threaten the usual storm. I wasn't ready to close myself in the boat yet and I thought Charlie probably needed a little space. I told her I was going to walk the finger piers for some exercise. She seemed relieved and said she had planned to get together with Doug for awhile.

As I neared the end of the middle pier, I discovered how imposing the Piranha Princess's lengthy yacht really was, and how intimidating. There was something smug about it. Even a smugness to the name—*Siren Song*. Ridiculously, I felt like hissing through my upper teeth at it. About to turn, I was startled by a touch in the middle of my back.

"Want to come aboard?" The sheer, filmy wrap did little to hide the ivory white bikini or glowing skin. A white band held most of the blonde hair away from her face but some spilled over one shoulder. She kept her eyes narrowed and I wasn't sure of their color. There was nothing special about her face except perhaps a haughty self-assuredness.

I said, "No, thank you. I'm walking the piers for exercise. And to walk off a heavy pasta lunch."

A breeze stirred open her wrap. Her taunting expression dared me to look. I didn't. She said, "You're on the *Willow*. With that urchin."

I drew myself as tall as possible and thrust out my chin.

She said complacently, "No offense intended. She's an industrious little thing. Sure you don't want to come aboard? I pour a fine wine."

My gaze took in the length of the yacht. "No. She's a bit too proud for my taste. No offense intended."

Hers was a tinkling laugh that parted the perfectly shaped lips to reveal white, even teeth. She stepped around me to approach the boat. I headed back to the main pier.

She called after me, "The invitation will stand, Lexy."

I stiffened but didn't break stride. How did she know my name?

Six

I waved a greeting to Meg, Fran, and Donna seated together at a table outside the office, the umbrella tilted to shield them from the western rays of the sun. Stepping on the bench, I hoisted myself onto the ledge and sat with my legs dangling. Carefully I avoided the *Siren Song* in my scrutiny of the boats. Thanks to Cap I could now tell a ketch from a sloop, a skiff from a bowrider, a dinghy from a flatboat.

Grunting loudly, Fran plopped down beside me. She said, "You may have to help this old lady up or down from here."

"Will do, but it's all relative. I thought I was young and in good shape until I had to keep up with Charlie."

"Saw the kid's new outfit when she passed by here. Meg says you must be some kind of a magician. She's run into Charlie's stubbornness about accepting things." Fran's voice dropped lower. "Told us about the run-in with Steve, too. How he manhandled Charlie. Said someone ought to send him to Davy Jones. That she knows personally there is a locker down below with Steve MacKay's name on it."

I got the feeling she was not making idle gossip—that she was preparing or arming me in some way.

In response to my sharp look, she added, "I've always lived letting the past go. Learned early on, though, that lots of people don't or can't do that. There's something rancid between Steve and Meg clogging the air. You just might be the fresh wind needed to blow things clear." She responded to my surprised expression. "I get hunches, like my granddaddy. Grew up on the stories about how he took his money out of the bank a month before Black Friday—the Depression. On a hunch. Kept his whole neighborhood afloat those early years. This here's my neighborhood. Want to do what I can to keep it afloat. For real."

I considered her words silently. Her tone changed again—lightened, needled gently. "So don't swim out too far with the Piranha Princess." I yelped like a startled puppy and she grinned, the gold tooth flashing. She said, "I saw her waylay you."

I was indignant. "Then you also saw me walk away."

"But she said something more to you. And you didn't turn around to answer. Bad sign, that. Means you didn't trust yourself to." I hissed through my teeth and she said, "Don't get all huffy-puffy. I'm not so old I can't remember what it feels like to be desired for an afternoon romp. She's a wave that might be worth riding—just make sure you get off before she grinds you into the sand."

"Fran!" I was appalled. At her words or at my thoughts?

Donna called out, "Fran, what nonsense are you feeding that young woman?"

"Nothing you would approve of, sweetheart."

Donna and Meg laughed. I tried to glare at Fran but ended up with a half-disgruntled smile. I asked, "How long have you two been together?" I was thinking of the morning's reference to Donna's granddaughter.

"A splendid fifteen years. We met early but we had to wait for…"

She gazed fondly at their boat. I finished for her. "…a second wind."

She nodded and I felt privileged to share the emotion in her eyes. I would have liked to hear the details.

A few minutes later Donna settled herself next to Fran. She said, "Meg's gone to get out the cards. There will be tables of bridge and maybe pinochle. Cribbage boards, too. You play, Lexy?"

"My family and friends are mostly into poker. But I've pegged many a cribbage hand."

Fran slipped down to the bench, then accepted my hand to step onto the dock, saying, "I could teach you pinochle easy if you ever want." To Donna, "Going to check on Tiger. Be right back."

Donna said, "Have you gotten stowed away okay, Lexy?"

"Yes. And I can't believe how at ease I've become already. I've only been here twenty-four hours." I smiled at her. "Must be the people."

She smiled back. "You have impressed Meg in that short time. Don't know if she would say anything to you yet, but she's worried about what's going to happen to Charlie when she's done with the *Willow*." She moistened her lips. "Or it may be that she's worried about Charlie being able to continue living here if Steve manages to steal away this marina." She tilted her head back to watch the swoop and glide of an osprey. "Was Fran getting in your face about the siren, Lexy?"

I felt myself blush and hoped it would fade before she turned back to me. I knew quite well she wasn't talking about the yacht. I managed a weak laugh. "I don't mind friendly advice."

"I'm sure you are more than capable of making your own choices. It bothers Fran that Damaris Del Riego is such a mystery. Other than rare but polite exchanges, she keeps to herself. Comes here two or three times a year."

I permitted myself a glance at the *Siren Song* and was relieved not to see a figure at the rail. "Are there other people aboard?"

"An older woman. Never leaves the boat. Fran calls her 'the lady's maid.' The crew always leaves not long after she docks. Large crew, too. More than a boat that size requires. When we see one or two of them dribbling back, we know she'll sail soon."

We sat quietly watching the osprey until he plunged toward the lake, blocked from our view by the boats.

I asked, "What's it like living with someone, Donna?" When she didn't answer, I turned toward her. The lines crinkling about her light blue eyes emphasized their alertness. I tapped my heels against the wall and felt ridiculously young. I wondered if I made Charlie feel like that.

She responded with a question of her own. "Is there someone special, Lexy?"

I nodded. "We've known each other for only four months or so. But the first time I saw her my heart started beating a staccato drum. Never felt anything near that with anyone else. Don't ever want to."

Donna kept her eyes glued to mine. "But the subject of living together has come up. Side by side living without let-up. You adjusting to her. Her adjusting to you. Nowhere to run off to anymore. Absolute scary." I stared at her in amazement. She added, "It's not me who knows about that. It's Fran."

"Fran! I wouldn't think anything could scare her."

"Well, I did when I came knocking on her door. Her version is that

I scared all the hot pee out of her and she was dehydrated for a month. Didn't like it the first time I heard her say that. Later I realized it was her way of saying how important it all was. This woman important to you, Lexy?"

"Very." Fran was approaching us. Tentatively I asked, "Would you tell me about it sometime? Knocking on Fran's door."

She said softly, "I would like to."

Fran looked up and past us. I peered over my shoulder and saw Charlie coming around the office. She carried a shoebox under one arm and her expression was one of inner concentration. She didn't notice us until she hit the dock and turned left. Her features tightened even more and she said a weak "Hi." She started on by but then paused in front of Fran. "Doug says you'd like me to check out your galley. See if it can be made bigger."

Fran replied, "We want it done if it can be, but there wouldn't be any hurry on the work."

Donna explained. "My family is coming down at Christmas and will stay with us in Mossville. But we want to see to it that my granddaughter gets a lot of boat time. Maybe you could also check out some storage space we don't need and see if it could be turned into another berth area."

"I can check it out whenever you want."

Fran said, "Make it Thursday. We're going out on the lake most of the day tomorrow. Hope to come up with some speckled perch for Friday. Figured if we're willing to spend the day moving, we will. Bluegill, too."

Charlie spoke with authority. "You'll need crickets for the bluegill. I could collect you a jarful tonight."

Fran was exuberant. "That's a deal. We'll share the catch with you." She stuck out her hand.

Charlie shifted the box to her other arm to shake with Fran and I heard a solid thud as the contents shifted. As Fran and Donna continued to speak of their fishing plans, I watched Charlie go along the dock and then use her key to enter the A-house. Several people were climbing from their boats and I assumed the gathering for cards was beginning. I sauntered after Charlie.

Using my own key, I entered the A-house. There was a wall of washers and dryers, deep sinks, tables for folding, racks for hanging. Even two ironing boards. I heard the unmistakable clang of a metal locker door and followed the sound to a smaller room. I had been in dozens of locker rooms like it—two tiers of gray lockers all around and low, narrow benches on the floor.

I knew without checking that the other doorway led to the shower room. Everything was clean and the odors, though natural for those surroundings, were not unpleasant.

Charlie flinched as she pulled her key from a locker and turned to see me in the doorway. She no longer carried the box. Her behavior was one part guilty and two parts defiant. I sidled around that by talking about all the time I had spent in locker rooms, and the teams I had played on.

"You play a sport, Charlie?"

"Never got into any of that. Wasn't around school much."

I looked her up and down. "You've got the build for a soccer player. Especially if you throw in what I've seen and heard about your energy and stamina."

She brightened. "Really? There's a...a girl I met a couple of weeks back. Comes with a bunch of kids with windboards. She hung around the *Willow* one day and talked to me while I was putting in the new railings." She avoided looking directly at me. "She plays soccer for a high school team. Be a senior next year. Said she'd bring a ball next time and teach me how to dribble with my feet." She walked along playing with the handles of the lockers while I leaned in the doorway. "How do you know, Lexy?"

I knew what she was asking. "How do you know if someone's gay? There's no formula. And for all the jokes, there's no such thing as gaydar, either. Sometimes you just know—instant, unquestioning gut reaction. That's been done to me recently." I was thinking about Fran this morning. "Other times you find someone is gay you never thought could possibly be or assume someone is who isn't. And then there's missing out because both of you are so careful to hide that you block each other's signals. It's hard enough for anyone to discover the right people to flesh out a life, but it's harder for gay people. And it's harder when you're young—too young to have made contacts yet or learned about places you can go." Charlie was listening intently. "I believe you have to make the effort accepting the difficulty and braving the risks. When you lose, you lose. But, oh, when you win...I'm not talking just about finding someone to love. I'm talking friends, people to work with, play with, laugh and cry with. Every one of us is made up of lots of different appetites, Charlie. Takes all kinds of people to feed them." I pushed away from the doorway. "End of lecture. We got more work to do?"

"Not until I go out cricket hunting tonight. Thought I might read some." She led the way to the front door.

"Good. What do you think about that road out there for some jogging?"

"To the boat ramp and back would make a good jog. Watch out for guys passing you with empty boat trailers. They jump back and forth a little." She grinned. "Thought I'd get a little lecturing in, too." She jumped down to the dock and swaggered off.

Forty-five minutes later and four trips to the boat ramp and back, I stood panting and sweating outside the *Willow*. I called to Charlie who appeared quickly, pursing her lips at the sight of sand stuck to my legs and shoes.

"I know," I said between heaving breaths. "No sand on your boat. Going to shower off at the A-house. Could you toss me a pair of cut-offs, shirt, and underwear? Do I need a towel?"

"Nope," she said over her shoulder. "What you need is in the shower room." She returned with everything wrapped neatly in the shirt.

I stretched over to take the bundle. "Charlie, there are alligators out there. I heard them barking."

"Sure. The closer to the point you get, the more chance you'll see them. They don't bother the marinas. And there's miles of a great hammock out there with all sorts of critters. Cap and a bunch from the little towns around are keeping an eye on the State plans. They don't want any real roads cut through it. We'll rent dirt bikes at Treder's one day and I'll take you through some of it."

"Does that mean I'll get to wear my hiking boots?" I teased. She made a face and dropped back into the cabin.

At the A-house I held the door for two women leaving with laundry baskets of clean clothes. One said, "Thank you, Lexy." Did everyone know my name? A different, softly accented voice calling after me strummed through my mind. Resolutely I refused to listen to anyone's siren song.

No one else was around. In the shower room I found towels and washrags in a closet. I chose the shower unit next to the outside wall. In front of the stall itself was a tiny area containing a bench and hooks for clothes. I had brushed off what sand I could before entering the building. Now I stripped off the sweaty clothes and let them fall in a pile. First I ran the water hot, turning and letting it beat everywhere, even tilting my head back and letting water stream through my hair. Wet, the red would nearly flee my auburn hair. After soaping and rinsing, I slowly turned the knob to cold and rotated several times sucking in my breath.

I disliked drying in the small space but did the best I could. Hearing no sound but the air conditioner, I pushed open the metal door. My body already cold from the shower descended into deep freeze at the sight of Damaris Del Riego. She was clad in a clinging, light yellow jumpsuit but it was her eyes that immobilized me. They were so pale as to appear colorless, almost as though they were composed of light only. There was an actress with eyes like that. I couldn't recall her name. I was grappling for thoughts to escape the mesmerizing power of those eyes.

The towel I held before me shielded only a portion of my body from her view. She took two steps and slipped it from my hand before I could command my fingers to tighten. Those amazing eyes swept my frame pausing longest between my legs. "You definitely are a redhead. You'll find me more blonde than red. Turn. I'll dry your back."

I turned as though I were a puppet whose strings she controlled. I was acutely conscious of the pressure of her hands through the towel. I bit my lip to stifle a response as she lingered in the small of my back then so carefully dried the roundness of me. She draped the towel over my shoulders and shaped the wet hair at my neck with sensual fingers. I couldn't stop the shiver.

Her voice was molten gold. "You would enjoy watching the fireworks from the deck of the *Song*. And I've promised you wine. A fumé blanc, I think. Crisp and delectable." She withdrew her fingers. I don't know how long I stood there unmoving. When at last I turned, she was gone.

Back on the *Willow* I was glad to find Charlie deep in the mystery novel. Damaris Del Riego had rocked me. The why of that was bothering me much more.

A matter of her sexual aggressiveness? An unmined vein in me? Wren's flight to minister to a former lover? I gritted my teeth at the unfairness of that thought and caught Charlie watching me.

"I'm going to fix us some supper, Charlie."

"I'm not used to eating as much as I did for lunch, so..."

"Don't worry. It's going to be light." I concentrated on filling two paper plates with chunks of orange, honeydew and sprigs of grapes. When I opened the refrigerator, I was pleased to see that Charlie had selected the gouda and baby swiss from my apartment fridge. I wasn't so sure about something else. I said, "Nice of you to include some wine for me." I held up a single-serve bottle from the four-pack of chardonnay.

"That can't be for us?" She was careful not to sound defensive.

"How old are you?"

She snapped the book shut. "I drank beer plenty of times with Big Charley. And not for a buzz. Because it tasted good with pizza and hot chili. Bet you didn't wait till you were twenty-one."

I couldn't dispute that but I wasn't going to hang it out in the open. "I like beer now and then, too. Especially with hot garlic chicken wings. And I like wine with fruit and cheese. I'll split one of these with you. Fair compromise?" Something else I wouldn't be telling Robbie Exline.

"Yep." She swung her feet to the deck and brought up the table. I added cheese to the plates and poured the wine into small paper cups. I couldn't stop an image of the delicate goblets the siren would undoubtedly use, and nearly spilled one cup. Charlie's quickness and agile fingers saved it.

I waited until we were finished eating before I asked, "Who's Big Charley?"

She kept her eyes lowered for a long time. "He was a good friend. Died a few months ago. He was past eighty. He's the one who taught me how to fix things." She was holding herself very still, her eyes wide.

I knew there was grief behind her words.

She tended to the clearing up. When she resettled, she touched the book but then said, "I'll tell you about Big Charley if you want."

"I'd like that."

She seldom glanced at me as she talked. "I've lived different places. I don't know where when I was real little. Or who the people were. Somewhere along the line I knew that I wasn't family with any of them like their own kids were." She shrugged. "No one was mean to me. I just knew I didn't belong the same way. I didn't know what my name was. Just remember being drilled to say Charity Johnson before I was taken to school for the first time. That was in New Jersey. I didn't know what the word charity meant then. When I found out, I hated it."

Charlie was speaking without feeling but I felt a rush of anger. She kept talking. "After the fifth grade I was taken to Kentucky. Out in the country. People there called it a hollow. I was left with an old woman. At least she seemed old to me. She lived in a cabin. Didn't talk much. I had to work a lot but she worked, too. Took care of a garden, the cabin, helped her can stuff. She taught me how to weave baskets. I liked that. Sold them in roadside stalls set up to catch the tourists coming and going from Mammoth Cave." As though she knew I wanted to ask, she said, "Didn't go to school much. Had to catch a bus for a long ride. Just didn't do it all the time. Someone came around to check once but nothing happened. Widow Johnson, that's what people called her, she fell on the ice one winter. Broke her hip. Her son and his wife came up from Alabama and got her settled someplace. Took me back with them to Alabama, a trailer park on a lake way bigger than this one. And shaped uneven. There were big mounds of trees between fingers of water in lots of places. It was something." She was lost in her thoughts for a moment, then resumed, "Anyway, I was put in a trailer with her father, Charley. He was way in his seventies but he didn't seem old. Because he worked all the time, I guess, and laughed and talked. Sometimes I think people called him to fix things just because they liked being around him. And because he didn't charge as much as he could of. Boy, did he know boats…and the lake."

She ran her fingers through her loose curls, forehead to neck, and her voice brightened. "He started taking me everywhere right away. He didn't exactly teach me how to do things. He'd explain what he was doing while I watched, then let me do some. He said I must have Indian blood in me. That I was real in touch with the insides of things. One day he fixed a truck for a guy and wouldn't take any money. Knew the guy was short and there was a baby coming. The guy said, 'You're a big man, Charley.' He said, 'Sure. I'm Big Charley and this here's Little Charlie.' It stuck—and I liked it." She drilled me with a hard gaze. "I intend to keep it."

"I'd say it's a good choice." I meant it.

"I don't know about 'Johnson' though. It's not like it's a real name to me or anything."

"Oh—well, you could get Robbie Exline to help you change your name legally."

"I could? Really?"

"When you know what name goes with 'Charlie,' yes, you can."

She got up suddenly and took a glass jar from a compartment. "He died one day when we were working on a boat. Heart just stopped. They sold his trailer. I wasn't ever going to finish high school so I headed out. Came down here. I'm going to go get those crickets now."

And she was out of the cabin and gone. I thought about all the ground she hadn't covered. I contrasted what I had heard with my warm, safe, loving upbringing. I said fervently, "You're not going to have to head out again, Charlie."

The *Willow* rocked gently as though in agreement.

Seven

On the Fourth of July I awoke to darkness but my body clock said dawn was near. I knew without checking that Charlie was up and gone. She had all but tucked me in last night after I fell on my sleeping bag marginally exhausted from two days of strenuous activities. She guaranteed that I would sleep through her leaving before sunrise, explaining that she had the first two-hour shift of watching the weekenders and Fourth-of-Julyers put out into the lake. She, Cap, and Doug would take turns this morning relaying descriptions and registration numbers of potential problems to the Marine Patrol—overloaded boats, too few flotation devices, potential alcohol abuse. After she related some tragedies she and Big Charley had contended with on the lake in Alabama and events Doug had seen happen here at Lake Arrow, I understood her seriousness.

I stretched and immediately regretted it. My muscles and sinews had been markedly challenged these past two days. Wednesday morning I had labored in apprenticeship to Charlie as she removed the *Willow*'s windshield and deftly replaced it with a larger, wrap-around, tinted one. Also she outfitted the cockpit with an easily removed hardtop that would provide protection from rain or too much sun. I marveled at her skills and enjoyed the pride she took in her work. Meg had surprised us with plates of her shepherd's pie for our lunch, saying she knew we would be in need of real workmen's fare. Then we spent the early afternoon with Doug stringing bright yellow rope through metal stakes to mark safe parking areas near and beyond the boat ramp.

When I had expressed my yearning for a shower, Charlie had snorted and said, "Not yet, Long Legs. You're going to smell of fish soon. When I delivered the crickets this morning, I volunteered us to help with the catch."

And help I did. While Charlie, Fran, and Donna chopped, slivered, and cleaned, I had toted coolers and bags of crushed ice from a large refrigerated shed on the south side of the office building. Then I lugged the coolers filled with fish fillets packed in ice back to the shed where Meg was receiving a delivery of meat for Friday's cookout. When at last I got my shower, I was glad of Charlie's presence there as well. I had kept thoughts of Damaris Del Riego in abeyance all day, but in the A-house I was fearful of discovering her with each turn I made.

Thursday had begun in a milder fashion. Charlie and I breakfasted with Fran and Donna aboard the *Second Wind*—coffee, sour-cream pound cake with peaches. While Charlie and Fran went below to discuss modifications to the interior, Donna and I stayed out of the way on deck. Tiger dashed back and forth trying to keep an eye on all of us. When Damaris Del Riego had saluted me from the much higher deck of the *Song*, if Donna saw she didn't indicate it. Charlie, scrambling up from below, however, did see.

The next thing I knew I was swabbing the bench that ran the length of the main pier while Charlie scoured the tables and benches on the patio. After that we joined Cap and Doug in unloading folding chairs and tables from their trucks, and setting them up along with large and small grills. Tactfully Charlie guided Meg toward wiping table tops rather than lifting and carrying.

Meg had said under her breath to me, "Managing little shit." But the two-color eyes had shone with warmth and appreciation. The day ended with our cleaning the topside of the *Willow* until it gleamed in the sun. Now, even after a solid, long night's sleep, I felt the effects of all my labors.

Marilyn had been right. Discovering new people and a new way of life was exciting and rewarding. Life along the piers had muted my irritation over the lost vacation with Wren. And I would eventually go back to my job at the *Ledger*, my research and interviews, notebooks and computer filings, more refreshed and eager. Not to say that there weren't undercurrents of concern. There were the threats to Cap's Marina. There was so much yet to learn about Charlie. There was still the undeniable lure of the siren.

I got up, groaning aloud, flipped on a light, and saw clothes laid out on the wide end of the berths. A note atop them read, 'Meg will have coffee and donuts by eight.'

I grinned at the clothing selection—dark blue shorts, tank top of red and white pin stripes, and my blue cap with the eagle decal. Obviously Charlie intended for me to be dressed for the occasion.

Topside I admired our handiwork in the pewter gray of first light. A sudden thought rushed through me. Wouldn't it feel good to share a place with Wren and accomplish things to our satisfaction? A second thought ambushed me. What if we disagreed on what would be satisfying? I switched my attention to the sounds of vehicles and voices coming from the nearby service road and the higher county road. No wonder Charlie had gotten up so early. People were already arriving, towing a variety of watercraft.

I turned my head eastward again and gasped with delight. The pewter gray was streaked with pink golds and yellow whites. Viewed through the silhouettes of masts and ropes and birds in swirling flight, the dawn was other-worldly. Then it ceased and the morning arrived. The poet Robert Frost said it best: 'So dawn goes down to day/Nothing gold can stay.'

I groaned aloud again as I climbed from the boat to the pier. I decided to be at the office when Meg arrived to help with the breakfast setup.

I removed the umbrellas from the long box under the window and inserted them in the tables. Seated and gazing out over the boats, I spotted Tiger stretching his long, black form on the bow of the *Second Wind*. Charlie had taught me that section was also called the pulpit. Soon I heard the crunch of automobile tires in the gravel of the parking lot, and walked around the building.

Climbing out of her car, Meg, also attired in red, white, and blue, greeted me. "Charlie got you up and working already, Lexy?"

I shook my head. "No. Actually, she let me sleep in. Left a note about your breakfast offerings. Thought maybe you'd let me sneak an early bite if I helped."

"A hearty yes to all that." She popped the trunk lid. "I'll unlock and start the coffee. You bring in the goodies. You'll find them a lot lighter than all the running and fetching you've had to do lately."

She was on base about that. The trunk was filled with white bakery boxes and the smell was heavenly. I was in need of a rare sugar fix.

"And I've earned it," I said defiantly to a squirrel that had scurried near. After I had carried in all the boxes, I closed the trunk lid, noticing the license plate. It was white with gold numbers and, also in gold, the phrase 'Pearl Harbor Survivor.'

As I arranged boxes on the card tables, Meg filled a large, stainless-steel cylinder with water. When she told me it would take about twenty minutes for the coffee to perk, I took her up on the offer of a glass of milk with my choice of pastry. She sat at her desk and I perched on the wide window ledge. Rapidly I downed a sugared donut, then asked about her license plate.

She said, "Thank you, Lexy." I raised an eyebrow not understanding the comment. She lifted her head proudly. "Most people ask about it by assuming I married a much older man and it belonged to him. The truth is it's mine. I'm the Pearl Harbor survivor."

"That's a story I have to hear, Meg."

"I don't mind telling it. My mother's oldest sister had gone into nursing and never married—which was kind of a black-sheep thing in those days. I suppose it still is in some quarters." I nodded. "I was the only girl of seven siblings and Aunt Viola was really good to me. Not long after I turned fourteen, she talked my parents into letting me go with her to Hawaii for the first two weeks in December. She had been advanced into nursing administration at her hospital starting the first of the new year and was taking December as a vacation. I was ecstatic. I had never been more than fifty miles from home." She paused. "It was 1941."

I shivered. "You were really at Pearl Harbor when they bombed?"

Her face was solemn. "Yes. We had been to Webster Field the day before. The son of one of Aunt Viola's nurses was there and we delivered Christmas gifts to him. He showed us around. I still remember how proud he was of the planes, so flimsy and tiny by today's standards. Of course few, if any, survived the bombing. Neither did he. That war had a specific face to me from day one."

I thought of Uncle Kurt and a land mine. "Vietnam does for me."

"Then you understand." She stretched out her long legs so like mine and ran her fingers through a pile of paperclips. "Aunt Viola and I were having breakfast and planning the day when we heard the explosions. Of course we didn't know that's what they were. They were just sounds out of place. Eventually we went outside and saw flashes and smoke. I'll condense the details. We ended up in a large building. To this day I don't know what it was. Gymnasium, warehouse, I don't know. My aunt put me to work tearing up sheets people brought in for bandages and later I washed blood away from wounds." She spoke through tightened lips. "Mostly less serious cases were shunted our way, but I saw two people die." I considered the effect that would have on a young girl who had led a sheltered life.

Meg concluded with a wan smile. "My aunt and I had always been close. After that it was the closeness of equals." She got up to go check the color of the coffee bubbling in the clear tube. "So the first time I saw one of those Pearl Harbor Survivor tags, I trotted down to the Department of Motor Vehicles and got myself one. Wish they'd had them when Aunt Viola was still alive."

Before I could respond to the story, people began coming and going. Plates were added to the tables. I was quick to snatch a large slice of fresh pineapple from one. Pitchers of orange juice appeared. A vase of red, white, and blue flowers was placed on Meg's desk. Small groups clustered inside and out. I was greeted, introduced, absorbed, passed on. I pingponged between the roles of participant and observer.

My back to three men, I listened blatantly after I heard Steve MacKay's name.

One man was saying, "Had breakfast in the diner yesterday. MacKay's man Ed Pike was in there bragging. Said Steve had great plans for Cap's place here. That he was going to throw out all us regulars and just rent space to boats for group fishing and for ferrying people to Jacksonville to go out on the gambling ships."

Another man said, "No wonder Cap's got diesel smoke coming out his ears. Steve's the worst kind of backflow there is. Got to be hard on Cap trying to understand how he could produce a son like that."

The third man chimed in, "Then there's Doug. Just like his grandpap without sharing one drop of blood with him. Go figure."

At that point I was approached by a clearly yuppie couple. The man smiled broadly—to show off his capped teeth, I thought.

He said, "You Lexy?" At my acknowledgement, he handed me an envelope. "Meg said to give you Charlie's money for fixing our scooter. Tell her we appreciate it."

They wandered off hip to hip, her arm around his waist, his hand tucked into the back pocket of her shorts. The Olivers, I assumed. I folded the envelope and slipped it into a pocket.

Fran and Donna appeared. Donna carried a plate of sliced pound-cake and took it inside.

Fran said, "Isn't the breeze great? Just enough to cool and keep away the bugs. Fourth of July or not, I don't think it's going to be the usual scorcher."

I replied, "Just hope we don't get the usual afternoon storm. We've been free of them for three days…"

"And today is going to make it four. Four on the Fourth. Tiger says so."

I was skeptical. "Tiger forecasts the weather?"

"Right. All cats do. He didn't spend more than ten minutes grooming this morning. When a storm's coming, he stays at it. Something to do with increased electricity in the air. Disturbs their skin. Makes their fur prickle. Something."

"So will lots of boats here be heading out before long?" I asked.

"Nope. We make it pretty much an in-port day. We eat, drink, be lazy, be merry. The Fourth of July is a good day for the saner and safer to stay off the water."

Already I could see what she meant—the multiple sails and merging wakes of motorboats, the numerous water scooters and water skiers competing for space. Out of the corner of my eye I caught sight of Charlie strolling down the dock, having come either from the *Willow* or the A-house. From the clothes I had given her, she had selected the larger, bright red shorts which dropped just below her knees and an equally roomy white crewneck. She also wore the twin to my blue softball cap, but turned around.

Donna had joined us. "My, my. Isn't Charlie the height of teenage fashion. Why do they want to wear their britches baggy and their hats backwards?"

I laughed, "Probably for the same reason I wore those horrible bell bottoms and shell necklaces."

"For me," Fran said jovially, "it was my father's white dress shirt hanging out over blue jeans with a string tie. Miss Priss here was probably in an angora sweater being petted by the captain of the basketball team."

Whatever Donna was going to say in retaliation was halted by

Charlie appearing on one side and Meg on the other. I was reminded that I very much wanted to hear how she and Fran had gotten together. Other things were tickling my reporter's curiosity as well. What had Charlie done to receive jail time? Who was Doug if he wasn't Steve and Cap's blood kin? And what was the particularly bad blood between Steve and Meg? Something else?—I had it. Meg had mentioned both she and Cap losing their mates close together.

But someone had mentioned three deaths occurring near the same time. I reminded myself that I was on vacation and no one was paying me to poke my nose in other people's business.

Meg was urging Charlie to get some goodies and the rest of us to get cups of fresh coffee. With mock authority she added to Charlie, "And you see to it that you take the day off, young lady. There are more than enough old farts around to lend a hand in what needs doing. Got that?"

Charlie grinned and said meekly. "Yes ma'am."

Meg gripped my shoulder. "And that goes for you, too."

I imitated Charlie. "Yes ma'am."

Fran and Donna headed for the fresh coffee. I asked Meg, "Is there a phone anywhere with some privacy attached to it?"

Instead of answering, she called to Cap who had recently appeared and was moving from group to group on the patio and below on the planking. White shorts and shirt emphasized his deep tan. A red, white, and blue bandanna tied tight over his head pirate style matched his rakish grin.

He punched my arm lightly. "Hear Charlie has turned you into a real swabbie." He took both my hands in his and turned them palms up. "Don't see any bone yet."

Meg said, "Lexy needs a quiet place for a phone call, Cap."

"She can use mine. Trailer's unlocked."

"Thank you," I said. "It's long distance but I've got a phone card."

Cap squeezed my hands. "Take all the time you need. And don't eat too much the rest of the day. We fire up the grills around four."

I didn't hear Meg's next statement as I started away from them, aiming to go around the building rather than through, but I heard most of his deeper reply. "...count on it... not our last bang-up Fourth... Steve...be hanged..."

About to cross the ribbon of road, I saw Charlie and Doug seated on the tailgate of his truck, a heaping plate of pastries between them. Joseph Quintana stood to the side consuming his share. Seconds later I found the cool quiet of Cap's trailer soothing. Quickly I spied the phone and tried the motel first but was not surprised when told Miss Carlyle was not in. Again I had to prod myself into calling the hospital and Nancy Marshall's room.

Wren's voice was warm in greeting me but immediately she said something away from the receiver. "Sorry, Lexy. I had to check if Nancy was just rambling or if she was saying something consciously. Usually she gives my hand a tiny squeeze when her mind is clear, but not always."

"Are you staying the nights there, Wren?"

"Yes. But don't be concerned. They've brought in a comfortable lounge chair for me."

Our small talk was strained. Wren was distracted by Nancy and an ongoing conversation with the nurse so that she kept putting me on hold. I understood but it made me feel so separated from her, and lonely.

Abruptly Wren said, "Got to go. Nancy's respirator is acting up."

I stared at the receiver in my hand a long time before hanging up.

Outside I sat on the trailer steps and watched a bluejay teasing a feisty squirrel. I pulled down the bill of my cap and hugged my knees. I wished the Admiral were here to bully me out of feeling sorry for myself. There was a tug on my cap. I looked up half expecting to see Marilyn. It was Charlie.

"Something wrong, Lexy?"

"No. Just weighed down by all the donuts I ate." I could tell by her still face and unblinking, bright brown eyes that she wasn't buying that. She had given me a fair portion of honesty lately. I owed her some. "I just made a long-distance call to Wren. It didn't go very well. Not her fault. She's involved in something necessary and I've just got to wait till it's over." I bit into the side of my cheek, needing the pain, guiltily knowing it was Nancy Marshall's death I was waiting for. I reached up and pulled a curl that was bobbing in the gap between the cloth and the plastic band. "Know your hat's on backwards?"

Her answer was to turn it sideways, but a concerned expression lingered. I stood up on the bottom step towering over her. I waved toward where we had set up tables, chairs, and grills. "Won't traffic be a problem when people start crossing back and forth for their food?"

She shook her head. "Doug says most people know to stop using the road around the middle of the afternoon. Besides, he'll be putting signs where this road turns off the county road. They'll point people about a half mile further where Cap mowed solid ground for parking to see the fireworks. Joe's going to keep an eye on them. He has to go to work soon."

A small truck went by with sailboards in the back. A car following stopped and a girl jumped out, waving them on. She called after them, "I'll catch up with you later." She tossed a soccer ball in a high arc toward Charlie. Almost without thinking I jumped in front of Charlie and rocketed the ball back with a flick of my head.

"Wow!" the astonished girl exclaimed. "You play soccer."

"Not much. And not in a long time. And I'm probably going to have a headache for doing that." I ran my fingers through my hair.

Charlie avoided my eyes as she introduced us. "This is Karen...Lexy Hyatt. She's helping me with some of the work on the *Willow*."

Karen was fresh-faced pretty—olive skin, turned-up nose, long dark lashes protecting inquisitive coal-black eyes. Two loosely woven braids of black hair were crisscrossed with red, white, and blue yarn. She was of medium height and athletically firm. Her smile was confident and engaging.

Speedily I removed myself and returned to the office. Fran was leaning against Meg's desk. She nodded toward the window and said in a low voice, "Something going on there?"

"I don't know, Fran." I sighed. "I wouldn't want to be going through all that again."

Fran patted her unruly tufts and curls, scattering them even more. "Oh I don't know. I remember having a fine time. And I sure wouldn't mind my hair being as naturally black again as that kid's. Stupid to dye it, I know, but I'm not going to look in mirrors and see a gray-haired old lady. Donna's a good sport about it. Says she doesn't mind us being an individually salt-and-pepper pair." She added as I looked about for Donna. "She's off exchanging recipes. How about some cribbage?"

We sat outside shielded by an umbrella and cooled by a marvelous breeze, a scarred wooden cribbage board at our elbows. We played several games with Fran besting me by two. I followed her gaze back to the distant *Willow* at one point and saw Charlie apparently showing off our handiwork.

I kept turning my head to check on them until Fran fluttered the cards in my face and said, "Leave them be."

A while later she said, "Look at that."

The two girls were coming our way just passing below the A-house. Charlie was dribbling the soccer ball tentatively with her feet as Karen walked backwards giving her encouragement. When Charlie nearly lost the ball to the water, Karen dashed to catch it and brought it up skillfully to her hands. They laughed together. When they reached us, Charlie said, "If Meg needs to know, I'm going sailboarding."

As I gritted my teeth to keep from cautioning her to remember the crowded conditions and to be careful, Fran said, "I heard Meg give you the day off. You girls go have a good time."

Surprisingly, Charlie tapped my shoulder and replied to Fran, "Then you look after Long Legs here. She's in a mood to get in trouble."

I glared unbelievingly into Charlie's concentrated stare as Fran chuckled and said, "Will do."

As they took off around the office building, Karen was saying, "We'll dribble the ball to the boat ramp and I'll teach you how to pass."

Fran's eyes continued to express amusement, but her tone was soft and contemplative. "The kid's special. Meg isn't real open about it, but I can tell she's concerned about what's going happen to Charlie. I think she'd like to talk to that Admiral of yours, and that other woman you won't admit is a cop, about arranging something more permanent. She and her husband never had any children. She lives six blocks from us in Mossville in a pretty big house. Don't know if that's what she has in mind but I wouldn't be surprised. Maybe you could get the talk going." She drew her lips in and looked toward the *Siren Song*. "Charlie right?"

"Fran," I warned.

She responded, "Okay, okay. You stayed out of Charlie's business. Guess I'd better stay out of yours."

Eight

I spent the afternoon cocooned in the cabin of the *Willow*. It was the kind of self-imposed isolation that I required every so often. If Wren and I were to live together, would she truly understand that need? Would she tolerate it with good humor? Or would she try to change me?

I ran from those thoughts by immersing myself in Sharon McCrumb's *Zombies of the Gene Pool*. I'd read and enjoyed her mysteries featuring Elizabeth MacPherson and Nora Bonesteel, but I had only recently discovered her *Bimbos of the Death Sun* and *Zombies*, mysteries displaying a knowledge of the American roots of science fiction and the cults of fans that developed early on. I was enthralled by them because they were peppered with references to writers, novels, and stories whose names and titles I recognized because they were on the bookcase of favorite works left behind by my Uncle Kurt when he shipped out for Vietnam.

If Wren and I moved in together, perhaps the stability and permanence implied by that would prompt my mother to offer me that bookcase and its contents. If...if...if...

I don't know when all the pastry I had consumed and the gentle rocking of the boat manipulated me into an unexpected nap, but when I woke with a start, the book sliding from my chest, golden shafts of late afternoon sunlight were streaming through the starboard windows. I splashed cold water on my face, combed my hair, adjusted my clothes, and went on deck. A light scent of meat being grilled over charcoal embers drifted my way. It drew me unresistingly.

Several men and women were managing the picnic preparations. One or two were at each grill prodding and turning. Others were carrying and arranging. Plastic bowls of salads were worked deep into trays of crushed ice. One table was heaped with boxes of paper plates, napkins, plastic utensils, buns and rolls. Another was bright with mustard, catsup, olives, pickles, onions. And another was weighted with large containers of potato chips. Several tubs of chunk ice cooled cans of beer and soft drinks.

Meg said in response to my checking all around as I approached, "Charlie isn't here. They came off the water a while back. Dougie joined them and they put up a net across the road just past the boat ramp for volleyball." She turned her head back and forth stretching her neck. "Rode down there with Cap to watch them a bit. It was good to see Charlie having fun. Don't think there's been much of that in her life."

"Not from the little she's told me," I agreed.

"Lexy," Meg plucked at the collar of her red and white checked shirt. "I'd like to talk to you sometime about what's going to happen to her."

"How about letting me get to Marilyn and Robbie first. I'm pretty much in the dark still. Then maybe a group meeting would be a good idea."

Meg was pleased. "But we'll have to be careful. Don't think the girl would want us plotting her charts for her. I just want to be sure there are grab rails in her reach."

"I think several of us feel that way, Meg." I tilted back my head and sniffed. "Things are sure beginning to smell good. What can I do to help?"

"I told you the answer to that this morning. It still goes. It'll be a good half hour or more before we clang the dinner bell."

"Then I'm going for a walk to limber up my appetite." I had taken only a couple of steps when Cap called to me from where he stood over a grill, "Snag you a beer, Lexy."

Scooping one from the ice with an "Aye aye, Cap," I headed south, planning to walk to the entrance point of the service road and back. I was tempted to walk in the other direction but didn't want Charlie to think I was checking up on her. Nor did I wish, considering Karen, to embarrass her or make her feel awkward.

When I reached the county road, I saw the signs Charlie had mentioned directing traffic further north for the boat ramp and parking. But what should have been the most easily seen sign was face down in the sand. I picked it up, jamming it into the ground as firmly as possible, then headed back. I had finished my beer and crossed to the diner which was closed, to toss the can into the trash. I decided to sit a minute at one of the picnic tables under the metal roof. From there I had a good view of Steve MacKay's marina piers. I supposed the empty slips represented boats out on the lake. Most of the other boats appeared to be unoccupied. I guessed that there wasn't much of a live-in community there.

"Hey, Lexy." Joseph Quintana sat down opposite me. "You lost?"

"Hi, Joseph. I took a little hike to stay away from the food until everything's ready."

"That's where I'm heading as soon as I check the signs one more time. Ed Pike's dumped them twice already."

I held up my hand. "You can save yourself the trip. I found one down just now and put it back up."

His smile softened the strong lines of his handsome face. "Thanks. They should be safe from now on. I heard Steve tell Pike to stay in the office till after the fireworks. Something about some special boats coming in and needing those rental vans." He jerked his thumb over his shoulder toward the marina office where six vans were lined up in front. Then he asked soberly, "Have you seen Doug?"

"No, but I heard he was down by the boat ramp playing volleyball."

"Good. I was afraid he would go off somewhere by himself after the run-in with Steve." He answered the questioning tilt of my head. "I was out front with Steve when the vans were delivered, getting keys while he got the paperwork. Doug went by and Steve flagged him down. Got on him about the signs but Doug just waved him off and started to drive on. Steve yelled something about not drinking too much tonight and wrapping his truck around a tree. Doug hit the brakes and jumped out of his truck. I started moving right away because I could tell Steve was looking to pound him into the dirt. I got in between them but not before he clipped Doug one and cut his cheek with his ring."

"Did that make trouble for you?"

"Not really. Gave Steve a chance to call me interfering brown trash. Nothing new. He likes asking me what kind of raft I floated into the Keys on. Doesn't do any good telling him I was born right here. I want to last the summer if I can, but I won't be back after that." He stood up and looked out toward the lake. "A three-month's chunk of money for work is all I'm ever going to want from him."

We walked back to Cap's together. Joseph was hailed by Doug from where he and Charlie and a group of sun-drenched teenagers clustered under the stand of low oaks.

Meg motioned to me. "My legs are as long as yours, Lexy, but they don't move as well. How about trotting down there and telling those kids they're welcome to eat with us. Maybe suggest they hang back till us old folks get our first helpings."

When I got near the group, Karen called, "You should have come play volleyball, Lexy. Bet you could block balls real in-your-face style."

I demurred. "Never got into volleyball. Preferred a softball field. You guys are invited to the picnic." There were stirrings and exclamations of pleasure. "But..." I still knew how to adopt a teacher's warning intonation and they stilled. "It would be polite to start at the end of the line." Heads nodded their understanding. "And..." I waited until all eyes were on mine. "No beer. I'll be watching—" I accepted their good-natured grumbling and started back.

Charlie caught up to me. "Did that come from Meg, Long Legs?"

"About the food, yes. The beer warning comes from me."

She was looking wonderingly at Meg standing with Fran over a grill.

She finger combed her short curls tightened by a day of water and sweat. "I won't let them mess up."

I squeezed her neck. "Hey, you don't have to take everything on your shoulders, Charlie. I'll do the watching like I said." I looked back toward the young people. "I like Karen. Gut instinct."

She ducked her head, then lifted her small, sharp face and said boldly, "So do I."

We grinned and went our own ways.

People filled their plates and scattered to various perches, some to the tables and chairs in the small parking area outside the office, others to the patio, the ledge, and the bench along the pier. Apparently there was some sort of unofficial rotation in the continued grilling and replacement of food. I took a seat on the steps of Cap's trailer where I could keep the tubs of beer in sight. Fran and Donna joined me. Cap and Meg and another man sat at a card table not too far from us. We watched the kids troop through heaping their plates. A couple of boys made fake swipes into the tubs of beer while grinning at me. Before getting her food, Charlie spoke with Meg. I was certain she was thanking her.

When I got up for seconds, I glanced at the sky over the lake now beginning to dim. Then I looked where a man ahead of me in line was pointing out the barge getting in position for the fireworks display scheduled for around nine-thirty.

I heard him say, "No moon tonight. And no clouds. Should be quite a show."

The woman next to him waved a hand toward the west. "Not a bad show going on there right now."

It was the kind of Florida sunset that always made me think of the aftermath of a battle—all dusky colors trying to stay separate but slowly bleeding into each other.

For a long time I ate and talked and laughed. I enjoyed being part of the unique camaraderie. I couldn't believe anyone would want to destroy such a community. Then in the weak light of dusk there was a flurry of movement.

As though a drill in which everyone knew his part, the entire area was rapidly cleaned and straightened. I was pleased to see the kids pitch in. Karen joined me in turning a long table on its side, folding the legs, and carrying it to stack with others.

Before releasing it, she said tentatively, "I don't really know you well enough to ask a favor, Lexy, but—"

"Try me, Karen."

"Okay. I've been attending a soccer day-camp outside Sanford. Sunday, late afternoon and early evening, we're going to have a mini-tournament of short games to kind of close things out. I asked Charlie to come watch. She wouldn't say yes or no. I think it might be because she doesn't want to ask anybody to bring her." Her voice trailed off and she sucked at her lip.

"I'll look into it," I said. "I know the area. Where are you going to be? The city park field or the old Sharks stadium?"

"The stadium field." We heaved the table against the others. "Thanks," she said brightly. "You're okay, like Charlie says." She dashed off.

I joined Fran and Meg who were fishing in icy water for the last cans. I was jolted by a sudden surge of rebellion rushing through me. "Damn those kids! They're making me feel like a den mother. The Admiral was plotting all along for me to link with Charlie like a big sister. Or worse yet, like an aunt. And Wren wants to set up housekeeping. I'm not ready to be a settled old woman!"

I was the one stunned by my outburst. Meg and Fran merely smiled tolerantly.

Meg said, "You're light years away from being old. Just turning a little corner is all. And you've been doing that probably since you started school. That's what life is, Lexy."

Fran put an arm around my shoulders. "She's right. The trick is to remember that you're turning those corners going on to something new. Something worth the movement."

Half disgruntled, half ashamed, I said, "But why does that movement have to include getting older?"

They both laughed. Fran squeezed my shoulder. "The fact that you say that means you aren't anywhere near being old yet. It's you young ones who fight the tick-tock of years so hard. Kids like Charlie and old-age pros like Meg and Donna and me don't give it a thought." She caught my line of sight. "No cracks about me dyeing my hair. That's vanity, not denial of age."

I had been nudged back into good humor, but a neon streak of discomfort continued to flash in a corner of my mind. I was embarrassed by my small tantrum—and relieved that no one seemed to be making anything of it. Everyone was scattering to secure viewing places for the fireworks. I hung back and stood in the middle of the road observing the first clear stars. I knew the blue-white twinkle in the southwest was Spica, part of the constellation Virgo. The steady reddish-orange glow above and to the right of it was angry Mars. I would have liked to believe Wren was looking up at the same sight.

I knew she wasn't. She would be hovering over Nancy Marshall. I tried to feel nothing.

The patio and pier below the office were filled with people. Meg had doused the usual night lights. I could see shapes settling on the decks of boats where lights had also been extinguished. I walked along the ledge toward the A-house and an empty bench I saw near there. Before I could sit down, the door of the A-house opened and I recognized the small stature of Doug MacKay. He had changed from swim trunks to jeans and a dark sweatshirt. He turned to lock the door without seeing me, then hurried around the corner of the building. From near the *Willow* the high-pitched laughter and chatter of the kids punctuated the evening.

I jerked my head toward the lake as the first rockets whistled skyward. A trio of red, white, and blue chrysanthemums blossomed against the darkness. People cheered and clapped. A barrage of white meteor showers and spirals followed, accompanied by staccato explosions like gunfire. In the fading glow, I saw a figure on the deck of the *Song* facing away from the fireworks display. It could only be Damaris Del Riego. My mouth went dry and I breathed more deeply.

In rapid succession, four more rockets whistled and exploded into strands of green falling down the sky like the wispy tendrils of weeping willows. They seemed to last forever and I saw something cascade down the side of the yacht. I knew it was a boarding ladder.

Unwilling to acknowledge my intent, I touched the shoulders of figures seated on the steps below the A-house and picked my way through them. Then I used the brightness of the steady bombardment of brilliant colors to make my way down the long middle pier until the *Song* loomed above me. Awkwardly I climbed the ladder.

When I achieved the deck, a lush voice from the shadows said, "Pull it up. Close the gate." I saw what was meant and did so.

I followed her to the port side where we leaned on the railing, our heads back, enjoying the blooming, streaking, revolving medleys of vivid colors. I glanced her way and watched the play of amber, rose, tangerine, silver on the long line of her taut throat. I felt her awareness of my desire to place my hand over that narrow ridge—and tore my eyes away. I concentrated on trying to connect the chaotic scattering of tiny boat lights over the dark waters of the lake into a semblance of star constellations.

I lost that concentration at the touch of her hand in the small of my back. I don't know who moved first, only that her body was molded to mine and I knew she was naked under the delicate wrap. As she gripped my head with both her hands and hungrily consumed my mouth, a tiny portion of my brain was glad that the on-deck cabin shielded us from the view of the marina community.

My hands lifted the flimsy material and I spread my long fingers over the sweet roundness of her. I pressed against the arch of her pelvis and was rewarded with a gasp that became a moan emptying into my own hungry mouth.

We drew back slightly, each of us breathing deeply. The bursting, blazing pyrotechnics went unnoticed. The popping volleys and booming cannonades no longer reached our ears. She tugged my tank top from my shorts and expertly unhooked my strapless bra. She folded it into the pocket of her robe. I tried to resist the command in those strange eyes, then closed my own and lifted my shirt over my head. I kept my eyes closed and bit back a cry as she stroked the upper fullness of my breasts before cupping them and pressing her thumbs against the hardened nipples.

I opened my eyes and discovered that Damaris Del Riego was a complete siren. She had loosened her robe and the diaphanous material was floating behind her in the strengthening breeze. She shrugged out of it in a graceful movement and it went skimming down the deck. Her hands were on my shoulders. Boldly I cupped her mound and worked my middle finger between the silken lips. In a rare moment of silence, I heard her sigh of pleasure. A small side-step brought her back to the railing. She spread her arms and gripped the steel vibrating with the reflection of exploding colors.

I removed my hand and peeled down my remaining clothes, kicking them back toward the cabin wall. My hands on her hips, I helped her lift her lower body to twine her legs about my hips. I kept my hands in place as I ground against her and sucked as much of a smooth breast as possible into my hot mouth. I'd have taken it all if I could. I achieved a rhythm of grind and thrust that brought long, kittenlike mewing from her. I felt more than heard the sounds as I brought my mouth to the hollow of her throat. I put my arms around her back to better brace her. She used my support to tighten her legs about me.

I was excited by the wetness of her. I increased the force of my movements and soon sensed the lifting within her toward climax. Trailing my mouth to a breast, I twirled my tongue about the nipple as rapidly as I was now rotating below. I strained to keep her from falling as she quaked with raw passion, releasing the rail to pierce the thin flesh of my shoulders with her nails.

Her thighs slid down mine and I pulled her upper body to me. She nestled into me, shivering, but I knew it had nothing to do with the breeze from the water or the thundering, brilliant finale above us. Her head was on my chest, her hair tickling my nose as I rubbed my face in it. We stood breathing against each other until there was only darkness and the smell of smoke lingering in the air above the lake. I felt her gather herself to step from my arms.

She took a hand and walked me toward the cabin wall where she drew me down onto an air mattress. Though the official fireworks had concluded, I heard sporadic firings from boats and along the shoreline.

My voice was a croaking whisper. "You were very sure of me."

Hers was a musical rustling. "I was very hopeful."

She stretched at my side as I lay on my back, one knee drawn up. She traced a finger down the center of my face, my throat, between my breasts, to the throbbing core of me.

Teasing in my hair, she said, "I've thought often about this glowing bush since I saw you in the shower, but I had no idea there would be so much fire-driven power." She swiveled and settled lightly on my chest, but her knees and legs pinned my arms against my sides with surprising strength.

I couldn't stop my needful cry as her arms cradled my thighs and drew them further apart. I felt her breasts on my abdomen and then she was blowing warm air along the wet crevice. I felt completely helpless, deliciously open to her. Voluntarily I drew my knees higher and spread myself even more. With a small triumphant laugh she parted the long line of my nether lips with the tip of her tongue, then began stroking deeper and deeper with torturous slowness. I couldn't control my shuddering or my blatant, raspy pleas.

Then there was the warm air again and my low moans at every exhalation. When I felt her mouth isolating the pulsating bud of flesh, I drew in my lips and bit down on them. But even that failed to stop my moans. Her tongue flicked at the bud from all sides, then began a circular motion that I thought would drive me to scream. Deep in the darkness of me the turbulence began.

It rocketed from all points within me, converging in the tiny morsel now being sucked between the lips of this mortal siren. My body became the night sky driven into light by the escalating splendor of sensation.

It was long after midnight when I stood on the pier with my back to the *Song,* and heard the scrape of the ladder going up against the side and the clink of the railing gate latching closed. The only other sound was the lapping of water. My blood still throbbed in my veins and my mouth tasted of wine—and of Damaris Del Riego. When exhausted and satiated beyond renewal, we had sat in deck chairs wrapped in terry cloth sipping wine. We said little. Her longest speech was the words she had just said to me. "That was the best I've ever had, Lexy. But it won't happen again. I won't deviate from a course I've charted—and I smell another woman. She'll be wanting you back. I would."

I began walking away. I didn't look back, for I knew she wouldn't be at the railing. We were done.

I approached the *Willow* hoping I could board without waking Charlie and uneasy about whether or not I would have to explain my absence. That hope was shattered at the sight of her in the aft seating. Surprisingly she offered me a steadying hand. My breasts bobbed hard as I landed on deck. I had bypassed chasing down the delicate robe containing my bra in a pocket. A trophy for the siren, perhaps.

It was too dark to read expressions and the blankness of Charlie's voice gave me no clue to her real thoughts as she asked, "Will you be going back?" She was facing toward the *Song*.

"No. It was a one-time thing."

"Do you have a lot of those?"

"Few and far between." I stepped around her and sat with my back to the yacht. "I don't know if it's a character flaw or a genetic defect." I was trying for a modicum of lightness.

She remained standing. "Will you tell her?"

I stayed silent a long while, then said, "I'm not refusing to answer you, Charlie. I don't know the answer yet. I'm kind of in limbo right now. And I'm a little scared about what's going to hit me at the light of day."

We both jumped as more random fireworks popped and cracked

and sizzled.

Charlie turned toward the hatchway. Her voice was gruffly humorous. "I don't know what will or should hit you, Long Legs, but the first thing you better hit tomorrow morning is the shower. I don't want Meg or Fran or Donna catching a whiff of you. Or of the Piranha."

I trotted after her down to the cabin feeling every bit the wayward kitten who had been seized by the scruff of its neck and given a good hard shake.

Nine

Mumbling and stretching, I came up slowly out of a heavy sleep. The intensity of the sex topped off with wine had produced the nearest I ever wanted to experience to a drugged stupor. Charlie was gone, I was still in my clothes, and the brightness of sunlight stabbing through the portside windows told me it was at least three hours past dawn. I had a date with a shower. I scooped up clean clothes and headed for the A-house, happy to see little movement about the marina though Meg's car was outside the office.

I was relieved to find the A-house empty. There was such a silence everywhere that I closed the door quietly. I wasn't prepared for the sight of Charlie at her locker and dropped my sandals with a clatter on the tiled floor. She looked me up and down shaking her head critically. I bent to retrieve my sandals and felt the imprint of the Olivers' envelope in my pocket. I had forgotten all about it. Good thing I hadn't lost it aboard the *Song*. Guiltily I handed it toward her. "Your money for fixing the Olivers' boat."

She gave me a weak 'thank you' and turned back to her locker. She pushed at the shoe box I had seen her carrying the other day to get behind it. Pulling out a small leather pouch made the box tumble to the floor despite her efforts to catch it. The top popped off. Even though the box was empty, Charlie stared at it open-mouthed. In a flash she was pawing the contents of the top shelf—even checked the bottom. Then she tossed me her key, bleated, "Close that up for me," and was gone.

I put the money in the pouch as she seemed to have intended, straightened things semi-neat, closed and locked the door. I had no idea what was going on.

I adjusted the shower nozzle to as hot as I could stand and soaped myself from crown to big toe. I wasn't trying to scrub away Damaris Del Riego. She bore no blame for my infidelity to Wren. I was attacking my exterior so vigorously to keep from searching my interior. I wasn't ready to confront motives, fears, decision-making…

I left my dirty clothes in my otherwise empty locker, deciding to do a load of wash later. Leaving the A-house, clean and acceptably aromatic, I found I could gaze at the *Song* with no feelings whatsoever.

Instead of descending to the pier, I strolled toward where Meg was standing at the rear of her car. I saw her toss a bundle in the trunk and slam it down muttering to herself. I heard the tail end "too old for this."

Meg straightened taller and flexed her back. Squinting into the sun, she greeted me with a lopsided smile. "Morning, Lexy. Come and enjoy the quiet with me over a cup of coffee. I held back some of Donna's pound cake."

"No arm twisting needed. I'm famished."

Meg arched a prickly gray eyebrow. "After all the food I saw you down before the fireworks!"

I hoped the flush I felt spreading over my cheeks wasn't visible through the tan I had been acquiring. I could hardly explain what I had done during those fireworks to activate my appetite all over again.

"It's all the trying to keep up with Charlie," I said limply. "Have you seen her?" I was still wondering about her sudden panic.

"Went by here a little while ago toward the work dock. Figured she was looking to team up with Dougie to go scoop out what fireworks debris they can. Other stuff, too. Some of the holiday boaters aren't very considerate."

Before we could move toward the office, Cap left his trailer and crossed to join us. He looked tired and sleep-deprived, but he made a strong effort to put a spring in his voice. "Well, another Fourth of July behind us, Meg."

"And safely, too. I hope it was that way all down the lake." Her tone and smile for Cap were tinged with sadness. He nodded once and touched her shoulder. Something private had just passed between them.

We all three lifted our heads at the sound of a siren approaching from the south. Soon a county green-and-white sped by. A moment more and the siren ceased its piercing wail instead of trailing away. Cap frowned. "Maybe we spoke too soon. Think they've stopped somewhere near the boat ramp. I'm going to steer that way." He took hard, hurried strides and his shaggy white hair jounced with each step.

Meg suggested, "Why don't you drive down?"

"I got a little deep in a bottle of rye whiskey last night. Need to sweat it out," he called back.

Meg watched after him concernedly. "He hid it very well during the picnic but we were mighty upset with how Steve marked up Dougie. When he disappeared after the clean-up, I..." She was interrupted by a car pulling in next to us. Her accent became more pronounced. "Well, Lexy, looks like you and Charlie have company. Invite them back to the patio for coffee if you want." She looked Cap's way one more time, then made for the office door.

Marilyn slammed her car door and boomed, "You less a landlubber after five days, kid?"

I replied rapidly, "I'm a whiz with a tack rag. I can worm and parcel a rope fast as Charlie. I know how to check a clove hitch for looseness. And I've learned to sleep on that oversized waterbed." Before she could bark fire, I added, "The *Willow* and I have become mates, Admiral." I smiled at Robbie who had opened her door but was still seated. "With Charlie, too. Hey, Robbie."

Her dark eyes flashed as she got out and said, "A deputy passed us going all out. We were afraid he was heading here."

"Nope. Went on down a ways. Meg's got coffee—unless you want to go to the *Willow* and wait for me to make some."

"Coffee now," Marilyn commanded.

We tagged after her to the patio, Robbie asking, "Charlie around?"

"Out on the water, I think. Can we do some talking?" I asked, and got a brisk affirmative nod.

In no time we were enjoying strong coffee and tasty pound cake with Meg who identified the baker of the cake. I pointed out Tiger doing his morning stretch and strut. I suggested that Marilyn might like to get the story of the cat's name from the ladies themselves. She rubbed her thumb along the back of her rings and I knew she had caught the emphasis in my tone. I ducked my head and picked at crumbs as Meg described Charlie's bo's'n manner of ordering me around. I could tell that both Marilyn and Robbie were pleased by Meg's tone and comments on Charlie's work ethic and behavior.

The office phone rang and Meg got up to start her workday. Marilyn said she would go check out the *Second Wind* and talk sailing—or what have you.

I wasted no time. "I want the background on Charlie, Detective Exline. Don't put me off."

"Okay, Miss Long Legs. I'll give you the pre-Florida first. There's not much. Charlie was a passed-around kid."

I leaned my arms on the table. "What does that mean?"

"Just that. At some point when she was too young to have any lasting images, her parents—or mother, or father, or grandparents—passed her to somebody willing to take her. For whoever knows what reasons—money, health, irresponsibility. Eventually they passed her along to someone else."

I said, "She told me a little of that but I assumed there would be some kind of family connection."

Robbie grunted. "Ah, Lexy. You've told me about your family—real 'all-American.' I'm classed with the single-parent group but my mother did all right by me—I had a mom, a real caring mom. Neither of us can really know what millions of kids go through as unwanted or abused foster kids. At least Charlie seems to have been one of the lucky ones." She reacted to my disbelieving expression. "That's right. Lucky. According to the psychologist at the Detention Center, Charlie doesn't appear to have been abused—physically or sexually. She was fed and clothed and sent to school some."

"So after Big Charley died, she really didn't belong anywhere. Didn't have any place to be." I was mostly musing aloud.

"Sounds like you know some things I don't," Robbie commented.

I didn't want to divulge any of Charlie's confidences. "Not important right now. I want to know about her problems with the law. Why was she in jail? I have nothing on that."

Robbie shifted to look out over the marina as she talked. "She was arrested for being a vagrant and stealing. She hit Orlando at the wrong time. You know the push by the City Council and all the other powers-that-be to get tough on vagrants. Send a message before the fall and winter hordes hit us."

"But she's a worker. She won't even ask for anything. I don't believe she'd steal something."

"She tried to work. Got some odd jobs for cash. But a real job takes papers. So does a place to live."

"I'm lost."

She explained. "Charlie doesn't exist on paper. No birth certificate. No driver's license. No Social Security number. Nothing. Doesn't know her real name. Doesn't have a birthdate. Doesn't know her exact age. Says she's eighteen. How many pieces of identification do you have in your wallet? In your car? At home? Charlie has zippo."

I was beginning to understand.

Robbie went on, "She was sleeping under overpasses, prying her way into empty boarded-up buildings. Took up with an old couple in Azalea Park who shared with her. When the food ran out she decided to take some from a supermarket. Figured they could absorb the loss without being hurt. To be honest with you, Lexy, I don't think she'd have stolen just for herself."

"Are you telling me she got jail time for a few groceries?"

Robbie sighed. "There's a little more to it than that. The manager spotted her going out the door with two plastic sacks full. He yelled and she ran. A patrol car just happened to be cutting through the lot. The cop hit his siren and started after her. All the noise and commotion scared a little kid waiting for his mother to open the car door and he started running. Charlie saw him and was afraid he was going to run out from the parked cars and get hit, so she dropped one sack and scooped him up. The uniform yanked the kid away and accused Charlie of trying to use him as a shield." Robbie paused. "That made her mad and she slugged him with the other sack—which had canned goods in it. Vagrancy, theft, resisting arrest, assaulting a police officer."

"Come on, Robbie!" I was angry.

"I know. And I think the judge did, too. The original sentence was three months to be followed by nine months probation. He was giving her a chance to regroup. I heard about her when I had to go to the Detention Center a few times to question some women and saw her in action. Checked with the psychologist that the judge had ordered for a follow-up. Told Marilyn about her. The psychologist and I started the ball rolling and got her out early. The judge was willing to shuffle the paperwork and let me act as probation officer." She grinned slyly. "Might even find a way to get her record expunged at the end of probation. Make a case that she might actually be a juvenile. She's doing well here, isn't she?"

"More than that. You need to get with Meg. I think she'd like to be in on getting Charlie more permanently settled."

Before Robbie could reply, we both turned our attention to the sound of another siren. Robbie got up and went to the corner of the building. Returning she said, "That was a crime-scene van and an ambulance. What's down that way?"

"A boat ramp Cap maintains for public use," I answered. "You're pawing the ground like an old fire horse, Robbie. Aren't you off duty? And out of your jurisdiction?"

"Just curious," she said defensively. "Hey, there's Charlie." She gave a wave toward the work dock.

When she reached us, Charlie's smile for Roberta was warm. She wore goggles pushed up to her wet hair, and there was the outline of a wet bathing suit under her oversized T-shirt.

Robbie said, "I hear you know how to put this one to work." She swatted at my shoulder.

"Part of the time." Charlie's voice was light with contrived innocence. "She manages to slip anchor, though."

I gave us both points for not glancing at the *Song*, and Marilyn coming up the finger pier from her visit to the *Second Wind* saved me from struggling with a reply.

She called to Charlie, "Ahoy, First Mate. Let's go check out the *Willow*." She had reached the ledge and Charlie vaulted down next to her. "Trim vessel back there. Nice women. They're coming to dinner at The Cat Tuesday," she said in my direction. Then said to Charlie whose spare, small frame held its own against her more solid bulk, "Has this redhead been keeping a neat berth?"

"Yep. Except for the sleeping bag she keeps in it."

There was laughter all around and for the second time that morning I felt myself flushing. We all turned at the crunch of car wheels on gravel. The green-and-white squad car had pulled in next to Marilyn's sedan. Cap and a uniformed officer got out. There was a whiteness in the wrinkles about Cap's eyes and mouth and a warning in the look he gave Meg who was just opening the office door.

"What's going on?" she asked uneasily. Marilyn and Charlie came up the steps.

The trooper touched the wide brim of his hat and introduced himself. His eyes darting from face to face, he said, "A fisherman bumped into a body. Mr. MacKay identified it as his son Stephen." Only Meg made a sound. He continued, "I realize there was a lot going on here yesterday and last night—at both marinas. We'll need to check with a lot of people to determine the young Mr. MacKay's movements."

I saw Charlie jerk and realized she thought he was referring to Doug.

Meg spoke up, to direct attention away from Charlie I thought. "I didn't see Steve yesterday but I talked with him on the phone just before the fireworks."

The trooper requested the use of the office for interviews and ushered Meg back into it. Robbie went over to sit with Marilyn and Charlie. Cap sat down with me. There was none of the jaunty seadog about him any longer.

"What do you know, Cap?" I asked.

"Not much. They just let me get a quick look to see if I could identify him." He picked at his teeth with a thumbnail. "Didn't expect to see Steve. Can't imagine him drowning. The fisherman told me that Steve's chest looked chewed some. Fish maybe." I shuddered as Cap continued. "They've got the Marine Patrol checking the lake for empty boats and talking to all-nighters." He raised his bushy white brows. "Lexy, they bagged a cap. Had an eagle on it. Like the one you were wearing yesterday. And Charlie."

I had no idea where mine had gotten to. I could have put it down anywhere. The last time I was sure of having it on was when I sat outside the diner talking to Joseph Quintana. I had tugged it down to shield my eyes from the setting sun.

Cap was still talking. "That trooper's wondering about me. Nothing I can do about it. No way I could explain how I could look at my dead son with so little feeling. Don't guess you could understand either."

I kept my voice low. "I saw Steve in action a couple of times, Cap. Once with Doug and once with Charlie. Didn't like what I saw either time. Are you afraid the police think it's more than a simple drowning?"

"Aye. They're bagging things. Put up that yellow tape." He nodded toward the office. "Asking questions. Meg will sail a smooth course with it. Not so sure about Doug. Wish I could talk to him first."

Marilyn came over and put a hand on my shoulder. "Just like Robbie's off duty and away from her own digs, so are you. Right?" She waited till Cap crossed over to speak with Charlie. "Charlie's been filling us in a little. Sounds like there could be some trouble. And she's real jittery. You know why?"

"She's had some run-ins with Steve." I hastened to add emphatically, "Not her fault."

The trooper dealt with the rest of us quickly. I was able to answer his questions honestly without having to reveal my observations of Steve MacKay's mean nature or recount the information I had collected concerning the inter-marina conflict. When he learned I was a *Ledger* reporter, he mildly cautioned me that nothing was being officially released yet. Somehow Robbie managed to wangle professional courtesy and was permitted to sit in on Charlie's interview. She told me that the trooper picked up on Charlie's contentiousness but may have blamed it on her recent arrest and probation rather than problems with Steve at the marina. After asking us not to stray too far, the trooper began canvassing up and down the piers. Marilyn and Charlie went to the *Willow* while Robbie joined Meg in the office.

As soon as the trooper shifted to the neighboring pier, Fran motioned me to come their way. I went below, having to bend my head until seated. The cabin was smaller than that of the *Willow* but homey. I had to give Tiger his share of attention as we talked and got the rumbling purr as payment.

"That cop had picked up a lot about the troubles between Cap and Steve before he got to us. People do like to share," Fran said with a grimace. "He's thinking murder, I bet, and I can't blame him."

"Why?" I asked immediately.

Donna answered. "Because Steve never went out on the water much. Except on those fancy power boats he used to ferry gamblers to and from

Jacksonville. And he never fished. He liked to brag about being a powerful swimmer, though. He was always telling about having to go in and out of the water one night to pick up people from a boat collision. The time I heard it, I saw those light spots in Meg's eyes go red hot. I thought she was going to bore absolute holes through him."

"It's their getting to Doug that I'm worried about," Fran interjected. "Cap's worried about that too."

I said, "I suppose they'll hear about the confrontation yesterday."

Fran leaned forward, gripping her bony knees. "You heard about that, too? George Treder saw it. He was the guy sitting with Cap and Meg last night. He owns that marine supply place just off the county road. He told them the Quinn boy stopped it right off, but not before Steve smacked Doug one in the face. We saw the proof of that. You know any more about it?"

I shook my head. "No. Joseph is the one who told me that much. Doug must have shaken it off, though. He went to play volleyball with the kids. He and Joseph stayed with them for the picnic."

"And the fireworks," Donna added.

I didn't correct her as I recalled a dark-clad Doug going around the A-house just as the fireworks started.

Fran said in a sugary tone, "Speaking of fireworks..."

"Fran..." Donna warned sharply.

Fran's voice oozed false meekness. "I was just going to ask if she enjoyed them."

I smothered my face in Tiger's warm body. I could feel the vibrating purr and was overwhelmed by a need for Wren, a desire to lay my cheek against the throb in her throat after I had satisfied her.

Donna touched my hair with a motherly gesture. "You're among friends, Lexy."

"I know, but it's Cap and Doug and Meg who are going to need friends, I'm afraid."

"And Charlie." Fran said softly. Her eyes said she'd wait for now, but would get back to the subject of me later.

Ten

When the Marine Patrol first brought Doug in off the lake, he was whisked into the office by the trooper and a detective before either Meg or Cap could speak with him. His paleness when he came out emphasized the blood-encrusted scratch on his cheek.

He then came over to where Cap and I stood together on the pier, and talked openly in front of me to his grandfather. The officers had told him of a death near the boat ramp and asked if he would volunteer information about his activities the evening and night before, in case he had been in a place to see something pertinent. He had told them about playing volleyball near the ramp, eating, then watching fireworks with the group of teenagers. He had explained about going out to the barge later with Joe Quinn to deliver food and drinks to the crew who had handled the display. After that he had dropped Joe off at the other marina to get his motorcycle while he had gone home to his grandfather's trailer.

At that point he was told that the victim was his father and was carefully warned that he didn't have to answer questions about his relationship with his father or the fight that had inflicted the mark on his face. He said to Cap, "The detective kept looking in a little notebook like he had stuff on me and my…Steve. Made me feel like he was hoping to trip me up. Told him I thought I'd better talk with you, Cap. Was that okay?"

Cap put his arm around Doug's shoulders and said, "Aye, mate. We're going to weather this storm. I wish I hadn't crawled in that bottle last night. Won't be doing that again." He looked at me and explained. "It's holiday times that hit me the hardest about Mary being gone. She always made them special. Meg understands. I should have stuck with her during the fireworks."

His voice was dull with sadness. "Should have gone to bed afterwards." He tried to lighten his tone. "Sometimes I'm just an ornery old seadog."

They walked away as I stood reflecting on Doug's omission of a stop at the A-house and a change of clothes. Harmlessly explained, I knew, except for my feeling that in rounding the corner of the building he had not been planning to end up down by the *Willow* where the teenagers were already clustered to watch the fireworks. My fingers itched for my own notebook and recordkeeping even as I considered Marilyn's admonition to curb my snooping urge—to remember that I was on vacation and away from my home territory.

But you are wrong, Admiral, I thought. You sent me here to join this community, to bond with the *Willow*, to reach out to Charlie. It just might be that steering a course through another murder investigation comes with the new territory.

I went to sit on the bench near the A-house, my arm crooked on the back, observing Cap, Meg, and Doug enter the trailer. I sensed that a powwow of sorts was getting under way now that the police had gone. They were facing far more than the relatively simple funeral plans for Stephen MacKay once the body was released.

I shifted my eyes to Marilyn's car where she and Robbie were saying goodbye to Charlie. I had declined to join them for a late lunch at the diner, believing that Charlie needed both a break from me and privacy with them. She shook hands with Marilyn and awkwardly tolerated a hug from Robbie. She watched them back out and pull off, then stared a long while toward the trailer before walking my way. I faced forward as she came from behind the bench to sit on the other end.

"The Admiral—Marilyn, I mean—thinks a lot of you, Lexy."

"She's been a good friend. Being a good one to you, too."

"You all are." Charlie clenched her teeth. "What if I let you down? Get in trouble again?"

"You don't have to prove yourself all the time, Charlie. And if there's trouble, you tell us and let us help. Is there?"

She was stopped from replying, if she was going to, by the Olivers skipping up the steps to the A-house and then swerving to sit cross legged in the scraggly grass in front of us. The man smoothed his fingers over the waves in his salon-styled hair.

He said, "Great job on the run-about, Charlie. We're going to slide her in the water now that the cops are gone." He looked at me. "I'm Wayne. This is Patsy. You're Lexy, right? We gave you Charlie's money yesterday. Did the cops corner you all too?"

"I couldn't tell them much," I said.

"Us either. Patsy went checking for more beer during the fireworks. She saw Cap on that little porch of his. Couldn't tell if he was coming or going. And she told them about you wearing that cap with the eagle on it. They had it in a plastic sack."

Charlie jerked her head toward me, her eyes wide.

Patsy Oliver spoke up in a rush that was more coy than angry. "Well, Big Mouth here told them more than that." She touched Charlie's knee. "He's supposed to be apologizing to you right now. He let it slip to the police about you and Doug tearing down the barricade Steve put up."

Charlie's face went blank and she drew her knee away from Patsy.

Wayne Oliver looked at his wife as he defended himself. "I didn't know anybody was dead. They just asked who we were and did we come here often and what did we know about people here." He whined to me, "I thought I was saying good things. I said how great Cap and Meg are and what a louse Steve is...was. How he blocked the road." He had the grace to look sheepishly at Charlie.

"Didn't mean to deep six you, Charlie."

They got up in unison. The quickening breeze didn't lift a hair of their identically frosted strands. "Playtime. See ya."

Charlie made a face. "Silly people." She sobered. "I didn't tell the trooper any of that." Her dark olive-brown eyes were anxious.

"Did he ask you questions when you should have?"

She mumbled, "Not really."

I asked another question, "What else is there, Charlie? What were you looking for in your locker so wildly."

"I need more time on that, Lexy. Please." I could hear the resolution, and I knew the plea cost her. I decided not to probe yet. She shifted direction "That could be my hat. I took it off when I went wind sailing. Then I hung it on a stalk when we played volleyball. I don't know about after that."

"And it could be mine," I said lightly. "Don't remember where or when I took it off."

She stared at the *Siren Song* but let it go, partially, saying instead, "Are you going to call Wren today?"

"I might tomorrow. How about I drop you off at Karen's soccer match while I go into Orlando to do that and tend to some things. Pick you up on the way back."

For a moment the anxiety and tension fled her face. "I'd like that." Then her expression sharpened. "Did she ask you to do that?"

"Not exactly. Just mentioned she wished you could come see her play—" I hurried on before she could mount an objection." I'm going to do a load of wash. Got clothes you want to throw in?"

She stood up. "I'll do it. I can read some more of that Stoner McTavish book while I wait." Her jaw stiffened. "Visit her world for awhile."

I fished keys from my pocket and tossed them to her. "My dirty clothes are in the basket in the head." I shoved my hand back into a pocket. "Oh, some in my locker, too."

"I don't need your key. I can pick the lock with a wire."

"Charlie!"

She grinned cockily. "I'm a big bad criminal. Don't you know?"

She skipped down the steps in a blatant imitation of the Olivers. Worried or not, she was tough and resilient.

I ignored the growl of an approaching motorcycle until I heard the sound of scattering gravel right behind me. Joseph Quintana removed a scarred white helmet and left his cycle to come sit on the bench with me. A somber stiffness to his face eradicated the deep dimples and deprived him of his youthful glow.

Without preamble he said, "I've been questioned by the police. They already knew about me stopping the fight between Doug and Steve yesterday. Tried to make it sound like no big deal. The fight I mean. I guess they've already been at everybody here. They're crawling all over Steve's marina now."

I nodded.

He continued, "I was supposed to work from noon till six but Ed Pike told me to get lost." His eyes, a thunder-cloud dark, were deeply concerned. "Did the cops hassle Doug and Cap, Lexy?"

"They questioned everyone. That's their job when there's a suspicious death. What other things did they ask you about?"

He took a deep breath and made an effort to relax. "What we did last night. I told them about taking food out to the barge with Doug after the show. Stayed out there talking for quite awhile. Watched other fireworks being set off up and down the shoreline. Then we came back in. Doug dropped me off at Steve's dock. He had to return the boat to Cap's. Later I saw him in his truck heading south while I was just about to head north to my home."

"Where was he going?" Now something else Doug had omitted.

Joseph shrugged. "Don't know. I figured it was all right to tell the police about it. That meant Doug was away from here part of the night. They asked me times and if I saw other people, but I couldn't tell them anything else. I just knew we came off the barge late and everybody seemed settled on their boats or gone." He added uncertainly, "I didn't mention seeing Mrs. Gilstrap's car 'cause I didn't actually see her. Just caught the car in my headlight for a second. Looked like she'd been down to the boat ramp."

That bothered me, but then I considered that Meg must have been looking for Doug or Cap before she took off home to Mossville. "Did you and Doug watch the fireworks with the kids down by the *Willow*, Joseph?"

He stirred uncomfortably. "Ah...no...I'm not much older than they are but once you've left your teens some of that silliness gets tiresome." He continued to look uncomfortable. "We watched the show sitting on the trunk of your car."

I smiled, understanding his discomfort. "No problem. I'm not one of those car-proud people. Any special rumors floating around Steve's place about what might have happened to him?"

He shook his head. "Not in my hearing. I was nearly grabbed off my bike the minute I got there. Two different guys questioned me. I didn't even know Steve was dead until the second guy told me what was going on." He brushed his fingers over the helmet. "I'm real worried about Doug, Lexy. I know Pike would pour it on about his troubles with Steve. The Houseboat queen, too, maybe."

"Houseboat queen? "

Ill at ease, he turned his face away. "Gina Lewis. She lives on a houseboat near the marina office. She and Steve had a private thing going. We were all in the diner one day and she laid it on thick, teasing Doug about her needing to get to know him better since she was his unofficial stepmother. Tore Doug up. He said some rough stuff to her. Then he and Steve took it outside but everyone in the diner got an earful."

I probed gently for more pertinent information while trying to ease the young man's concerns, but gleaned nothing new. Joseph placed his helmet on his cycle, thanking me politely for talking with him, and went toward the work dock, saying he'd hang around in case Doug wanted to talk. I went to my car and retrieved a trusty orange notebook from the back seat. Sitting sideways in the front with the door open, I jotted notes on everything I could remember seeing and hearing about Steve MacKay and his confrontations. I steeled myself to be an objective reporter and included Charlie.

A drop of sweat caused the ink of several words to run, so I heaved myself from the hot car. As I was putting the notebook safely out of sight in the trunk, I saw Meg crossing from the trailer to the office. I closed the lid and looked up. The low branches of the oak were thickly interwoven. They would have effectively blocked most of the fireworks from view. I ran my fingers along the edge of the trunk and wondered why the two young men really sought such seclusion and privacy. The questions were piling up. I smacked the trunk top in irritation and decided to join Meg.

When I entered the office, Meg was sitting at her desk staring at the computer screen. Strain and worry had deepened the lines on her face but the eyes she lifted to mine were clear and determined. There was almost a fierceness in them, heightened by the green portions.

She said, "Even in death Steve is tormenting us. But I'll not let him win this way either. I told him on the phone yesterday that if he ever touched Dougie again, I'd sic the gambling authorities on him." She picked at the hair over her ears. "I figured there might be something to the rumors that he permitted high-stakes poker games on the boats ferrying people to and from Jacksonville."

"Did he admit to that?" I perched on a corner of the desk.

"Of course not. Just laughed. Told me to go watch the fireworks because it would be my last Fourth of July here. God forgive me, but there is some satisfaction in knowing that it was his last." She gnawed at her lower lip. "Wouldn't want you to pass that on, Lexy. Cap's caught up in some father-son feelings right now. Don't know what Dougie is feeling. Probably same as me. Both of us lost too much to Steve to feel any charity toward him even in death."

I wanted her to enlarge on that last statement but the phone rang. She spoke only single-word responses. I walked out to the patio, politeness winning out over inquisitiveness, and saw Charlie and Doug by the *Willow*, a laundry bag at her feet. Her gestures and quick movements indicated anger.

He kept shaking his head and holding his hands out in a placating way. Then he pointed to Joseph's motorcycle. Charlie gave an expressive shrug, hoisted the bag, and stomped off to the A-house.

Doug walked more slowly up the dock. He was about to pass by below me, but I spoke to halt him. "You and Charlie got a problem, Doug?"

His cheek muscles tightened and the veins in his neck bulged. "Nothing important. Have you seen Joe?"

I waved toward the work dock. "Maybe down there."

He gave me a curt nod and moved on. Meg tapped on the window and I returned to the office.

"That was Cap on the phone," she said. "Wants me to go into town with him to check with the lawyers about keeping Steve's place operating until we know what's what. He doesn't trust Ed Pike to run things without supervision. We've no right to impose on you, Lexy, but could you keep an eye on things here so that I don't have to lock up?"

"It's not an imposition, Meg. Charlie's washing our dirty clothes. This way I won't feel like I'm dumping on her. Domestic chores were never my forte."

Meg drew herself tall, stretching stiff shoulders. "Mine either. Even though I was the only girl, I lobbied to earn my allowance doing outside chores. Surprisingly it was my father who agreed. Worked out a compromise actually. Set up a rotation where we all did inside duty a week at a time." Warmth and sadness flickered across her face at the memory. "Can't say for sure when I'll be back."

"Not a problem. I've got a good view and plenty to think about."

I stood at the front window noticing the encroachment of afternoon shadows on the dock. Many of the slips were empty—the weekenders having put out on the lake as soon as they were released by the police. Here and there were small knots of people talking, no doubt, about Steve MacKay's death and its possible ramifications.

A man in crisp white trousers and shirt politely edged around a couple such groups apparently on his way to the *Song*. A sign that the yacht would be leaving the marina soon? If so, I felt no pang of loss. What I felt was a cross between distress and embarrassment at my behavior. At the time the uncommitted sex had been a liberating rush, a jettisoning of tension. Now I wished I could rewind and play over it.

"I need you, Wren." The hot breath of my whisper ricocheted off the window pane back into my mouth.

I dropped into Meg's chair and noticed the small framed photograph propped next to the computer. Cap and Meg, perhaps twenty years younger, smiled at me. Cap's arm was around a robust woman whose wire-frame glasses above plump cheeks made her look like a younger Mrs. Santa Claus. A lean square-jawed man rested a hand lightly on Meg's shoulder. Overwhelmingly, I ached for the touch of Wren.

Movement outside caught my eye as a police car pulled up to Cap's trailer. A trooper and the detective I had seen questioning Doug got out.

When no one answered his knock, the detective came across to the office.

"Where's Andrew MacKay?" He flashed his ID at me.

"Gone into town. I'm not sure where or when he'll be back."

His eyes darted everywhere but at me as he talked. "Do you have a key? We have a search warrant. I don't really like to order doors battered in unless it's necessary."

"His grandson is around somewhere. I'm sure he'd let you in if it's really required."

Now he looked at me. Something about the set of his face with its expressionless eyes and the compact body declining toward softness reminded me of the large placid dog my parents owned. A deceptive image, I was certain. He opened the door and called to the trooper, "Check around for the boy," then lifted a hand and jerked his thumb indicating that I was to give him access to the desk. I hesitated until he produced a paper and declared with excessive politeness, "The warrant covers all property of Cap MacKay's Marina."

He searched the desk and the file cabinet. I stood in the doorway of the storage room while he searched it thoroughly as well. The trooper returned with Doug, explaining that he had already checked the work dock, outer storage, and Cap's sailboat.

Doug, his voice thin with strain, said, "If you'd tell me what you're looking for, maybe I could help."

The detective ignored him. Pointing out the north window toward the A-house, he asked, "What's that building?"

I explained and he dispatched the trooper to search it after requiring Doug to provide keys. I tensed remembering that Charlie was there.

At the detective's blunt command of "Now the trailer, boy," Doug bristled and I saw the veins again bulge in his neck.

I gave him a warning frown and he followed the man out silently.

Scant minutes later Charlie, a study in controlled fury, rushed in, her sharp facial bones tight against her skin. "What's going on? That cop had Doug's keys! He was opening the lockers. I told him he was messing with people's private stuff and he threw me out! Can he do that?" She gulped a breath.

"They've got a warrant, Charlie. He can do it. Some judge issued the warrant because they convinced him there was probable cause for finding something related to Steve's death."

"Like what?"

"Any number of things. Paperwork that shows Cap or Doug might profit from Steve's death or that's connected with the feud about the land. Something that could be a murder weapon."

Her hand that had been rummaging in Meg's plate of paper clips stopped abruptly. "Murder weapon! I thought he drowned."

"No one really said that. There might have been something about his body that made them go looking for things. Signs of a blow to the head, being punched out, marks on his throat..."

She relaxed some but methodically pulled apart a large clip. "Oh. Where's Doug?"

"He and the detective are over there in the trailer." I watched her first bite her lower lip and then moisten the upper with her tongue.

When she started to scratch on her palm with the point of the clip, I took it from her. "Talk to me, Charlie. You're worried about something specific. What is it?" I was careful to keep my voice level and calm. Five years of contending with the defense mechanisms of teenagers had taught me how to maneuver.

She glanced out one window at the A-house and then the other toward the trailer. "I'm scared they're looking for Cap's gun. Doug saw him cleaning it after Steve put up the barricade. That's one reason we took it down. And Doug kept thinking about Cap having the gun, so he took it and gave it to me to put in my locker till he could decide what to do with it." She lifted a very perturbed face to plead for my understanding. "He just wanted it out of the way, Lexy. Steve was getting meaner and meaner in how he talked to Cap, his own father."

I ran a finger down the bridge of Charlie's nose, pausing in the indentation of a long-ago break. She needed a reassuring touch but not a cloying one. But most of my thoughts were on the image of a dark-clad Doug stealing out of the A-house at the commencement of the fireworks—and of Charlie staring in consternation at the empty shoebox that had tumbled from her locker.

Eleven

I sensed a Sunday lull enveloping the sleeping marina as dawn inched its way up the sky. I threw back my sheet and sat up staring at Charlie's empty berth, uncharacteristically disheveled. I hadn't heard her leave.

Yesterday, even after my initial attempts at being calm, I had come on rather strong about the gun—about Charlie accepting it in the first place and then about not telling me, or at least Robbie, after she discovered it missing. Later, in bed aboard the *Willow*, tossing and turning and struggling to sleep, I admitted contritely that it was concern for her that had made me lecture her. Her only response had been a neutral grunt. The rigid form, her back to me, only suggested her own sleeplessness. I knew any further attempts at conversation would be fruitless so I grappled for sleep. I mulled over my increasing anxiety concerning Steve MacKay's death and potential explanations. I didn't like any of them.

My confrontation with Charlie over the gun had never gotten very far anyway. She had used Meg's return to cover her leaving.

Meg hadn't picked up on the tension between Charlie and me because her mind was on Doug's account of the police search. I bit back what I suspected about that search, arguing with myself over whether or not I was being protective of Doug or Charlie—or even Meg and Cap.

I lay back down to better appreciate the almost imperceptible rocking of the boat and to review what little Meg had told me. After Cap's wife had died and Steve had inherited her half of the original marina, Cap had drawn up a new will leaving his half to Doug. According to Meg, that had not set well with Steve. But Steve had refused to have a new will of his own drawn up.

Meg had said, "I think he was reacting like a lot of younger people.

They feel like it's tempting fate to make a will. But in Steve's case I think it was also a matter of refusing to admit that he would ever die." Her voice had gone dull and cold. "He was never touched by the deaths of others either. His mother, his wife, my—" She had shaken herself. "Got to stop speaking ill of him."

I had asked about the status of Steve's marina and she had explained. "Cap's lawyer did some unofficial checking with the firm Steve used and they admitted he had never done a will through them. If none turns up, that would mean it would all come to Dougie." She had laughed sardonically. "Wouldn't that make Steve choke on those brimstone fumes!"

My thoughts were more bleak. First the gun—now the possible inheritance. The police and prosecutor would see it as means and motive, assuming Steve had been shot. I wondered if Robbie could scrounge for some details and if she would reveal them to me. I intended to find out.

I had shared some leftover party food with Meg and, in an unspoken agreement, shifted to light conversation. But our silences were laden with our private worries. Like Charlie, I had used the entrance of others to cover my leaving. Retrieving my running shoes from the trunk of my car, I had sought oblivion in mindless jogging through the late afternoon heat, stopping only when the mosquitoes rose from the vegetation to forage for blood.

Now I wondered where Charlie was this morning. Doing something on schedule or avoiding me? I dressed, made coffee, and went on deck. I was met by one of those meek sunrises devoid of flaring colors, just gray strengthening into blue. Every so often a truck or car passed by on the service road towing some water vehicle. I sipped the coffee slowly while cataloging my moves for the day. I knew I wanted to start with a solid eggs-and-bacon breakfast to replenish the energy consumed by the stress of yesterday and the manic jogging.

"Trying to read the grounds in the bottom of the cup?"

With pleasure I leaped to extend a hand and assist Fran aboard. "No gypsy blood in me, Fran. Wish there were. I could use some crystal ball skills right now."

Her hair was still tousled from sleep, but her dark blue eyes snapped with alertness. "Nah. You don't want that. It would take all the fun and challenge out of life." At my glance down the dock, she added, "Just me. No Donna. She listens to church music on the radio every Sunday morning. All that organ folderol makes me nervous."

She accepted my offer of coffee and I gave her my cup to hold as I zipped down below, noting as I did how much better I maneuvered aboard the boat. If only I could get to maneuvering as well around Charlie. Returning topside with her coffee I asked, "Seen my shipmate?"

"Nope." She tested the coffee and nodded approval, then ran her tongue over her gold tooth. "Since she's not here I'm going to pass on something I saw the other night. I'm from the football school that says the best defense is a good offense. If you and your Admiral and your cop friend intend to look out for Charlie, you need to know."

I waited uneasily for her to chug some coffee and continue. The reporter in me that usually leaned forward eagerly for news, held still.

"I was walking the main pier here real late Friday night—more like Saturday morning because it was way after midnight. I quit smoking a lot of years ago but once in a great while I have to have the taste of tobacco again. Usually something sets it off—like all that firecracker smoke hanging in the air. I keep a supply of nice slim cigars on hand." She laughed at my raised eyebrow. "Donna never nags me not to, but I always light up away from the boat. Actually Donna doesn't mind the smell. Tiger's the one that fusses. Anyway, I was snitching my pleasure in private when I noticed that Meg's car was still here. And I could see a little light spilling from the storage room into the office. Then it went out and I figured she was bedding down on the cot there instead of going home so late. She's done that before. I was going to walk the service road while I smoked but I saw someone coming up it, maybe from the boat ramp. I could tell it was Charlie. I know her size and way of walking too well to miss her. She went aboard the *Willow*..." She paused to swallow more coffee. "I'm probably telling you something you already know."

"'Fraid not. I didn't know." I couldn't stop my head turning toward the *Siren Song*. "I wasn't here. Damn! I should have been! She might have told me things then." I snapped my mouth shut, not wanting to say too much.

"Don't beat up on yourself, Lexy. Charlie had a good day Friday. She may have been walking off the highs, winding down." Fran glanced toward the *Song*. "Or she may have been walking off some teenage confusion—over her situation as well as yours." There was nothing accusatory in her tone.

I mumbled, "She wasn't too confused over mine. She waited up to lecture me. She turned her nose up at the smell of me."

Fran's hearty laugh surged out over the water. "Like Tiger, I'll bet, when we come in with the smell of another cat on us." Her pitch dropped a notch. "But sometimes it just has to happen."

I knew she was no longer speaking of cats. I asked, "What about atonement?"

"Never been into that. I don't think it's a healthy approach to life. I prefer to do things because they're right—not as compensation for past actions or behavior."

I thought about that. Would I want Wren to return from Atlanta feeling that she needed to compensate me for flying to Nancy Marshall's bedside? No. Would she want me to make love to her driven by the need to compensate her for the hours with Damaris? Not my strong-minded Wren. Though I knew it wasn't as simple as that, I felt better. I lifted my cup toward Fran. "Thank you."

She lifted hers in reply.

I refilled our cups and we sat in the cockpit seats. Fran gave me a lesson in the controls and instrumentation. Even though I could not foresee ever taking the boat out on the lake, I concentrated on absorbing the terminology and understanding the technological aspects. It was a toss-up whom I wanted to impress more—the Admiral or Charlie.

"Planning to ditch me ashore and make a run for it, Long Legs?"

I jerked my head to see Charlie propped casually against a piling.

Fran said, "Not with me aboard, she's not. Give this old lady a hand, Charlie."

Swiftly Charlie moved to assist her. Fran squinted into the sun and winked at me. "Organ bombardment should be over by now." With a snappy salute she headed for the *Second Wind*.

Charlie looked at the two cups I was holding and said, "Put those down and I'll buy us breakfast at the diner."

I knew a peace offering when I heard one. "Ah, Charlie. You read my mind. I need a greasy-spoon fix. Can I order the lumberjack's breakfast?"

She grunted, "They call it the stevedore here. Use those long legs to catch up with me." She took off down the dock. She wasn't going to sugarcoat it. I caught up with her in front of the office and shortened my stride to match hers. On our walk to the diner she volunteered that she had been scrubbing down the storage shed, planning to paint it the next morning.

"Now that there's no need not to," she said.

I chose to let that go unchallenged.

Charlie was greeted by name as we slid into an empty booth near the door. The elderly waitress who looked like she should be at home relaxing instead of serving other people on swollen ankles and slightly bowed legs, put a Coke in front of Charlie and gave me a glass of water. Two sun-blackened, stringy-haired men took the booth behind Charlie. She frowned as one slammed against the back, jolting her. I caught snatches of talk as I studied the menu.

"...left the wife and kids to fight over stale donuts...heard they're biting near the reeds on the other side...snuck off enough yellow pine and nails to do me a back porch to the trailer..."

We ordered and I let Charlie run the conversation as my peace offering. She told me the colors she was planning for the shed, that she wanted to get aboard the *Second Wind* for some measurements, and that she needed to rake the ground where we had picnicked. She teased me about the size of the breakfast I ordered, and I chastised her for drinking Coke. When we fell silent eating, it was hard not to hear the comments from the booth behind as they demanded unnecessary service.

"...this here spoon's dirty...get me a new bottle of catsup...this syrup's gone to sugar...my coffee's cold, bring me a fresh cup..."

I gritted my teeth in anger as one jibed, "Old bitch. See that turkey wattle hanging off her neck." A moment later he gobbled as the waitress walked by after refilling my coffee. Charlie appeared not to notice. Finally they settled in to eat and I managed to forget about them.

We finished and Charlie plucked the bill from the table, reminding me it was her treat. I talked her into letting me leave the tip and she watched me put down twice the usual amount. I didn't trust the rude pair to leave any. I stood at the door as she paid and requested a large

Coke to go. The two men crowded up behind her complaining that they thought the dumb waitress got their bill wrong.

Outside Charlie paused to remove the lid and straw, tossing them in a trash can. Then she whirled the wrong way just as the two men exited the diner. She stumbled and bumped into them, spilling sticky Coke on both. I watched in amazed admiration as she played the contrite bumbler to perfection, apologizing and swiping at their wet shirts while spilling ice on their sandaled feet. They cursed and backed away, then headed off, spitting epithets.

Charlie flipped the empty cup into the trash. Her chin jutted as she locked eyes with me.

"Feel better?" I asked.

"Yep," she replied.

"So do I." I put my hand up and we high-fived.

We started back to Cap's in a comfortable silence. Nearly there, Charlie said, "Is dropping me off at the soccer field still on?"

"Of course. How about we leave around one o'clock?"

"That's good. Lexy…what…I…what do I do about the gun being gone? Doug won't tell me anything."

I controlled a relieved sigh that she was talking about it. "Getting with Cap about it is on my agenda. You just hang loose 'til I know more."

I stood at the corner of the office building and watched her head down the finger pier toward the *Second Wind*. At the sound of voices near the trailer, I turned and saw Cap on the porch, Doug on the bottom step. He was nodding at whatever Cap was saying, then turned and set off with a resolute step.

Cap saw me and motioned me over.

"Got something for you, Lexy. Doug found it under the step here this morning."

He handed me my cap. That meant the police had Charlie's. I had been hoping they had mine, blown off the *Siren Song* while I was very much otherwise occupied. "Thanks, Cap. Got time for a little talk?"

He drew one corner of his mouth to the side, emphasizing the deep dimple. "Maybe about my pistol that's missing?"

I sighed with a whoosh. "It helps that you know that."

He took a chair and I folded myself onto the top step. Cap said, "The minute Doug told me about the search warrant, I checked for it. Thought the cops had taken it. The boy dangled from the yardarm till Meg left, then he told me the truth of it."

"Just what did he say?" I added quickly as he narrowed his eyes, "This is Charlie's friend asking…this marina's friend. Not a reporter. I'm still on vacation."

He accepted that. "Doug says he wasn't worried about me shooting Steve but that he was afraid Steve might be here going at me and remember about the gun. Doesn't matter which version is true. He wanted it out of the way. Once he took it, he wasn't sure what to do with it. Knew it was registered to me. I got it a few years back when we had a problem with some lake pirate stealing in at night and cutting motors off the unmanned boats." He pulled a bandanna out of his pocket and began twisting it. "When he said he gave it to Charlie to hide, I wanted to keelhaul him. Told him so."

"Did he tell you the rest of it?"

Cap pulled the bandanna taut. "What rest of it? He said he was going to get it back."

I told him about Charlie finding the shoebox empty. Again I kept quiet about Doug's furtive trip to the A-house during the fireworks.

Cap stood and hit his fist on the railing. "That polliwog!" His face pleaded for my understanding. "He's gone to take over the big marina. Lawyer says it's all right for him to assume control as next of kin until something official comes down the channel. I can't go down there and fire a cannon 'cross his bow in front of Ed Pike." He gripped the railing. "But I'll catch him when he comes in."

I asked, "Will Pike be a problem?"

"He's more blowhard than anything. Without Steve to back him up, he won't do much more than just get in the way. And make a lot of noise doing it. Doug wanted to fire him right off but I convinced him that Pike is needed to keep things afloat for the time being. He's bringing Joe Quinn in full time. That'll give him his own backup." His face was sorrowful.

"Cap, I'm sorry for the troubles. And I know you're feeling pain over your son's death."

"Aye. But our being a family started to die a long time ago. I never knew what was missing in him but I could never see him through eyes as hard as Meg's. Maybe I should have. Then maybe this weekend wouldn't have happened. She always said..." He stopped and looked over my head. "Here she comes now. She's going to worry about Dougie being at the helm alone." He rubbed the decorative knob of the railing with his palm. "Going to be proud, too."

Twelve

"I'm going to detour through Mossville, Charlie, and take a back road to the stadium field." Even though no explanation was requested, I provided one. "I've been invited to Fran and Donna's when Wren gets home. They gave me directions so I thought I'd check them out in daylight."

"Is she coming home soon?"

A brief sigh slipped past my lips. "I don't know anything about the timing yet. I may call her this afternoon. Want to know more about soccer before we get to the field?"

Her agreement was eager but her shrewd eyes indicated she recognized my swift change of subject. I explained what I thought would be helpful for her to know about the sport. As we neared Mossville, I pointed to a scattering of oaks, gums and pines. Clusters of silver Spanish moss embroidered their branches, spilling loose tendrils toward the ground.

I said, "Easy to see where the town got its name."

"Meg told me about it. She said a bunch of people from Virginia came down here after they lost their whole town in a Civil War battle. There was lots more trees then. They started making mattresses and pillows stuffed with the moss. Guess they figured it was kind of advertising to name the town for it."

I found Fran and Donna's home easily. It was a modest white clapboard in the middle of a long residential block. A small porch bordered by azalea bushes faced east. A large magnolia dominated the front yard and a line of cherry laurels marched down one side. I drove by slowly then sped up going a few blocks and making a couple of turns. I paused before a corner house on a double lot. It was sandy brick split-level. The grass was neatly cut but the bushes and flower beds were overgrown or scraggly.

Charlie gave me a curious glance. "That's Meg's place. Doug showed it to me. Yard needs work."

I agreed. "Don't imagine she has much time for it. Her arthritis would be a problem, too."

I let it go at that and drove on. Soon we left the town and I was enjoying holding the car to the pavement as I had to bank left then right through a stretch that made me think of an elongated corkscrew.

The black of skid marks and deep ruts in the soft dirt of the shoulders warned me to watch my speed. As I rounded a particularly sharp curve, Charlie pointed to a towering sweet gum a few feet off the pavement on the other side at the middle of the curve.

"That's the tree that got Doug's mother."

I slowed considerably. "What does that mean? What happened? When?"

She told me in hushed tones that barely rose above the whir of the air conditioner. "Not long after I went aboard the *Willow*, Doug asked me if I wanted to ride into Mossville with him. He had to get some stuff from the hardware store. He showed me where he lived as a little kid. Meg's house, too. Then he drove this road and pulled over by that tree back there." She smoothed her fingers up and down her shoulder belt. "He knew I'd picked up on the bad feelings between him and Steve and I think he wanted to let me know why. He grew up knowing he was adopted but that it didn't matter to his mother or Cap and his grandmother. He was family to them." Her voice hardened. "But he said that for as long as he could remember, Steve made it real clear he didn't want him, didn't think of him as his." She glanced my way. "I didn't have it that bad, Lexy. I knew I didn't really belong to the people I was with, but they didn't shove my nose in it every time I breathed."

I said, "I think Steve was one of those people born with something missing on the inside. The way some people are born with something physical out of kilter."

Charlie continued, "Doug said Steve was just as rough on his wife. He didn't beat on her with his fists. He did it with words. The way I heard him do to Doug. She started drinking. Doug said it was like she was just half there most of the time. Cap and his wife started keeping Doug a lot. He knew why even though he was just a little kid. Then one night when he was around twelve he woke up hearing Steve and his mother going at it bad. Said he had never heard his mother carry on like that. She had always just kind of folded up inside and stayed quiet." Charlie finished in a rush, "But that night she left. Ran out and got in the car. She never made that curve back there."

We each lapsed into our own thoughts. I didn't like the way things were stacking up against Doug. From my encounters with troubled youth as a teacher, I knew that anti-social behavior too often resulted from pain incurred in childhood. I could understand Doug wanting to destroy Steve MacKay, but I could never condone it. Mostly I worried about Charlie being drawn deeper into the quagmire—either by her concern for Doug, Cap, and the marina, or by official discovery that she had held a gun for awhile. I really needed Robbie to get me some behind-the-scenes information. Another reason I wanted the privacy of the phone in my apartment.

Charlie touched my thigh. She said perceptively, "You don't have to worry about Doug or me, Long Legs. He's got back-up and I've been taking care of myself for a long time."

"You're not by yourself anymore, Charlie." I was surprised by my own vehemence. I lightened my tone. "Have a good afternoon doing something new and different. Tell me about it later."

She grinned mischievously. "Might be something I wouldn't want to tell."

I faked a punch to her chin, then concentrated on the increasing traffic as I neared Sanford. There was lots of Sunday traffic around Lake Monroe and the entrance to the zoo. Dust swirled as I followed a dirt road toward the back gate of the stadium where dozens of brightly clad figures grouped, then scattered, then re-grouped like the ever-changing patterns in a kaleidoscope. I nosed the car to the fence.

"Look at the munchkins!" Charlie was pointing to a corner area inside the fence. I guessed them to be around six years old. Patiently, their teenage coaches were trying to keep them in line for practice kicks while their interest was on the boys' match surging from goal to goal in uneven bursts of speed.

Suddenly Charlie drooped in the seat, shy and hesitant. I knew she was uncomfortable not knowing for sure where to go or what to do. Finally she put a hand to the door and said, "Guess you need to go."

She got out of the car. I was pleased that she had dressed with care from the clothes I had given her—tan shorts with a cinnamon polo. I was relieved to see Karen leave a yellow-clad gaggle and head for the fence. She waved to me and greeted Charlie with a wide smile. She said something, and Charlie came around to my window.

"Karen says things will go on here till about six o'clock. You can pick me up here then or…or if you need to be later, I can go get pizza with her team." She played with the sideview mirror.

"I've got a lot to do so you go stuff yourself with pizza. She tell you where?"

"Yep. Cardone's. Five blocks up Front Street."

"I'll find it." I started the car and called to Karen, "Rocket that ball!" She gave me a thumb's up.

A short time later I stood in my apartment feeling somewhat alien. I had become accustomed to the brightness, the fluctuating sounds, the fluid movement of the marina. I resolved not to tell Marilyn and have to suffer an 'I told you so.' Sitting at the desk, I toyed with a pencil, darkening the number of Pinecrest Hospital written on the pad. Then I punched in Robbie's voice-mail number and left a message.

Just as I finished making a cup of tea, the phone rang. Robbie, her voice coated with fatigue, said, "Just completed the paperwork on an all-nighter and then some. I hate holiday weekends. They make the crazies crazier." I felt guilty about having called to seek information but she opened that door before I could. "Let me put my feet up on your couch. Provide some iced tea, Lexy, and maybe we can swap some war stories."

"You cut to the chase in a hurry, Detective Exline."

She gave a throaty chuckle and there was more vitality in her voice. "I've already had to share one murder investigation with you. I learned it's okay to give you a little ground." Then more seriously, "And we share some common ground on this one. Be right there."

I knew she meant Charlie.

Robbie arrived as I was placing a large pitcher of iced tea and a frosted glass on the low table in front of the couch. Her light blue slacks and blue and white windowpane blazer were rumpled. Plumping both pillows on one end of the couch, she slipped off her shoes and settled against the pillows with a weary sigh. When I returned from the kitchen with my tea and a sack of goldfish crackers for nibbling, she was rubbing the cold glass over her forehead. I settled cross-legged in front of the table.

Robbie scanned my soft shoes, white jeans, and purple and white striped shirt. "Damn if you're not dressing like a sailor!"

"Don't tell," I huffed. "What have you found out, Robbie?" At her hesitation I added, "I'm still on vacation and I've made friends at that marina."

She nodded in understanding. "I had to be at the morgue this morning, and shared in some case talk. Steve MacKay died from a bullet severing an artery in his chest...they think—"

"Think! Not know?"

"That's right. Seems fish or what have you did some nibbling. So no clear entry wound and none at all in the back. The M.E. thinks further examination will back up his guess that it was a bullet that tore through the artery. And he thinks MacKay could have been bumped around enough in the water for the bullet to be dislodged and drop out—if some fish didn't swallow it."

I asked with little hope, "No chance he drowned?"

"None. The M.E. says it was probably a low-velocity handgun—and a lucky shot. But he's not sure he'll ever be able to commit to anything real specific."

"Time of death?"

"A coin toss, he claims. Figures MacKay was in the water anywhere from four to eight hours. Dead when he went in." Robbie munched some crackers, then said, "Ziegler did some trolling for me with State and County late yesterday and got a little. County's been sniffing around the marina for illegal gambling. State investigators have been around, too. Maybe the gambling again. Or something else."

"Don't they talk to each other?"

Robbie countered, "Do you clue in other reporters? When your job, reputation and money are tied to successes, you don't help someone poach on you. Not the way it ought to be. Not a perfect world." She shrugged. "Anyway, looks like there's going to be a second circle of people connected with MacKay's legal or illegal enterprises who could come under police scrutiny. But they're going to be looking hardest at first-circle people." As I hissed through my teeth, she added, "I would. What I picked up around the marinas yesterday emphasized the bad blood between Steve MacKay, his son, his father and probably everyone at Cap's. They'll be around soon with a search warrant."

"Already have." I told her about the search late yesterday afternoon including Cap's ownership of a gun now missing, but not Doug's appropriation of it and its passage through Charlie's hands. I told myself I was protecting Robbie from a compromising involvement.

She crunched ice and asked, "How's our girl today?" She was pleased to hear where Charlie was. "She's been an adult most of her life, Lexy. Needs to be a kid while there's still time."

"I think Meg Gilstrap might want to offer a her real home. But I don't think we had better push Charlie toward it. She needs to come to things by her own means. And there's too much choppy water to steer through right now."

"Now you're talking like a sailor! You'll be saying 'shiver me timbers' next."

We laughed and relaxed as our talk became a tad more personal. After Robbie left, I returned to the desk and the phone number that would bring me to Wren. My mouth was dry and my stomach uneasy. How could I have so casually climbed that ladder and accepted the body of Damaris Del Riego? I tried to argue that Wren was at the side of another woman, but contritely stomped on one foot with the other to punish myself.

Deep down I knew that I had sought the night with Damaris for the pure physical excitement, unconnected to any commitment—and to punish an unknowing Wren for deserting me. I spoke aloud, "So what are you going to do about it, my witless friend?" I answered myself, "I don't know yet. But I will find a way to make it right. Wren is that important. We are that important." I tapped in the number of Pinecrest Hospital.

Ten minutes later I was hugging sorrow and joy to me. The leap in Wren's voice when I identified myself had dissipated my fears. The pain below her words when she described holding Nancy Marshall's slackening hand as the coma deepened made me ache to share the burden with her. I had asked questions that gave Wren the opportunity to relate the good memories of her time with the dying woman. We shared our uncertainties about death.

Wren's closing words sang in my mind. "Lexy, when I come back, I want to come to you on the *Willow*. I want the newness of it."

I had responded with a simple "Yes."

I considered what to do with the rest of the afternoon. On an impulse I decided to call the *Ledger* and leave a message for the Iron Maiden. I smiled to myself, realizing that a few months ago I would never have dared do so. Barbara MacFadden, long ago dubbed the Iron Maiden by a staff in awe of her steely appearance and rigid demeanor, was a legend. She was a veteran of World War II where, despite her youth at the time, she had been efficient and effective in the realm of information gathering and interpretation. I knew she had been stationed in Europe during the early Cold War years, eventually being posted to the Pentagon. Now, with the speed and range of computer access at her fingertips, she was a formidable researcher in the private sector of journalism.

As a neophyte reporter I had approached her cubicle only in moments of extreme need. More recently she had been an ally in my efforts to assist Marilyn Neff and The Cat through a murder investigation.She had helped me hone my journalistic skills. Perhaps it would be wise to enlist her expertise on the part of the people of Cap's Marina. I punched in her extension number and, at the conclusion of the recorded message, made my request. I asked her to run a check on any noteworthy events relating to the two marinas and a string of names of everyone I could think of connected with Steve MacKay.

On a quirky afterthought I included Damaris Del Riego.

I puttered about my apartment for awhile finding inconsequential things to do. As the afternoon lengthened toward early evening, I headed out in my car again, intent on no specific destination. At least I didn't think so until I neared the large, sprawling airport and turned off the busy entrance lanes onto a narrow road winding about the outer perimeter. I backed the car safely into the grass and faced the huge wire fence beyond which lay an approach runway.

The only other time I had been here was in darkness with Wren. As jets thundered to screeching landings, we had shared our first kisses. Now the pain of wanting her throbbed in concert with the roar of the jetliner quaking the air above my car. I watched the plane strike the runway, then speedily diminish in size. I pressed my forehead to the steering wheel. After a moment I stretched my legs as best I could and leaned back against the headrest. The periodic rumble and vibration became almost soothing. I gave myself up to a light sleep…

I jerked upright, yelping as I struck my knee on the steering column. I started the car and checked the time. The soccer crowd would be flooding the pizza parlor just about now. I relaxed my body but mentally chased after the fading images of a dream. I caught only one.

I was watching a soccer match. Charlie was on the field in a yellow outfit like the one I had seen Karen wearing. She was working the ball toward the goal and was about to take her shot. Suddenly the goalie metamorphosed into Steve MacKay, his chest ripped and bleeding. Charlie's foot connected with the ball and sent it rocketing toward the goal. Steve drew a gun and fired. The bullet exploded the ball which came screaming toward me in the stands. I put out my hand and caught it. The crowd roared.

I knew those sounds were of another plane landing but had been woven into the fabric of my dream.

I struggled after other images but they were already gone—not that I expected them to mean anything more than this one had. I wasn't disturbed by the dream, considering it no more than a mish-mash of things in my mind. I wished that solving MacKay's murder could be as simple as capturing dream images.

I shook my head, put the car in gear, and headed back to Sanford and Cardone's.

I found the pizza parlor awash in adolescent energy. Three booths in the back were filled with yellow uniforms and Charlie, wedged between Karen and a blonde Amazon, looking marvelously carefree. I took a front table and ordered two slices of white pizza. Waiting for it, I opened the orange spiral-bound notebook I had carried in and perused the notes I made yesterday afternoon. I added notes on the police search, Charlie and Cap's information on the gun, Fran's seeing Meg and Charlie up and about late Friday night, and about the authorities looking into gambling. I added a lot on Doug—taking the gun but apparently not yet explaining where it got to, possibly inheriting Steve's marina, no doubt blaming Steve for his mother's death.

I decided I needed to corner Doug myself—or maybe go to Meg first for background on the mother. And there was something else. I skipped back a couple of pages and found what I was looking for. Joseph had seen Meg's car coming from the boat ramp right after Doug took off toward Mossville. That made lots of people moving about in the dead of night. I grunted out loud realizing I was one of them. And where was Steve MacKay during those times? At what time did a bullet tear through his artery?

With all the boats and people around for the holiday weekend, how was the body slipped into the water without anyone seeing?

I was about to close the notebook when I noticed something else Joseph had told me. I had put a question mark after his reference to the 'Houseboat queen.' With Doug taking charge of the big marina, I could semi-legitimately nose around there, maybe get something from the woman supposedly attached to MacKay. I ate my pizza considering questions I wished to ask various people. I shied away from labeling them suspects.

The chair across from me was snapped away from the table and Karen dropped into it. "Hey, Lexy. Why didn't you come back and join us?"

I winked at Charlie who was leaning on the back of a side chair.

"And just where would I have put these long legs? You soccer mesomorphs were taking up all the room."

Karen tossed her thick, dark braid. "Bet you think I don't know what that means."

Charlie said, "I don't."

Karen answered smugly, "Means we have medium-size, compact, tough bodies. Right?" She didn't wait for a response. "But did you see our goalie? She's six-one. And what a reach! Not many balls get past her."

"How did the games go?"

"We played four different teams. Twenty-minute matches. Lost one, tied two, won one. Good enough."

"What about you personally?"

Charlie answered. "She scored the winning goal."

Karen grinned. "Had to look good for my fan."

I paid my bill and we walked out together. "Drop you off home, Karen?"

"I'd appreciate that. I have wheels sometimes but my brother and I have to take turns."

As we approached my car I said, "You two get in the back. I'll play chauffeur." I didn't know if Charlie's wide-eyed look was panic or surprise.

I sucked in my lips to stop a smile.

I put the radio on a rock station. The two girls conversed in low tones, Karen now and then giving me directions. My instincts told me there was some hand-holding going on but I carefully kept my eyes from the rearview mirror. At Karen's house, she gave me a warm and polite goodbye. I waited till she was safely inside and Charlie up front with me before driving away.

Charlie chattered about the matches, helping with a group of little kids, meeting other teens. As we neared the two marinas, she asked, "Did you call Wren?"

"Yes. A good call. She wants to come to the *Willow* when she gets back. That going to be okay?"

"Not for me to say."

"Yes it is, Charlie."

She tapped the dash in rhythm with the music which I had turned down.

"I would like to meet her." After a pause, "You can trust me, Lexy."

Without looking her way, I put up my hand. For the second time that day, we high-fived.

Thirteen

"You missed a spot, Long Legs."

I stepped back and saw the area barely touched by my paint brush. Charlie and I were giving the storage shed a coat of white paint. Later Charlie planned to do the door and trim in a bright gold. I looked down at my paint-spattered legs. "How come you don't have paint all over you, Charlie?"

"'Cause I don't flop the brush around all over the place. You even got some on your cap."

"Is there anything you don't do well?" I was half admiring, half irritated.

"Lots. I sure can't work the ball with my feet like all those guys I saw yesterday—even the munchkins. I can't read the wind as well as Cap—but I'm learning. And I can't hit the mark with a heaving line like Joe Quinn can." She paused in her brush strokes. "I guess with Steve gone and Doug running things, he could use his real name now. He told you what it was, didn't he? I've heard you call him Joseph."

"He told me the day we met. Did you see him and Doug during the show Friday night?"

Charlie dipped her brush in the bucket and her short, deft strokes spread the paint evenly. "Some. I was on the ledge above the *Willow* and I looked around and saw Joe sitting on the back of your car. Doug was standing there talking to him. Right after the first rockets went up, I turned back but Doug was gone." She gave me a hard look. "You checking up on Doug, Lexy?"

"Just trying to find out where everyone was that night. Maybe find out what they saw."

"Or what they did?" She rushed on. "I know it needs doing. But can't you leave it to the police?" Her mouth tightened. "I know you can't let someone kill even a louse like Steve and get away with it. But I don't want it to be anyone I know."

I understood that sentiment only too well.

Charlie resumed painting. She said, "I kind of saw him after the fireworks. I was saying goodbye to Karen and the others and heard the motorboat crank up. It had been tied off behind the *Willow*. I knew Doug and Joe were going to take food out to the barge."

"Did they come back to the same place?"

"No. Wouldn't expect them to. Doug would have dropped Joe off at the other marina and then tied off down there." She motioned with her brush toward the work dock. "There was lots going on after the fireworks, Lexy. Some of the people bringing their boats off the water, using the service road again. People here were moving up and down the piers, going on and off each other's boats. I sat on the bow of the *Willow* and watched."

What she didn't add was that she was waiting for me. I felt the stabbing guilt again.

Charlie continued, "I dozed for awhile but woke up when the breeze stopped. I needed something to swat at the mosquitoes with. That's when I noticed I didn't have the cap you gave me. Took a flashlight and went looking for it. Checked where we played volleyball and around the boat ramp." She answered my question before I could do more than open my mouth to ask it.

"I didn't see anybody. 'Cept Fran down below the office. I could tell by her shape. But I didn't know she smoked. I saw the red glow."

I smiled to myself, remembering Fran's comment about recognizing Charlie by her shape. I explained about the occasional cigar.

"Cigar, huh. That's neat."

I reacted quickly. "Don't you get any ideas, young lady. The *Willow* is a no-smoking zone. You're a no-smoking zone." A week ago I wouldn't have dared issue an order to Charlie. Now she took it with just a bit of a 'we'll-see' expression.

She spoke seriously again. "I went diving with Doug Saturday morning. You know, getting trash just outside the marina waters. He was just fine. Didn't act any kind of weird. He even teased me a little about

Karen...in a nice way."

I had forgotten about that. Would Doug have taken Charlie out there knowing they could encounter his father's body? I'd hope not. But what if he actually wanted to? And Charlie would be along as his cover for the event.

I thrust my brush too deep in the bucket of paint and got some on my fingers.

Charlie shook her head at me while saying, "Good thing we're almost done. You use up too much paint on yourself. At least it'll shower off easy."

She was right. A short while later, showered and smelling clean, I sat in the office with Meg. I told her about seeing her house as we passed through Mossville on our way to the soccer field.

She said, "It's a big house for just me. It's plenty big enough to include Charlie and give us both room for privacy. She's going to need a set place to be." She leaned forward. "And Dougie taking over the big marina leaves Cap and me really needing her. I'm sure Cap has it in his mind to work out something solid and permanent." She must have read something in my expression. "Don't worry, Lexy. Not going to run up any signal flags just yet. Too much else needs to be settled first. And I know better than to just throw something at Charlie." She smiled conspiratorially.

Cautiously I seconded her idea, made some favorable comments about Mossville, then zeroed in on where I wanted to go. "On the way out of town, Charlie pointed out the tree where Doug's mother died."

Meg's smile faded. "I've wished lightning would strike it. It isn't close enough to the road to warrant being felled, but it's a constant reminder to Dougie. Janice was a sweet girl. Wanted to be a good mother. But she didn't have any toughness, any inner strength." She clenched her jaw. "If she had, she would never have married Steve MacKay. Or he wouldn't have been interested in her. He wanted a woman he could jerk around. My husband Ben and I saw that in him. I think Cap and Mary saw it, too. They did their best to shield the girl, and Dougie. There just wasn't any way to do it all the time."

"With what I saw and picked up about Steve, I'm surprised he went along with adoption."

"That was Mary's doing. She got him to agree. Thought the presence of a child might soften him. But on the way home from the christening, Ben said he felt sorry for the little tyke, that Steve would never let him be a son. He was right."

"It's a shame the mother got into alcohol."

Meg wiggled her stiff fingers against the desk edge. "It wasn't alcohol. I know Dougie thinks that—mostly because Steve was always talking about his drunken sailor of a wife. But it was actually drugs. I always thought Steve himself started her on them. I'm sure he supplied them. For her it was a softer escape than drinking would have been."

"Do you know what drove her out of the house that night?"

"No. Dougie could only say that Daddy was yelling like he did a lot of times. But this time Mommy was yelling, too. Sometimes I think she let herself hit that tree. But Ben didn't. There had been a light rain after a long dry spell..."

I finished the thought, "Light rain, oil on the road...Florida ice."

Meg nodded. "I hope Ben was right. I don't want to believe she would have deserted Dougie like that. Cap and Mary took him. Steve didn't care."

She lowered her eyes and seemed to recede. "Two months later Mary was gone. Some new strain of flu that hit just as winter was jumping into spring. Then...then Cap and Dougie became real shipmates. Moved a trailer here. Started this marina."

I was sure she was going to say something else. But the sharpness of the gaze she turned on me warned me off from asking. I approached from a different direction. "Did you see Doug after the fireworks?"

She brought herself up straighter and taller in the chair.

"I'm just trying to place people, Meg. I've found that sometimes someone is at a place to see something that they don't register at the time."

She relaxed a little. "I didn't see him, or Cap either. I figured Dougie was with the young people down by the *Willow*, but I was concerned about not seeing Cap. Worried about his heart with all that had been going on—especially with how angry he got over Steve hitting Dougie. That's why I called Steve earlier. Tried to make him understand about Cap's condition. Wasted my breath, of course." She leaned back and crossed her legs at the ankles. "I decided to spend the night here. There's a cot back there. I went to the trailer to tell Cap. Mostly I wanted him to know I was nearby if he needed me. But I heard him talking to somebody. Thought it was Dougie and didn't want to insert myself just then. After I made up the cot, I checked that way again. Dougie's truck was nowhere up or down and Cap's lights were still on. This time I knocked. Knocked good and loud. I'm surprised you didn't hear me all the way down on the *Willow*."

I was relieved that Meg didn't appear to know of my late night escapade on the *Song*.

Meg went on, "I had old-woman willies. Got in my car and went looking. Drove by Steve's place, then down to the boat ramp. Finally went to bed. Didn't sleep too well. Woke up stiff and cranky."

The patio door opened and a sudden gust of wind sliced through, lifting a piece of paper from Meg's desk. I caught it even with my ear.

"Nice snag, Long Legs. Guess you really did earn that ball cap." Charlie, carrying a bright red cooler, had entered behind Fran. Both of them had on frayed cut-offs and loose T-shirts.

Fran said, "Charlie and me are going to start tracking down materials she needs for the new galley and berth. Donna said to tell you two she's got plenty of tuna sandwiches." She tapped the cooler at Charlie's side. "We've got our share."

I pulled off my cap and tossed it to Charlie. "Hang on to that one."

As they started out the front door, I called, "Fran." She looked over her shoulder at me. "No cigars."

She looked puzzled, but at Charlie's indignant "Lexy!" she understood. "Don't worry. I'm not going to pass on my bad habits."

As Charlie followed Fran out the front door, she yanked the cap smartly sideways.

Meg chuckled. "You brought—what's the saying?—good vibes here with you, Lexy. Charlie's relaxing more with all of us."

"I think she's allowing herself to believe in us." A near pain coursed through me. What was going to happen to Charlie's faith if one of the people she was beginning to believe in turned out to have murdered Steve MacKay? Maybe I should leave it to the police. I rose and tried to shake off the feeling.

I said to Meg, "How about some of those sandwiches? I've been running on coffee only."

"You go on," Meg replied. "I had a late breakfast with Cap and Dougie. Planning some business strategy. And a funeral. Haven't found out yet when the authorities will release Steve's body. It's going to be a private graveside service. Cap wants me there. Don't really want to be, but I guess I owe the living more than the dead." The phone rang. As she reached for it, she said, "Go feed those long limbs."

Several people spoke to me as I made my way to the *Second Wind*. Even Tiger had a meow for me as I scrambled aboard. At that point I discovered I still had the piece of paper from Meg's desk in my hand. I stuffed it in a pocket, slid back the hatch, and descended into welcome coolness. Tiger dashed between my feet, leaped gracefully onto a counter, and nosed an empty tuna can.

Donna said, "Now, Tiger. You've already licked every can clean." She smiled at me. "No Meg?"

"Declined on the basis of a late breakfast." I picked up another empty can from the floor. "I didn't have any." I tried for little-girl meekness.

"Then make yourself comfortable and eat. I've got a light fruit punch with or without a smidgen of wine." She finished with a questioning lilt.

"With," I said.

She poured punch into large ice-filled glasses and removed the plastic wrap from a large platter of triangle sandwiches, the crusts neatly removed. "We'll eat down here. There's not enough breeze right now to keep the bugs away."

She placed a bowl of pickles and olives and a stack of napkins next to the platter, motioning me to help myself. "Use your fingers. I hope I sent enough Gatorade with Fran and Charlie. Even with the clouds coming in again, it's going to be hot, sweaty work."

I mumbled through a mouthful of sandwich, "What's so hot and sweaty about shopping?"

Donna's eyes twinkled. "That was their cover story for Meg. Charlie stuck her head in here early this morning wanting to know if we'd give her a ride to Meg's place the first time we were going home for part of a day. Said she wanted to clean the flower beds, trim the shrubbery. Fran suggested this afternoon and offered any yard equipment needed and a second pair of hands."

"Don't tell Fran I asked, but is she up to that?"

"Fran's like Charlie'll be some day. Just as capable but with the good sense to go a little slower and practice a little caution. And don't underestimate Little Miss Dynamo. I'll bet she has Fran supervising from the porch most of the time. Glad to see her and Meg beginning to inch closer, Lexy. It'll be good for both of them."

I nodded, reaching for another sandwich. "Donna, would this be a good time for you to tell me about knocking on Fran's door?"

For a second her face became soft and dreamy—actually beautiful. "It would be a fine time," she said.

I listened with interest as I alternately ate and petted Tiger.

"My first job out of high school," Donna began, "was in the accounting department of a plant in Toledo. It was the early Fifties—placid times. Before long I was dating Nick Polaski, an assistant manager of the department, and daydreaming about marriage, one of those three-bedroom homes mushrooming on large tracts of land at the edge of cities, having children. It was part of my job to deliver paychecks to the foremen on the floor every Friday. The plant made small kitchen appliances, a growing business in those days. There were quite a few women working the lines. They all wore coveralls but you couldn't help noticing Fran. She was different."

"Why do I not have trouble believing that?"

Donna laughed cheerily. "For one thing, you could tell she never put any starch in her coveralls—and she wore motorcycle boots. She didn't wear a hairnet either. Couldn't really. She had short, coal-black hair flowing back from her face. No neat side part or sculpted bangs like all the other girls." She touched her silver. "Me included. She had an old fishing hat that she would cram on her head whenever the foreman fussed. She'd start teasing me when I'd arrive at the top of the steps, calling out things like 'Hey, Ginger Rogers, tap dance that money down to us,' or 'make a June Allyson entrance—slide down the railing.' I loved her grin. She would do it with her whole face. She had that gold tooth even then."

Donna refilled our glasses and I noticed how neatly manicured and painted her fingernails were. I could visualize the proper young woman she would have been. She continued her narrative. "One day I came out the main door and stood under the overhang looking up at the clouds. You could tell they were about to open up and my car was way off past the middle of the lot. Fran zoomed up on a motorcycle, an Indian Chief. Don't know if you have any idea, Lexy, how out-of-the-normal that was for then. She had on an army surplus jacket, no helmet. Told me to hop on and she'd get me to my car before the rain. That night I kept thinking about how it had felt to hold on, pressed tight against her back, my cheek feeling the movement of her shoulder." She gave me a direct look. "I had no idea what I was feeling. I came from a conservative family, went to sock hops and movies, dated nice boys. I had never heard the word lesbian. There was nothing in the books, magazines and movies I encountered to clue me in. Nothing on television. Heck, there was hardly any television at all. It wasn't that I was naive. I was just unknowing."

"It hasn't gone out of style, Donna. A lot of young girls still struggle through their awakenings alone, without knowledge or simply unsure."

"Well, my struggle didn't get very far. About a week later I found Fran waiting by my car. She gave me a slow smile and asked if I'd like to follow her to the new drive-in to sample their pork tenderloin sandwiches. We sat in my car and had a good time talking." She sighed. "I didn't know it but we were seen by a couple of women who worked in the same area I did. One of them cornered me in the washroom the next day. I can't tell you exactly what she said—we spoke in circles in those days. I understood just enough about her references to 'that kind of woman...unnatural things' to be embarrassed, confused. It spoiled the pleasure I had experienced with Fran. After that I avoided her, wouldn't look her in the eye when I had to be near. She was a good person. Let me go without making it any rougher on me." Donna began speaking faster. "I married Nick Polaski. Two children came right away. It was a decent marriage. We liked each other, loved the children. Nick opened his own accounting office and after the children were both in school, I worked it with him. Unfortunately, Nick fell into that statistical category of men who died from sudden, unexplained heart attacks before turning fifty. Our son had just come to work in the office. He still has it and I still receive income from it. My daughter finished college and married. I drifted along, a relatively young widow, concerned with the office and the lives of my grown children."

She paused, her face set in reflection, and I said into the silence, "What happened to change that?"

"Something quite simple really. Our longtime secretary started taking some college courses and suggested I might like to do the same. Said it was exciting to get her brain stirred up again. I decided to give it a try. I was tired of numbers and ledgers and wasn't particularly interested in babysitting grandchildren, so I signed up for art history and a course called Literature and the Independent Woman."

I chirped knowingly, "And discovered a whole new world!"

She echoed my mirth. "Oh, yes. And the class discussions! The first time I heard one of the younger women say, 'As a dyke, I can tell you where Willa Cather was coming from,' I stared in amazement, mouth open."

"And did she tell?"

"Absolutely. After she winked at me. I went straight from class to the library. One of several such excursions. Talk about a rush of information. There was more than I could absorb."

"Were you rattled?"

"Surprisingly, no. I felt like I was opening windows to fresh spring air. And part of what was good was that it wasn't destructive of the life I had lived. Given the parameters of my background and knowledge, I had had a good life—lucky in a marriage of companionship if not passion. But more and more I came to know there was a me in need of acknowledgment, of release, deserving of it."

An impish gleam brightened her eyes. I said emphatically, "You went looking for Fran."

"That, too, was remarkably simple. She was right there in the phone book. I would later find out that she had stayed at the plant, become floor supervisor."

As Donna pointed commandingly to the last sandwich, I scooped it up with one hand while Tiger butted the other to remind me of my duty.

"Did you call her right away?" I asked.

"No. All sorts of questions stopped me from doing that. What were the circumstances of her life? Was she settled in with some woman? Would she even remember me? Would I be making a fool of myself?"

Donna tilted her nose upward rolling her eyes. "What in the world would I say?" She brought her head down. "You'll laugh when I tell you what I did do. I started driving by her apartment building now and then, parking nearby sometimes. Finally I saw her. Older, heavier, but moving with that same air of being at ease with herself, and the hair nearly as black. I decided it was right then or never. I gave her a few minutes, then went into the building entranceway.

"Hers was the second door on the right. She answered my knock and stared at me critically when I didn't say anything—couldn't say anything. Then her lips did that slow smile I remembered and she said, 'You still delivering paychecks?'"

"And that was that?"

"No, no. It was months before we got all the wrinkles ironed out. At first we played the friendship game. I had her to my home, introduced her to my family as a friend from my days at the plant. She took me fishing and boating which I immediately fell in tune with." She huffed exasperatedly. "But she made no moves toward me and I didn't know how to initiate anything. I began to think she wasn't interested that way. Much much later she told me how scared she was all that time. First she was scared I'd back off again. Then she was afraid of giving up her freedom, of being unable to live happily committed with someone. Especially someone who had lived a straight life. She had spent her life moving from one casual relationship to another, never interested in permanence. And she was concerned about whether or not I could make the shift from the life I had known without harm or loss."

I spoke with strong feeling. "Obviously everything got settled to the satisfaction of you both."

Her face was infused with pleasure and warmth. "Satisfaction doesn't touch it." She wet her lips. "The only wrinkle that never got smoothed out entirely was my son. He tries to put on a good face when necessary but he's never been able to fully understand or accept us. I don't see him or his family often. My daughter, however, and her family are happy to accept Fran and me as a family unit as well. Perhaps you'll meet them when they come down." She smiled widely. "To my granddaughter Kristen, we are Gran and Aunt Fran. And she gets a lot of mileage out of the rhyming."

"I would like to meet them." I meant it. I concentrated on petting Tiger my thoughts sliding to Wren. She was knocking on my door and, like Fran, I was afraid to make a move. I was acting like a sailor letting her boat be pitched by winds and tides, unable to put my hand on the tiller.

"Lexy," Donna said gently, "about you and your young woman. Don't trap yourself into a corner with too much thinking. When I realized that was what Fran was doing, I commandeered her vacation time and put us in a cabin on a lake for two weeks. I told her it was time we found out how we felt about each other. Reasoning will take you only part of the way."

When I left the *Second Wind*, I felt bolstered in both body and mind.

Wren had said she wanted to come to me on the *Willow*. I would receive her there. Until then, Charlie and the events of the marina were going to get my full attention. I tucked my fingers into my pockets and, ridiculously, felt like doing a Popeye hornpipe jig up the pier.

My fingers touched the paper that had flown from Meg's desk. I removed it and started walking purposely toward the office, but stopped when I read what it said. In careful block letters someone had written DDR—CALL MIAMI IMMIGRATION. And there was a number. I looked up and, surprisingly, saw Damaris Del Riego speaking with Cap on the patio. The note must have been intended for her.

She gave Cap a dazzling smile and a crisp salute, then flowed like water down the steps. Her hair was a reddish gold aureole. She wore white slacks below a shimmering, silvery blue tunic. I stood unmoving in the middle of the narrow pier forcing her to stop in front of me. I was pleased, and relieved, to discover that I could observe her beauty and swirl the remembered taste of her in my mouth without being consumed by a renewed desire to experience her.

I extended the piece of paper. "I believe this was intended for you. I picked it up when it fell off the desk."

She read the note. Her strange eyes flew from the paper to my face with a chilling effect. There was a forced casualness to her question, "Have you been playing secretary as well as deckhand?"

I explained about the gust of wind and going off to answer Donna's lunch invitation without realizing I still carried the slip of paper with me. Her smile was truly warm and I wondered if I had imagined the chill in her disconcertingly colorless eyes. I turned sideways and she walked past me, but not before sweeping my form knowingly with those eyes.

Cap waited for me and patted a place beside him on the long dock bench. "Striking woman, that. I'll be sorry to see her go."

We were both watching her progress toward the *Song*. "She's leaving?"

"Aye. In a few days. She was just telling me that." He began telling me in detail how well Doug was doing so far. He added, "No sign of temper or strain. And he's going slowly. He's letting things run themselves as much as possible while he sounds the depths. Even Ed Pike's minding his tongue. Wants to keep his job, I figure."

Meg came out of the office and to the ledge above us. She said to Cap, "I've done what I can with that stack of notes you brought over from Steve's desk. Some made sense and were easy to deal with. A few I still don't know what they are referring to."

Cap replied, "Well, just hold on to them. Doug went through the whole stack and the ones I brought to you were ones he wasn't sure what to do with."

Meg turned back to the office and was gone before the full thought formed in my mind. Had I erred in thinking the note had been meant for Damaris? If it was one that came from Steve's desk, what had been his intent?

Fourteen

Considering the late afternoon heat and humidity, I was walking much too rapidly toward the larger marina. The undulations rising from all metal surfaces distorted the scenery, muting sounds. No birds swooped or squirrels scurried—instinct serving them better than human judgment. My long, hard strides were in response to my possible error in judgment at having given Damaris the note and also an urge to seek a solution along the multiple piers of Doug MacKay's new domain.

Wanting to avoid Ed Pike if he was in the office, I walked on to the diner, crossed through the outside seating area, and slipped down to the dock. The stillness was more than a matter of oppressive heat. Many of the slips were empty and most of the boats in port were covered, closed, uninhabited. I knew I was seeing a marina that was more a commercial enterprise than an active community. To what degree would Doug seek to change that? Would he have the opportunity? I added a hot sigh to the searing air about me.

I approached the houseboat moored at the first finger pier past the office. Rectangular and box-like, it looked dumpy and awkward. Something about it made me think of a treehouse squatting on water. I listened to the earthy voice of Bonnie Raitt coming from inside while I puzzled over my approach. I didn't want to shout for attention in case Doug or Pike were within hearing.

I shrugged and stepped easily onto the deck, then rapped my knuckles on the glass doors along the starboard side.

The music faded away and a hand pulled back enough drape for me to be viewed and measured. Squeaking, one door slid across the other and I breathed in the escaping cool air. The woman, now holding the drape further back and eyeing me quizzically, was probably around forty.

She wore a bathing suit beneath a thin, white T-shirt and I could tell the battle of sag and bulge was just around the corner. She wasn't a natural blonde and her shoulder length hair was brittle from too many experiments. But the smooth planes of her face were a golden tan that emphasized the whites of her large eyes, making her look mildly startled. A look that no doubt drew the men. I remembered how Ed Pike had watched her out the window on the day of my arrival.

I spoke first, deciding to be direct. "I'm Lexy Hyatt. I'm staying at Cap's. And am a friend of Doug. I'm trying to help them piece together what happened to Steve."

"And you've decided to talk to the mistress."

I wasn't prepared for her directness. I shifted my weight and made a defensive sound.

She curled a lip and did a good imitation of Mae West. "Come into my parlor." Then a trifle sadly. "I haven't talked to anyone since the police. Unless you count Ed Pike and, believe me, I don't count him. I'm Gina Lewis, in case you don't already know."

I stepped into what could have been a small apartment living room. I nodded at her offer of iced tea and she drew back a paisley curtain revealing an impressive kitchen. She talked without prompting as she prepared and served our drinks.

"I hadn't seen much of Steve lately even though we humped the light fantastic every now and then." She flashed a smile that was more than half chagrin. "We used to do that a lot. But that was before I realized there wasn't going to be any wedding ring ever and before he got pretty much all he was going to want. No big deal."

I wasn't too sure of that. "Did you see Steve Friday?"

"I heard more than saw. I was getting settled on the back of the boat to watch the fireworks when I heard Cap's voice and peeked around. I saw them standing just out there below the office. Cap hadn't been by here in a long time." She became cautious. "You know the scuttlebutt?"

"I know some. The argument about the road, the barricade, family problems…" I let my voice trail off.

Gina picked up, "Steve didn't have it in him to be part of a family. When I saw that, I didn't get the wedding-bell blues. I figured I wasn't missing out on anything if it included a guy like he'd turned out to be.

I've been planning to move on to another marina soon before tourist season sets in. Get a change of scene. Maybe even lock grapnel anchors with the right sort."

I prodded her back on course. "Did you hear anything Cap and Steve said to each other—by chance?"

She grinned. "Honey, I listened with both ears. It was mostly about Doug. I'd heard he'd taken a real hit from Steve. I didn't know what that was all about, but Cap sounded like he was after a hit of his own. He told Steve that if he ever laid a hand on Doug again, he'd find a way to pierce his bulkhead and send him to the bottom."

"How did Steve answer that?"

"He laughed and said Cap was the one going down. And he'd be taking Doug and Meg with him. He told Cap to tell Meg not to tie up his phone by calling him again. That she was as dumb as her do-gooder husband, and that she'd end up eating bottom slime like Cap would if she tried to keep worthless spawn like Doug and Charlie afloat. Mean thing to say. They're good kids."

I asked, "Did Cap have a come-back to that? Do you know what Steve meant about Meg's husband?"

"No on both counts. Actually nothing else was said. I peeked around again just as the first bunch of rockets went off. I could see Cap's face in the light. He looked as hard as coquina rock. Then he turned his back on Steve and took off. Last I ever saw of Steve was the back of his head. I drank a pitcher of martinis watching the fireworks—then slept me a good sleep. I woke up next morning to a cop pounding on the glass."

We were seated on the couch and she touched her cold glass to my bare knee, saying, "Guess I don't sound much like a grieving...whatever."

I responded honestly. "I haven't heard much grief expressed by anyone. Not much of an epitaph. Did you ever talk to Doug any?"

She looked regretful. "No. I teased him once in the diner before I knew how things were between him and Steve. No getting on with him after that. I don't know what to say to him now. He may not be grieving for Steve either but I hope he can let go of his anger."

I hoped that, too. I hoped even more that the anger hadn't exploded into murder.

I stayed through a second glass of iced tea—as much to give Gina Lewis some company as to seek information. I was certain there was a fairly shrewd woman behind the facade of artlessness. I wasn't sure how far to trust her apparent conclusions, however. She seconded Meg's belief that Steve had been engaged in illegal gambling practices but categorized it as minor, a matter of making a little 'bait money.' Casually she voiced her own belief that it might have been an old con man's ploy of directing attention to one activity in order to successfully carry out another and more important one. She claimed to have no idea what that might have been.

I brought up a plethora of other subjects but Gina volunteered little of any value. She agreed that the *Siren Song* was an impressive yacht but made no reference to Damaris Del Riego. She praised the good looks of Joe Quinn and his pleasant manner, adding, "I don't know how he put up with Steve's racial tripe." Then said with cold laughter, "Hell, I had to put up with my own brand from him. You do what you have to do until you're ready to crank the engine and take off." She described Ed Pike as a camp follower of power who would take off on his own soon. "Doug's smart not to fire him. He's the kind that deals in payback."

When I asked if he was likely to keep weapons around, or if Steve might have, she replied, "I don't know how much you've been on the water, Lexy, but pirates still exist. They'll steal your sails and seat cushions, cut free your anchors and outboards—sell them at flea markets or out of the back of trucks. So a lot of people pack guns aboard their boats."

When I tilted my head and lifted an eyebrow, she merely tapped my knee again and took my empty glass. I said a polite good-bye.

After the dim, cool interior of the houseboat, the white glare was almost intolerable. I leaned against a piling and rotated my right shoulder, long ago injured by too many ground tumbles, diving for fast-dropping fly balls. The increased stiffness and dull ache said rain on the way. So did the distant rumble of thunder. I hoped Fran and Charlie were heading back from their attack on Meg's yard.

I looked toward the office but the windows reflected the harbor scene.

I decided to see if Doug was within or, if not, tackle Ed Pike in as mild a way as he would let me. I hadn't forgotten his abrasive manner when I had mistakenly sought Marilyn's boat here.

I found Doug at the desk punching up data on the computer with a rapidity I envied. The large chair swallowed his slight form, but he glanced up at me with a smile and an air of fledgling authority. He might not grow into the chair but he was on his way to developing into the job.

"Where have you come from, Lexy?"

In case he had seen me from the window, I admitted to calling on Gina Lewis in her houseboat. He ducked his head over some computer sheets, and I said slowly and softly, "I'm trying to discover things that might help you all, Doug. Okay?"

He raised his head and some of the tension eased from his face. "Of course that's okay. I'm a little uncomfortable there. Not sure what I ought to be doing about her. And I don't feel like asking Cap or Meg."

I said, "She seems a decent sort. Why don't you treat her like anyone else keeping a boat here. Sometimes it's a good idea to pretend not to know that you know things you both know. If that makes any sense. Gives everyone a chance to reassess their positions. Besides," I pulled up a gray metal chair and sat down, "I think she was planning a course change where your...where Steve was concerned." I smiled inwardly at my increasing use of water terminology.

"I'll give that idea a try. Charlie's right. You have a good way of seeing things."

"Speaking of seeing things..." I tried to keep my tone from sounding ominous. "I saw you coming out of the A-house at the start of the fireworks. You'd gone for the gun you'd given Charlie to hold, hadn't you?"

Doug flinched and swallowed, but he didn't look away. "Cap's already given me a tongue lashing for that. Charlie and I have gotten to be mates. I didn't look at it like I was using her or getting her in trouble. Guess I should have." His voice squeaked a little. "Things between Cap and Steve were...were escalating. I snatched the gun from the trailer, then didn't know what to do with it. Anywhere I might put it, Cap or Meg could come across it. They even use my truck sometimes. So I asked Charlie to put it in her locker." He whipped his fingers through his hair. "I could tell she didn't want to, but I pushed. Told her it just wasn't safe for it to be where either Cap or Steve could reach it when they were going at each other. She didn't believe me about Cap but she did about Steve—so she took it." He gave me a straight look. "Truth is I was more afraid of me reaching for it."

That surprised me. But a second thought arose before I could stifle it. Was he being clever to admit that? I hardened my tone. "So what was your intention when you got it from Charlie's locker?"

He waited the space of three breaths before answering. "All the while I was playing volleyball, I was thinking about what he had said and how he had hit me. The being hit wasn't so bad. It was his saying not to get drunk and wrap my truck around a tree..." Pain shadowed his face and his voice trailed away.

I leaned forward. "I've heard the story, Doug. I understand."

"He didn't care that she died. He didn't care when Grandma died. He didn't care that Meg's husband died." He stared at me defiantly. "I don't care that he died. When I got the gun from the A-house, I intended to go threaten him, warn him to back off from all of us, from trying to steal the marina. But when I held that gun in my hand, I scared myself. I knew I had to get rid of it." He stared at the computer screen.

"So what did you do with it?" I asked bluntly.

Doug's long sigh was like letting something loose. "I tied it to a cement block and sent it to the bottom of the lake halfway out to the barge." He shook his head slowly from side to side. "If I'd known what was going to happen to Steve, I wouldn't have done that. I'm not a fool all the time. I know how the cops look at the gun being missing." He turned back to me. "I told Cap I'd go tell them what I did but he said not yet. For us to wait and see how the wind blows."

I considered that without replying. I wished I could ask Robbie about it but knew that would be stretching friendships, or sisterhood, too far. I thought about what he had said, then asked, "So what did you do during the fireworks while you still had the gun?"

Again he waited before answering. "I went looking for Steve. Thought I might find him around the office...or the houseboat. Even though I felt uncomfortable with the gun, I hadn't decided to let go of it yet. It was kind of like I was daring myself." His lips trembled slightly. "I'll never know what I would have done if I'd found him alone."

"But you did see him? Where? When?"

"By those vans in front out there. All the regular lights were out but it was easy to see when some of the rockets exploded. I used a parked car for cover and watched him herding bunches of people into the backs of the vans. Ed Pike was doing a lot of shoving."

"Who were they? Where'd they come from?"

"I don't know. From the office was all I saw. Seemed to be a lot of them. Steve drove off in the first van. Pike in the last one. I don't know who drove the others. I stood there watching them go, holding the gun under my sweatshirt. I didn't feel right. There was a dumpster nearby and I almost tossed the gun in it. Then I thought about somebody finding it and getting hurt—or hurting somebody else. That's when I decided to deep-six it when Joe and I went out to the barge."

"You didn't get your truck and follow the vans?"

Doug jerked forward, scooting the chair back. "No. I never thought about doing it."

I stretched out my legs, uncomfortable on the small, hard chair. "I've talked to a lot of people about where they were and what they saw Friday night. Someone mentioned seeing you drive up onto the main road and head south."

He appeared to relax, drew the chair back to the desk. "That would have been a lot later. Joe and I talked with the fireworks guys awhile, then I brought him in to the dock out there to get his motorcycle. I took the boat back to the dock. I was all keyed up—not ready to go to the trailer—so I got in my truck and took off." He finished very quietly. "I drove the road where my mother died. Parked by the tree. I do that sometimes."

He bowed his head and I left him to his thoughts. I ruminated over what I had heard. As both a teacher and a reporter, I knew that questions answered and information offered weren't necessarily the truth. Statements were often whitewashed, slanted, or downright lies. Even if Doug had given me truth, Steve MacKay obviously returned to the marina area at some point. And as far as I knew, no one could verify Doug's movements the rest of the night after Joseph saw him driving off. I needed to check with Joseph about the gun being dropped overboard and with Cap about whether he heard Doug come in and what time.

Doug brought me back with a question of his own. "Are you playing detective, Lexy, or charting a story for your paper?"

"I've been answering that question a lot lately. I'm on vacation but I'm also involved—especially through Charlie. I'm not one to turn my back on friends if finding the truth will help them."

"There's going to be one person it won't help—" His voice was flat, almost resigned.

I had no comeback for that. The shrill ring of the phone covered my awkward silence. As Doug responded with information about available slips and prices, I motioned that I was going. He nodded and gave me a bland smile.

Outside a deep rumble of thunder made me look up. Black clouds were beginning to boil up from the west. Thin, lighter ones were already dimming the sun although the temperature had yet to drop. I started off but halted at a guttural command. "Hold up there, hiker."

I turned to see Ed Pike flip a cigarette into a scrawny bush. He approached with a rolling, cocky walk. "Found your boat, haven't you? What's your business here?"

"Talking with your boss." I knew I should have put some warmth into my voice, but the man set my teeth on edge.

He barked a nasty sound. "I know a detective who'll probably have something to say about that before long. I gave him an earful Saturday. That runt in there threatened his daddy more than once."

"We all say things in anger we never intend to follow through on."

Pike sneered. "Someone did this time."

"From the way I hear it, lots of people had problems with Steve MacKay. Maybe even you had some. He couldn't have been all that easy to work for."

So much for being moderate and diplomatic.

His fleshy face was quivering and thick brows hooded his eyes in a scowl. "I was his right-hand man, first mate, going to be a partner soon. Gave him some good ideas—none that namby-pamby in there would ever listen to. Or that blowhard grandfather of his."

"Like maybe permitting gambling on the excursion runs to Jacksonville and back?" A small voice in my head asked me what in the hell I thought I was doing, but I kept on going. Pike's kind was more likely to give up something in anger or off balance than bite at a gentle, teasing lure. "Or cramming people in vans while everybody else is watching fireworks."

He took a menacing step toward me and I drew myself tall turning slightly sideways. I was wishing I had listened to some friends and taken up one of the martial arts, or at least done some workout routines.

Suddenly there was a triple blast of a car horn and Charlie's voice. "Hey, Long Legs. Need a lift?" She and Fran were in an old station wagon idling in the middle of the road.

I returned my eyes to Pike as I called out, "You bet."

He said, "You've got a long nose to go with those long legs. Keep it out of my business."

Fifteen

Fran, Charlie, and I stood outside Meg's office lifting our heads to the breeze stirring our hair and billowing Fran's shirt. I noticed Charlie was the more grimy and sweat-stained. She was chattering happily about their accomplishments. Fran rolled her eyes whenever Charlie said 'we.'

"You should see it, Lexy. We dug out all around the trees and bordered them in black dirt and mulch, ready for plants. We marked off some places for crape myrtles and azalea bushes and holly if Meg will okay it. Then we cleaned out all the flower beds but now they look really empty. Fran's going to talk to Meg about what kind of flowers she might want—if she does, of course." A return to shyness there. "I'm hoping she'll want some rain lillies. The shade around the front porch would be great for them."

Fran said, "I'm sure she'll be glad to leave things in your capable hands, Charlie." To me, "Hope you ate up all the tuna sandwiches. Ever since Donna read about how good salmon and tuna are for the health-conscious older woman, we've had more than our share. At least I have. Suits Tiger though." Her grin took any sting out of the words.

I acknowledged having eaten the last one. Charlie excused herself and headed for the shower. I said to Fran, "She's not going to say anything to Meg?"

"She asked me to do that. And I understand. That fifty year gap in ages doesn't mean a thing when it comes to being afraid of losing the ones you care about. it makes you more careful when it comes to making new connections. I don't know that because of anything either one has said, but I smell it as sure as the coming rain."

I nodded agreement, then looked skyward. "I was hoping for some jog time. I wanted to see if it would pound some details into place."

"You've got time. The clouds always slow down as they approach the lake. And the early lightning bolts will be way out on the water. Head for the *Willow* when you see the first one."

"I'll test your theory, then. Thank you, Fran, for the time you gave Charlie."

"No thanks needed. She's been walking a lot taller since you came on deck. Been good to see."

Fran entered the office and I started off at a slow trot. I had on soft shoes but figured they'd work for a run in the loose ground of the dirt road leading to the boat dock. I encountered no traffic and took the middle of the road between the ruts. Hearing the loud, clear whistle that I recognized as the marina's resident osprey, I jogged in place at the dock and watched his slow wing-beat as he passed overhead. The black and white design of the underfeathers of the wings and tail were very distinct. Suddenly he swooped to the level of the water and skipped off with a fish firmly secured in the long talons.

I called out, "Bon appetit," and hit the road again. Fran appeared to be right about the clouds as only wispy gray-whites were gathering over the lake. There was a large patch of cattails spreading in a low section off to my right away from the lake. I kept hearing an interesting bird call from that area but never spotted the songster. There was a buzzing note followed by three clear different pitches. I tried to imitate it a couple of times so I could ask Charlie what it was. I never doubted that she would know.

As I reached the stand of oaks where my car was parked, I heard a piercing whistle and saw Charlie walking the ledge from the A house to the *Willow*. I answered her wave as I turned for another lap. I thought about the wave I had received from Wren a week before as she was pulling out of the driveway. How I longed to receive another as greeting—to pull her to me and taste the vanilla flavor of her throat, embed my fingers in the soft, lovely hair...embed my fingers in her. I stumbled and broke my stride. "Behave, Lexy," I muttered through short breaths.

I increased my pace and tried for the runner's slackness of mind. I lost track of my laps until, as I was turning at the boat dock, I saw a thin streak plunge from a black cloud and strike the lake. I was startled, too, to note how dark it had become due to the massing of thick clouds and the nearness of dusk. Time to heed Fran's advice and head for the *Willow*.

I had gone about a third of the way back when a large drop of rain struck my cheek. I lengthened my stride but slowed at the sight of an old battered light blue pickup heading toward me. I shifted to my right along the edge, but the truck matched my move. Considering that he might be trying to avoid the ruts, I swung over to the left. The truck countered that move as well.

I stopped and tried to see if I recognized the driver, but the windshield was dulled by a thick layer of dust. Both doors opened and two people in nondescript jeans and shirts got out. Halfway towards me, I realized that their strange features were the result of nylon-stocking masks. Retreat seemed wise even though I had no idea what was going on. The rain was beginning to pelt down in earnest. I turned swiftly and headed for the dock hoping that someone would be coming in to escape the rising wind and rain.

No boats were in sight. I glanced toward the county road high up and a good distance away. One of the men moved to block that route. I leaped onto the dock, considering the water as an escape route little as I liked the thought of gators lurking in the weeds nearby. But a blow to my back sent me sprawling.

I came up on one knee, squinting into the rain. "Okay, guys, what's going on here?" I made a concerted effort at calm and control. "I don't have any money, no car keys, no valuables."

"You got a long nose, bitch. Maybe getting it broken will make you more careful where you stick it."

I tried to stare defiantly at the two distorted faces but double shafts of lightning and resounding thunderclaps made me flinch. Ed Pike, thought.

But neither had his width or paunch. Again I decided the water was my only chance. I rolled and dropped from the side of the dock Immediately the wind-driven water churned me, striking my head against a piling and I saw stars.

Then hands were roughly grabbing my shirt. I fought but was dragged partially onto the dock. One of the men tried to get a grip on my short, wet hair to force my head back, but failed. I regretted my clipped nails as I tried to dig them into the flesh above his boot.

He jerked his leg from my grasp. Still dizzy from the blow to my head, I attempted to grip the planking before I remembered that the water was my best bet. The rain was now coming down in torrents.

muffled voice yelled, "Let's get out of here! We've delivered the message."

From above me, a deeper voice snarled, "Not good enough."

My scream was lost to the thunder as he brought his heavy workman's boot down twice on my hand and arm. I dropped back into the water. Weakly I reached up and clung to the planking with my good hand. Soon I heard the truck gunning its way up to the road. I tried to lift myself onto the dock with one arm but the wind and rain drove me back. I got my arm around a piling and held myself tightly to it, now and then resting my head against the dock. I had no idea how long I would have to hold on.

Time had no meaning but eventually I lifted my head to what I thought was a shout cutting through the noise of the storm. I opened my mouth to shout back but choked on the rain. Then I heard the high-pitched call of my name. It had to be Charlie. I shouted her name as loudly as I could but it was thrust back into my face by the wind. I was about to try again when I saw her slight figure charging onto the dock. She hurled herself onto her knees above where I bobbed in the rough water.

My teeth were chattering. "I need some help, Charlie," I cried out as she grabbed my injured arm. I managed to say, "It got hurt."

Without a word she slipped into the water. She boosted me until I was half on the dock, then heaved my legs up so that I lay on my side. I felt her scramble up behind me. Gently she brought me to a sitting position and had me lean against her. We were both breathing hard, our heads lowered against the sting of the rain.

Weakly I said, "You're going to have to take another shower." I must have been groggy from the blow to my head.

Grimly she said into my ear, "I'm afraid to leave you here. Think you can lean on me and walk?"

With her help I got to my feet. She got a good grip around my waist and I gripped her shoulder with my right hand. My left hand was hanging down and beginning to throb with pain, or maybe I was just becoming aware of it. Neither of us had breath for talking as we struggled through the rain and wet sand toward the marina.

When we finally got to the paved road, I tried to swerve toward the *Willow*, but Charlie said in a hard voice, "No. Meg's car is still here. We're going in there." And she headed me to the office.

Meg must have seen us out the window as we approached. Moving faster than I had known she could, she rushed to us and took over my support. Charlie held the door for us saying, "I don't know what happened to her. She wasn't in when the storm hit and I went looking. I found her in the water at the boat dock. Her left arm's hurt."

Meg took me into the back room and removed my wet clothes, being as careful as possible with my injured arm. She yanked a blanket from the cot and wrapped me in it, drying me as she did so. I was conscious of her efforts through a haze of dizziness and pain. I was conscious, too, of Charlie hovering close.

Meg said, "Got a change of clothes here that will fit you, Lexy, if you can do without undies."

"Sure, Meg." My teeth were still chattering. I sat on the cot and Charlie began toweling my hair. I jerked and grunted.

Quickly she said, "What?"

"I hit my head on the dock."

Carefully she checked my scalp. "There's a big lump here, Meg! The skin's not broken but she needs a doctor."

"I know," Meg said calmly. "The rain's letting up. There's a clinic in Mossville that can take x-rays and see what needs doing."

"You're not going without me." Charlie was adamant.

"Of course not. You take an umbrella and scamper to the *Willow*. You need dry clothes, too."

Charlie whirled toward the door. I croaked, "Charlie." She stopped and turned. "Thank you for coming and getting me."

She made a face. "You're starting to be a halfway decent deck hand. I didn't want to lose you." She gave me a stern look. "Don't you tell what happened till I get back."

"Aye, aye, Skipper."

Charlie returned, bringing dry socks and shoes for me. As she knelt to put them on, I plucked at her still wet hair. She gave me a wan smile but her eyes were dark with concern.

In Meg's car, I moaned as I placed my left arm on the armrest in the middle so that Charlie could maneuver the seatbelt about me. On the way to Mossville, with Charlie leaning forward from the back seat, I related what had happened. I omitted my suspicion that Ed Pike was behind the attack, not wanting to either alarm them or set them off.

As we entered Mossville, Charlie said, "You have to tell the police." Rapidly she added, "Jeez! I can't believe I said that."

I would have laughed if it didn't hurt so. "Not much I could tell them. I've seen dozens of pickups like that one and I couldn't identify the men."

Meg pulled up to the door of the well-lit clinic, and Charlie helped me out. The automatic sliding doors swished open, and Charlie forced me into one of the waiting wheelchairs. At the counter I gave pertinent information, glad that I had memorized the number of my group insurance plan, though the receptionist wasn't pleased that I didn't have the card with me. She pressed a buzzer just as Meg joined us.

Down a corridor a middle-aged woman pushed through wide swinging doors. She walked with a determined tread, her smock flaring over broad hips. She accepted a paper from the receptionist, glanced over it quickly, looked scrutinizingly at my left arm cradled against my waist, and started pushing me toward the swinging doors. Over her shoulder she said to Meg and Charlie, "You two wait out here."

The x-ray technician was fast and efficient. He shot my head from the front, back, and side after determining the area of the blow. The procedure for my arm and hand was more painful. Then I was taken to an examining area closed off by thick curtains and my arm immersed in ice water for the swelling.

I welcomed the numbing effect. Alone with my thoughts, I tried to conjure up my earlier brief conversation with Ed Pike. I was sure it was the business with the vans that had goaded him.

My wait lengthened, interrupted only once by a nurse informing me that an orthopedist was on his way. Eventually a surprisingly young man arrived, dressed in casual slacks and shirt. Though he greeted me pleasantly, I was sure he had been called away from something much more entertaining than the x-rays in his hand. He placed them against a light box on the wall and pointed out the fractures of my thumb and wrist. "Clear breaks," he said. "Easily set. These'll mend clean."

Despite all my years of playing sports, I had never broken anything, so the casting procedure was new and interesting—until I considered the weight, time, and inconvenience. The cast went up nearly to my elbow and my fingers wiggled out the other end. I sent vituperative thoughts Ed Pike's way. I was given a sling for support.

Then the doctor, or intern I suspected, explained, "You also have a mild concussion, Miss Hyatt. It should involve no more than a slight headache for a few days, but I'll be giving you instructions and signs to watch out for in case of complications. You shouldn't be alone for a few days."

"No problem there," I replied. I knew without question that Charlie would be glued to my side.

He patted me on the shoulder and said, "The nurse will be in shortly with written instructions and some medication for later. Feel free to contact the clinic or your regular doctor if you spot any complications. Otherwise take it easy for awhile. The cast can come off in six weeks." He glanced at it as though quite pleased with his handiwork.

I thought it was a good thing that I had nearly two weeks of vacation time ahead of me still. I wondered what it was like in the wilds of the mountains right now. Then I thought of Wren isolated as well in cold clinical surroundings…

When wheeled to the reception area, clutching my papers and medication in my right hand, I was mildly startled and irritated to see Robbie Exline squatting on her haunches in front of Charlie and Meg. Charlie was speaking rapidly and Robbie was listening intently. At the sight of me, Charlie's first reaction was a flash of sheepish discomfort quickly replaced by defiance. Over her head, Meg frowned me a silent 'don't-fuss' warning.

I took a deep breath and relaxed my tightened lips.

Robbie pivoted and put her hand on the arm of the wheelchair. "I've gotten the story and they're right. It needs reporting, at least to the local authorities here." She overrode my beginning objection. "Even if you can't identify anyone, it needs to be on record in case that changes. Can you walk?"

I heaved myself from the chair but was glad of her steadying hand as she rose with me.

She said, "Then come around the corner with me while I call for a uniform to take a statement. Professional courtesy should speed things up."

There were a couple of chairs next to the pay phone. We sat in them after she placed the call. Robbie was direct. "Okay, Lexy, what else? Wha didn't you tell Meg and Charlie? With what's been going on at that mari na, I don't believe that was a random attack."

With only a brief hesitation, I told her of my encounter with Ed Pike earlier in the afternoon and my suspicion that he had sent the two men to convince me to back off. "I don't want to tell that to the police, Robbie. I don't have any proof and I don't want to alert Pike. I'm sure it's my knowing about the people being put into those vans that spooked him—but I don't know why."

"How did you know about them?" She had become Detective Exline.

"Heard it from a couple of people."

Her eyes became narrow slits. "You're protecting people again, Lexy," She sighed. "Okay. I'll go along with that right now, but the attack itself really does need to be on the record." She tapped my cast. "And don't you go off by yourself again." She dropped her voice. "And especially don't get after Charlie for calling me."

"Don't worry. I probably owe her my life, Robbie. I was too dazed from hitting my head to think that I might have been able to work my way around the dock to the other side. It's possible I could have gotten up the concrete incline where the boats are backed in. I might have drowned if she hadn't come looking."

We returned to reception where Charlie took my papers and medication, and perused them. The policeman arrived, and I gave him the same abbreviated version I had given Charlie and Meg. I convinced Meg that I could walk to her car while Charlie accompanied Robbie to hers. I saw her nodding vigorously to whatever Robbie was saying.

When she slipped into the back seat, I said, "You were right to call her."

She gave a long, relieved sigh and Meg winked at me.

Starting the car, Meg informed us we were going to spend the night at her place. I was winding down into real fatigue and a wider, softer berth than the *Willow* provided was more than tempting. Once we arrived, Meg led us to a small table in a large, cheery kitchen. "I doubt that either of you had any supper. I'm going to fix you something light and warm to sleep on. No arguments." Within moments she placed buttered toast and hot chocolate before us. She cut my slices in half, then left us alone.

Charlie dove into hers. I withdrew my arm from the sling and rested it on the table, then followed her example more slowly. I lifted my cup and inhaled the lush, sweet odor. Suddenly my eyes flooded with tears, a few slipping down my cheeks. I put the cup down with a thunk, nearly sloshing the dark contents over the side, and swiped at the tears.

Charlie half rose. "Lexy! What's wrong?"

I motioned her to sit back down. "It's all right. Just an ambush of sorts. A few months ago I got pushed around in a parking lot. Wren was there. She took me home and fed me hot chocolate, too." I paused and tried to swallow the lump out of my throat. "It turned into a special night." I took a sip of the sweet liquid, savored the taste and the warm trickle down my raw throat. "I miss her."

"Do you tell her that when you call?"

"I try not to. She's dealing with something hard. I don't want to add to it."

Charlie reached across the table and touched the fingers jutting from my cast. "If someone was missing me, I'd want to hear it."

I looked into the face older than its years, and into the eyes wiser. "Looks like it's your night for knowing best." We smiled as equals.

Meg returned and refilled our cups, having a cup with us. Charlie opened my medication and placed two tablets next to my cup. "The paper the doctor gave you said to take these before going to bed." I obeyed.

Meg said, "Charlie, go find the bedroom with the twin beds. See if the shirts I laid out will serve as nightwear for you two." She chuckled, "There's a bit of difference in your sizes. And make certain there are enough towels in the bathroom. Click on the nightlight if I forgot." With Charlie gone, she said, "Won't hurt to give her a look at the house. See what it might feel like to her."

"You've made a good team tonight, Meg. I know I've never been handled so easily or well." I laughed ruefully. "I'll probably be mad as hell about it tomorrow."

Instinctively Charlie allowed me to manage the bathroom and changing of clothes by myself. But once in the bed across from me, she lay facing me and propped her head higher by placing her arm under the pillow. I knew she would watch me until I slept.

Sixteen

I swam up out of a deep sleep without opening my eyes, gradually registering that I was lying in a twin bed in Meg Gilstrap's house. Eyes still closed, I mentally skimmed through the jogging, the attack, my rescue by Charlie, the clinic. I felt the weight of the cast and touched its rough surface. I shifted and stretched, getting in touch with my body again and testing for dizziness which, thankfully, did not occur.

Finally I opened my eyes. The bed across from me was empty and neatly made up. The clock on the wall said five after ten. Gingerly I pushed back the top sheet and carefully swung my feet to the floor. Still no dizziness, but I was stiff and sore and there were bruises on my legs.

Meg spoke from the doorway. "Don't rush things, Lexy."

Even smiling hurt. "I slept well, Meg. I need to be up and moving now. Where's Charlie?"

"Joe Quinn came in for her on his motorcycle. She liked that. She's going to manage the office and chores this morning while Cap meets with the funeral director and I keep an eye on you. Someone will bring her back here later with some of your stuff."

She waited while I went to the bathroom, then helped me into a pair of her jeans. I padded barefoot after her to the kitchen. The table was against a large window overlooking her backyard. A brown thrasher was energetically scratching the dirt under a tree and a cardinal strutted on the windowsill.

Meg said, "I hope strong coffee and cereal is acceptable."

"I don't want you waiting on me, Meg."

She screwed her face into mock irritation and I hushed. Her face relaxed into pleasure. "Charlie and I sat here and had a good talk early this morning. When I called Cap to set up Charlie running things till I could come back in, he said to go ahead and tell her she had a permanent job when she was finished with her obligations to the *Willow* and Marilyn."

"How'd she take it?"

"Like she was scared to show she was pleased—but she was. I rather imagine she's had things yanked out from under her more than once. I held off mentioning she could live here. Don't want to come at her with too much too fast. Roberta Exline gave me her card last night—put her home phone number on the back. You agree that it might be all right to call her about these plans?"

I caught something in her eyes. "And maybe report on me while you're at it?"

She rested her chin in the cradle of her fingers and chuckled the sound that I was beginning to connect with her—a warm, harmonious communication. "That blow to your head didn't dull anything, did it?" In a flash she became serious. "Those men had to be after you for a reason, young woman. I don't buy that random attack bit. You asking questions about Steve's death is the only reason I can figure."

I concentrated on sipping the hot coffee but there was no escaping her penetrating gaze, her green flecked eyes boring into me. "Okay, Meg. They were delivering a message—but I can't be positive of the source. If I'd let the guy break my nose like he wanted, I wouldn't be stuck with this." I tapped the cast. "They won't be back. I'm going to act as if I got the message." I didn't add only where Ed Pike was concerned. From now on, I would go around some corners to get at him.

She seemed to accept that. "Charlie's nose was broken once upon a time," she said thoughtfully.

"I could see that."

Meg went on. "She was expressing worry this morning about your breaks healing without any lasting harm. She fingered the crook of her nose and, when she caught me watching her, tried to shrug it off. Said she didn't know if it had been broken or if she was born that way. It hurts her not to know things. It could have been something as simple as falling out of a swing—or it could have been caused by a fist. Probably just as well she doesn't know. There are things it's a damn sight better not to know." Her southern inflection had increased.

I reached out and touched her forearm to keep her from rising. "Something for us to talk about, Meg?" I tried for a light tone. "I've sure got the time."

She shook her head no but settled back into her chair. "Not your fault, Lexy, but you nearly drowning in that storm brought back some bad memories. I haven't shaken free of them yet—even though it's a nice, bright day." She continued rapidly, "But it isn't only what happened to you. It's Cap talking funeral plans. It brought back the last funeral I attended. Ben's—my husband. At his funeral I found out how he really died. Never been able to shake free of that either." Her face was forlorn, the wrinkles deeper.

I urged her again to talk with me—to let me earn my keep by at least listening to her. Gradually she relented, toying with her coffee cup and glancing out the window now and then as she talked. Her voice was too soft for what she related, which made the images she created all the harsher.

"Ben died on a Labor Day weekend ten years ago. Last holiday of the summer. The lake was full of people—boats of all kinds and sizes. There was just the big marina then. Ben and I were sticking close to Cap. Mary had been gone about five months and he didn't have a real good feel for life again yet. Concentrating on Dougie helped but it didn't heal. He had let Steve take over more and more. Steve also was part-owner of a good size excursion boat running up and down the lake. Dinner, dancing, just enjoying the lake scenes—that kind of thing. Ben was sure he was permitting high stakes poker games in the cabins. Probably was."

Meg brought her eyes back to me. "You got a little taste of the lake under storm yesterday. That Labor Day we were hit by a thunder squall right at noon that exploded on the edge of a temperature drop that no weatherman had foreseen. The wind was ferocious. And there may have been a waterspout. The lightning seemed to stay in the clouds but the thunder was rumbling through the air all around us. We could see sailboats and canoes flipping over. Small power boats were trying to keep from hitting each other as well as capsized craft—and picking up people from the water. Even the excursion boat that had been about to enter the harbor was pushed out of the channel. Cap said later that the other owner's teenage son had been at the wheel. We could see some people getting washed off the lower deck. Cap, Ben, Steve and others put out in power boats to get all the people they could." She paused. "Eleven souls died that day."

She got up from the table and refilled our cups. "There were a lot of us all along the piers helping people out of boats. I was too busy, and scared, to think about Ben being in danger. Then there was Cap telling me they'd found Ben's boat—people in it and clinging to it. No Ben. Marine Patrol found him the next day. Autopsy showed a combination of heart attack and drowning. That's all I knew until the day of his burial."

She fell silent. I watched her come up out of memories much as I had come up out of sleep a short while before.

She continued. "After the graveside service, I was approached by an Asian couple and a younger American. He served as an interpreter. They understood English well enough but had difficulty speaking it. They were what had been called boat people—Vietnamese refugees eventually relocated here from Thailand. They often fished Lake Arrow, and had gone out that day not knowing about Americans flocking to water on certain holidays. They had been in a rowboat. The storm hit and they picked up a family from a capsized sailboat. Their boat was filling with water when Ben pulled up. He had a bunch in his boat but he threw them a line so he could tow them in."

Meg stopped again and the quiet of the kitchen was charged with her inner tension. "Steve, according to their description of him and his boat, came alongside and shouted at Ben to let them go. To follow him out to the excursion boat. That there were more important people out there to save. When Steve powered off, he bumped the rowboat and it foundered. Ben went into the water to help people get a grip on it." She clutched her cup in both hands. "He swam a couple of strokes back toward his boat, but then he started thrashing about and went under. He never came up. The Asian couple wanted me to know how good and brave my husband was. And how deeply they regretted his death."

I reached across and removed the cup from her gnarled fingers. I tried to take both her hands in my one. There was nothing to say but she read my eyes and felt the sympathy of my touch.

She gave me a wan smile. "It was time I told that to someone, Lexy.

Thank you. I tried to make clear to them how much their words meant to me, and I told Cap that they were two of those saved by Ben. I couldn't let him see all the rage and hatred I was feeling toward Steve at that moment. It wouldn't bring Ben back. And it would only add to Cap's pain. So I consigned Steve to a black hole as far as my feelings were concerned. But I think he knew how I felt—and maybe why."

Meg and I puttered away the next few hours by her showing me the house, exchanging family and job stories, talking of Charlie. At midafternoon we heard the rumble of a motorcycle. I opened the door to Charlie laden down with one of my nylon carry-alls, then I stepped off the porch to speak with Joseph.

He removed his helmet and I rapped on it. "Doesn't look much like a chauffeur's cap."

He grinned and his dimples deepened. "Charlie weighs so little I didn't even know she was aboard." He rapped my cast. "She says you had an argument with the boat dock in the middle of the storm."

I hadn't had a chance to caution Charlie and was pleased at her circumvention of the truth. I said, "Something I'll never do again. I'm not happy with this." I adjusted the cast in the sling and wriggled my fingers the little bit I could. "Joseph, I've been talking with Doug. He told me he dropped a gun over the side Friday night on the way out to the barge."

Panic and concern warred in his dark eyes. "Ah, why did…I mean…" Then he spoke a phrase in Spanish that I was sure was far from polite. "I hoped that wouldn't come out. Pike's been telling tales to the police. They're true but he makes them sound worse. If they find out about the gun… You're not going to tell them, are you?"

I ignored the question. "Then he did drop it in the lake?"

Joseph compressed his lips. "I did. Doug was driving the boat. He told me to tie it to a chunk of broken concrete he'd brought along. When we hit a stretch empty of other boats, I pitched them."

"Could you point out where?"

"Not very close. Even if I could, that storm yesterday really moved the water around. Even that chunk of concrete would have gotten shoved around or covered over with bottom sludge." He smacked his hand across the top of the smooth helmet. "Doug has a temper. He's not a killer."

"I believe that, too. But the police are looking for that gun. The truth is a better defense than appearing to destroy evidence. He involved Charlie by letting her handle that gun. And now you, too."

I could see him absorbing that. I added meaningfully, "A good friend would talk to him about it."

Joseph donned his helmet, shielding his eyes from my probing. He muttered, "I'll think on it." He wheeled the cycle around and took off with a roar, skidding at the edge of the driveway.

I found Charlie in the kitchen filling in Meg on her day. "And Cap says he'll cover the rest of the day—and tomorrow if need be." She grinned at me. "He said it would probably take two of us to keep you below deck and out of harm's way. Oh, Marilyn wants you to call her."

My stomach plummeted. I didn't relish fending off Marilyn's aggressive concern. "What did you tell her?"

"I didn't have to tell her anything. I guess Roberta told her 'cause she knew about your arm and staying here in Mossville. Mostly I just said 'yes ma'am' and 'no ma'am' to whatever she said."

I laughed. "And probably stood at attention while you did it. I've been there, Charlie."

Meg said, "There's a phone with some privacy in the living room. Use that."

I knew Marilyn would be at The Cat supervising the kitchen preparations for the evening meal. A server caught my call and I waited a minute before Marilyn picked up. She started an immediate bombardment. "What in the Sam Hill do you think you're doing! You're supposed to be watching out for Charlie—not the other way around! You ought to be ashamed of yourself making that tiny child drag you out of that lake!" I held the receiver slightly away from my ear until she ran out of steam. Her tag line was, "I'm just yelling because you'd be missed around here, kid."

"I know, Admiral. I'd miss being here. Things are okay. I know where my problem's coming from and I'm not testing that wind again."

Despite her effort to maintain her bluster, Marilyn snorted a half laugh. "Damn if Robbie isn't right. You're talking like a sailor. Seriously, Lexy, I want you and Charlie safe. Come back in. Bring her with you."

"You may not know Charlie well enough, Marilyn, but you know me. Neither of us is going to turn her back on people who have become special."

There was silence—then an exasperated sigh. "Don't suppose I expected anything different. You watch your back, kid. Don't make me have to face Wren with worse news than a broken arm. I've got a message for you."

My heart soared. "From Wren!"

"No—a Barbara MacFadden. She says she's a researcher at the *Ledger*. Wants you to meet her at a place called The Billet tonight or Thursday night."

Back in the kitchen, I said, "Meg, I hate to be such a nuisance but I need another favor. A ride in to Orlando around six o'clock." At her critically raised eyebrow, I hastened to add, "Things will go quiet and easy and not take long." I adopted an exaggerated wheedling tone. "I'll throw in supper."

She yielded. "All right if that quiet and easy part is true. I'm not used to staying in all day. i could use an outing."

Charlie looked up expectantly. I tried to speak placatingly. "Sorry, Charlie. I have to meet someone at a bar, so I can't take you."

Her disappointment was palpable and Meg moved to dispel it. She asked, "Do you know how to get in touch with your friend Karen, Charlie?"

"I have her phone number."

"Well, Sanford isn't far. Why don't you call her and see if she's got the time and transportation to run over here. There's fixings for sandwiches in the refrigerator or there are take-out places in town."

Charlie brightened, shyly thanked Meg, and headed for the phone in the living room.

Meg said to me, "I'm sending you to your room for awhile. Some rest, if not a nap, is called for before we set out."

Obediently I returned to the bedroom Charlie and I shared. My bag was on the bed. I checked the contents and found three changes of clothing—slacks, jeans, and shorts with appropriate shirts. Also a plastic sack of toiletries. Efficient Charlie. I lay down surprised both by the fatigue I felt and a longing for the gentle rocking of the *Willow*.

The dream began slowly. I was standing like a scarecrow among cattails, bound to the T-bar of the stake. My forearms dangled while birds strutted back and forth across my shoulders and upper arms. I wore only Meg's jeans. Ed Pike rose from a mud puddle and began aiming a gun at me. I could see it blaze and smoke as he fired but heard no sound. The small birds flew to attack him, and the osprey swooped down to seize the gun from his raised hand. I watched it dive toward the lake and then loop a figure eight before releasing the gun. It made a gigantic splash that reached all the way to drench me.

Still unable to hear, I saw a motorcycle rise from the lake. The rider was female and naked except for a helmet. She circled Pike, spraying him with sand until he was covered. Then she let the bike drop on the mound and removed her helmet.

The strawberry-blonde hair flowed free and Damaris Del Riego stood burnished by the rays of the setting sun. She took slow steps toward me.

The tips of her erect breasts were blood-red spikes. I wanted to impale myself on them. The silken triangle was gilded the brass-yellow of fool's gold. I wanted to smooth my cheeks against it. But those strange silvery eyes froze me, chilled my desire.

I turned my head in response to movement on a high grassy dune. Wren stood there, regal and commanding, her hair a halo of golden fire, her velvet green eyes as clear and inviting as though she were at my side. I felt my nipples harden, heat rise from between my legs. Then a robed figure, the face blank of any features, appeared and began to draw her down the back of the dune. I strained against the ropes binding me. A rising wind pushed against me. Shadows jutted and bulged as the sun lost the battle with the night.

I dropped my head and sank below dreaming.

Seventeen

For the second time in one day, I rose from the depths of sleep, this time seeming to float effortlessly toward wakefulness. I stared at the ceiling and sorted through what I could remember of my dream. I understood what was withholding Wren from me but I also knew she would return. I would be waiting.

In the bathroom I gave myself a one-armed spit bath from the basin, for the first time in my life regretting my height. Most definitely I was not looking forward to the inconveniences of the next few weeks. I hoped I could find a way to extract several pounds of Ed Pike's considerable bulk in payment.

Again I found Meg awaiting me in the bedroom. She said, "Heard the water running. What outfit do you want? And don't glare so about needing help. You've been quick to provide it. Learn to accept it more graciously."

Her technique differed greatly from Marilyn's, but I was properly chastised. Reluctantly I replied, "Yes ma'am." I cocked my head at the sound of youthful voices drifting up the short flight of stairs as I handed Meg the sage green slacks and the pencil-striped, green and white Oxford shirt.

She explained, "Karen's here. Brought enough Chinese food to feed six people, but the way they are digging in I expect it to be gone soon. Brought a movie, too. That'll give my VCR a chance to be used. Dougie and Cap gave it to me for Christmas." Her face was free now from the sag and the deep wrinkles that had accentuated the story of her husband's death. "Those girls bring real life into the house. Stir it up in me, too."

I said, "That's part of what I still miss from teaching."

Once again I followed Meg to the kitchen. The table was nearly hidden from view by many white cartons. Charlie's eyes swept my frame approving her choice of clothing while Karen's went immediately to my cast.

She said, "Gee, Lexy, I'm sorry about your accident." She looked at Charlie. "How come that cast's so clean? It needs to be signed."

I held my arm over my head. "Not yet. Where I'm going tonight I need to be neat and trim. Maybe when I get back." At their exchange of sly grins, I regretted that last comment.

Charlie said appeasingly, "Have a bite, Lexy. Meg took an eggroll."

I chose a crab rangoon and dipped it in sauce, leaning over the table to eat so that I wouldn't spot my clothing. I said playfully, "Well, I suppose Charlie should be the first to sign my cast, considering she rescued me yesterday."

Swiftly Charlie began shoving empty cartons together, her head bent away from all eyes. She grumbled, "You'd better get on your way. And don't stay out too late. And you ought to have that arm in the sling."

Meg chuckled and said, "We've got our orders, Lexy. Let's shove off." Over her shoulder she said, "Not that you could possibly have any room, but there's microwave popcorn in the pantry to go with the movie."

Despite heavy traffic as we neared Orlando, I was comfortable with Meg's driving. She was a skillful, easy driver who kept her eyes on the road and other cars rather than glancing my way as we talked. I gave her directions in plenty of time for turns or lane changes, but I told her nothing of where we were going. I wanted The Billet to be a surprise. Though I knew she didn't qualify for entrance any more than I did, except for Barbara MacFadden's invitation, I thought I could square things—and with more than my broken wrist and needing a driver.

Nearly there I had a sudden thought. "Meg, I want you to know we're not going to a gay bar. I just realized you might think that."

"Aw, shucks. I thought I was in for a new experience." She exaggerated the drawl.

I was pleasantly surprised. "Then I promise you that experience another time, another bar. Okay?"

"Don't think I won't hold you to that, young woman." She followed my directions into a gravelly expanse in front of a long rectangle of gray cement blocks. I pointed her to the end where a faded sign swung in the breeze and a few cars gathered. She said, "Looks like I'm still in for some kind of adventure."

We entered and I let Meg survey the interior of The Billet. I loved the warm lighting of the many lamps, the tables and chairs that looked like escapees from farm kitchens, the military jackets and hats living out retirement on the tall wooden racks. Meg breathed a soft "Oh my stars and garters—or should I say stars and stripes. I feel like I've stepped back in time." I realized that, unlike me, it was a time she had known.

I led the way to the bar where the craggy-faced Schooner greeted me, "Hey, it's our female Ernie Pyle! What action you covering this time?"

"Now, Schooner, who says I'm covering anything? I'm on vacation."

"Sure you are. Babs is over there in the last booth. Came in carrying a folder and said you'd probably be in. Add that to your wing in a sling and I smell active duty behind enemy lines. Don't bullshit an old campaigner like me. Beer or wine, ladies?" She sneered a bit. "Getting some young vets in here lately. They're wine sippers. So I stock some of the silly looking stuff."

Meg opted for beer. While I waited for Schooner to draw us two tall drafts, Meg skimmed the hodgepodge of snapshots, yellowed newspaper photos, magazine glossies filling the wall space behind the bar—all women in uniform. Then we each picked up a glass, and she followed me to the high-backed booths along the far wall.

The Iron Maiden, her back ramrod straight against the wood of the booth, didn't move a muscle as I slid in opposite her. Meg slid in after me, eyeing the silent woman warily. Barbara MacFadden's eyes, a deep purple in the dim light, stayed on my cast and sling. Tonelessly she said, "I don't consider that an improvement over a black eye. Connected with the mysterious death at the marina, I presume."

I tried to glide past her comment by introducing the two women, so very different yet obviously of a similar age. I still had trouble saying 'Barbara' though I had been granted its use in The Billet.

Barbara's face relaxed minutely as she acknowledged the introduction and asked Meg, "When?"

Meg understood. "Early yesterday evening. I've managed to keep her tied down twenty-four hours, but she is a determined skiff when she smells the wind. I'm seeing to it she drags me along as an anchor—old and rusty though I may be."

The Iron Maiden actually smiled. I took advantage by saying, "I hope you'll consider that Meg has a right to be here in her own right. She was at Pearl Harbor when it was bombed." Instantly the normally stiff face became active with interest. I added, "She has quite a story to tell."

Meg looked as shy as Charlie could. Barbara scanned the room, then looked back at Meg as she pushed a folder toward me. "I suggest we join another table. I see two women over there who also survived that bombing. They'll want to hear your story and share theirs. We'll leave Miss Hyatt to her copy."

I knew when I had returned to subordinate status. Before they were halfway across the room, I was intent on the contents of the folder. I pulled the small lamp closer and inspected the copies of newspaper articles and features first. One, dated about twelve years earlier, included a picture of the excursion boat Meg had mentioned that morning in a feature on Lake Arrow. MacKay's Marina was mentioned along with the two owners of the boat—Steve and a Patrick Nagel. The efficient Miss MacFadden had included blank paper and a pen so I jotted down the unfamiliar name.

There was a picture of Cap and the smaller marina in an article on the increasing number of central Floridians living aboard their boats. Cap was quoted in several articles on environmental protection of the lake and surrounding lands. I found Doug's name listed as second-place winner in a sailing contest.

The largest group of related clippings detailed the Labor Day tragedy. It was as Meg had said. The storm had been sudden and vicious—completely undetected by meteorological devices until it struck. It hit the northern half of the lake full force and spilled over onto areas east of it. A farmer was killed by flying debris from a demolished shed, a greenhouse employee by shattered glass, and four people in road accidents, plus the eleven on the lake. Only the name Benjamin Gilstrap meant anything to me.

I checked for Meg and saw her in animated conversation with Barbara and four other women at a round table. Hamburgers and fries were being served all around by a young woman wearing camouflage pants, a white T-shirt, a towel over her shoulder, and sporting a buzz cut.

I would bet she was another stray being salvaged by Schooner. She stomped my way and slid a basket of food toward me.

"Another beer—ma'am?"

I tried not to smile at her awkward rendition of 'ma'am.' I said, "Please. Who sent this to me?"

The young toughie looked back at the table of six women. "I'd say the one with gray hair but that wouldn't tell you anything. That one that looks like she might be your grandmother."

I was glad Meg hadn't heard that. When she returned with my beer, the server brought a knife and cut my burger in half. Schooner's instructions I was sure. I nibbled at the food as I began checking computer sheets of information—my right hand having to do double duty.

I knew I wasn't reading published material and wondered what source the Iron Maiden had tapped. Carefully I read an article maintaining that the major entry point for drugs into Florida might have shifted to the less obvious Jacksonville where they could be dispersed both northward and downward through the state. The writer claimed that increased patrol of major highways and air routes made the use of waterways and marinas highly likely. There was a list of marinas suitable for the exchange of drugs and money, with or without owner knowledge,due to rapid turnover of slip occupants. The marinas were also suitable because of a good migratory location or a brisk business in fishing, sightseeing, or ferrying. MacKay's Marina was on that list.

The next pages I took from the folder confused me. They read like a textbook summary of the political and social upheavals of the past two decades in Central America. There was a bewildering array of designations and initials—Contras, Sandinistas, Christian Democrats, UNO, FMLN, ARENA, EGP, ORPA, URNG. Some of the names I recognized from a too-thin knowledge of the events, others meant nothing. The tangled thread of who espoused or opposed what, who was backed by or repudiated by whom was such a rat's nest that I couldn't differentiate the good guys from the bad. And that included the CIA and the United States government.

I lifted my eyes, puzzling over why the information had been included, and focused on Barbara seated directly across from me. I had not felt her enter the booth. Looking for Meg, I spotted her sitting with three other woman, one of whom was dealing cards around.

"Pinochle," Barbara said tersely. Then in a slightly warmer tone, "A pleasant woman. And solid, I think." She stared at my cast resting on the table as I let the sling dangle from my neck. Caught in the lamplight, the eyes she lifted to mine were cold and piercing. She said nothing.

I lost the staring contest and told her exactly what had happened.

She said, "I assume that if you appear to have learned your lesson, you are safe from further retaliation."

The corners of my mouth twitched at her emphasis. "Aye that."

She cocked an eyebrow.

I nearly giggled. "Sorry, Captain. I've been on the water too long ."

Her laughter was a seldom heard sound. It reminded me of Tiger's purr. She asked, "Anything helpful there?"

"Maybe." I lifted the pages I had been puzzling over. "I don't understand these."

"That is background for what I wish to give you verbally." As I put down the sheets and reached for the pen, she said sharply, "No notes. Just listen. You concluded your recorded request for information with a woman's name." I nodded, knowing she was referring to Damaris Del Riego. Barbara continued, "The name reactivated a memory from when I was concluding my military career in Washington."

I massaged the back of my neck and leaned back to listen.

She kept her voice low. "The issues in Central America have been and are extremely complex. For the most part, the wealthy and well-born prefer the regime that will protect their interests, but they are not without their idealists. Persons who want to improve all aspects of life for everyone, who care about individual rights and justice. Dario Del Riego was one such. He came out of college wanting to spread education to the masses, including the Indian peasants, and to improve the economic and justice systems. He refused to stop his efforts even when his family disowned him, even after a period of imprisonment and torture." Calm though her voice was, I heard the anger. "He was killed returning from a teaching session in a village."

I ran my fingers along the edge of the table. "His relationship to Damaris?"

"Older brother."

"Did she support him or go along with her family in disowning him?"

"That I cannot answer. Her name was in his file simply as a family member." Her eyes narrowed. "However, I contacted a friend in Washington and called in a marker." I straightened with interest but she added, "It isn't much. After her brother's death, Damaris Del Riego sampled several American universities—never graduating from any. Then she became a feature of resorts up and down the southern hemisphere. Now she appears to live a quieter nomadic life aboard her yacht drifting in and out of major and minor ports."

"But someone is attaching significance to that," I said alertly.

"My marker wouldn't buy me that information, but I think I correctly inferred that no especially strong interest is attached to her."

I leaned on my good elbow. Someone was interested enough to want to check with Immigration. Steve MacKay—if he wrote that note. Maybe Ed Pike. And what had I done by giving it to Damaris herself? And what was she doing, if anything, as she drifted from port to port? And was there any connection with Steve MacKay's death? I hissed in irritation at the little I knew.

"Are you involved with this woman, Lexy?" There was no accusation or criticism in her tone.

Still the question startled me—both in that the Iron Maiden asked it and in that she had read something in me to prompt the question. As with my arm, I gave her the truth. "A very brief fling or momentary lapse. Right now she is just a fringe player in what has happened at the marinas. Perhaps of no importance." I rubbed a knuckle hard across my brow.

"You are worried about who killed this man."

"Yes. He was not a good man, and he harmed a lot of good people. I don't want that harm to continue even after his death."

"I understand. Is there any other way I can be of help?"

I tapped the papers on the Central American upheavals. "Tell me more about this. If I get the chance to talk to Damaris Del Riego before she leaves, I'd like to know enough to sound informed. And do you have any idea why she would need to check with Immigration—or be checked on by someone else?"

"For her part it could be quite mundane, a simple matter of necessary paperwork. Someone else's interest," Barbara mused, "could be mere curiosity, or concern over the possibility of drug smuggling, or of birds, fish, artifacts. Then there is the brown slavery that has become so lucrative."

"Brown slavery?"

She explained succinctly. "All over this country, people from Central America are working the crops—groves, truck farms, orchards. Many are legal and have green cards, but a large number are smuggled in for the express purpose of working for little pay in difficult conditions. A colleague of yours has been investigating locally and his articles will start appearing next week. Not far from here tomato workers are being paid forty cents a bushel but they have to rent trailers to live in at a thousand dollars a month. You can imagine how many have to live in one trailer to manage that. And the food they have access to is very expensive. It's a difficult life to escape. It's the old story of owing your soul to the company store."

I was stunned. "Brown slavery," I repeated. Suddenly I thought of the people being hurried into the vans during the fireworks. Where had they come from? How had they arrived at the marina? What was their destination? Could it be that Steve MacKay's death had no connection whatsoever with the people I had been so pleasantly sharing my vacation with? Some wind went out of my inner sails. What about Damaris? Could she be connected?

I described the scene outside the marina office for Barbara as Doug had for me. She said nothing but her brisk nod indicated further investigation on her part. She signaled the gruff young woman to bring us coffee. The 'Yes, Captain' was more natural sounding than the 'ma'am' for me had been.

Barbara said, "Schooner has drilled her well in all our ranks. Probably the first time she has enjoyed learning something. She doesn't know yet that Schooner is lining up an adult-education program for her."

The coffee arrived, and I listened and scribbled notes as the Iron Maiden went into detail about conditions and events south of the United States.

Eventually Meg rejoined us, apologizing for interrupting. "But," she said, "I promised Charlie I wouldn't let you stay out too late. And it's after eight o'clock."

As though emphasizing her words, a wave of fatigue swept through me. I decided that I wasn't up to explaining who Charlie was right then. I thanked Barbara for the folder of material and the information. She and Meg each said polite but warm goodnights.

On the ride back to Mossville, I learned that Meg had been granted an honorary membership in The Billet due to her Pearl Harbor experience. Also, two of the women she met were coming soon to Cap's Marina to go out sailing with her. Another was going to check out the marina as a place to keep her boat and live aboard part of the time.

As we entered town, Meg said, "I've managed just fine these past several years, but it feels good heading home to a house with someone else in it. Sure hope I can sell Charlie on it as a permanent home."

I replied, "From all I've seen, Meg, the odds are in your favor." I smiled into the darkness. "Karen being only twenty minutes away helps those odds, too."

"Like that, is it?"

"Perhaps on its way. But whether it goes well, or badly, or just fades away, Charlie will need someone to talk to."

Meg said, "I would expect that to be you."

"I won't always be on hand as conveniently as I am now. Roberta Exline, either. I know we'd both feel better with you in the immediate vicinity. Think you can anchor both Charlie and me?" I rushed on, "Though I'm planning to slip anchor a little bit tomorrow."

"Lexy..." she said anxiously.

"I need to get back to the marina, Meg. I promise to take it easy and stay in view of people."

She sighed. "All right. But only because I know Charlie will stand a reliable watch."

We pulled into the driveway, the headlights catching Charlie and Karen sitting on the steps. Goodnights were said, and Charlie walked Karen to her car. I declined help in getting ready for bed. Within moments I was drifting off to sleep, lulled by voices from the living room.

Eighteen

I sat in the rear of the *Willow* while Charlie checked everything above and below deck, fore and aft. I thought about seeing Ed Pike getting out of a brown truck in front of the diner when we rode in with Meg earlier. His bumper sticker said 'Keep Honking—I'm Reloading.' I could still taste the acid that had flooded my mouth.

Charlie bobbed up from below. "Made you some coffee, Long Legs. Can you handle it with one hand?"

"Sure." It was good to hear my nickname again. She hadn't used it since my encounter with the two masked men and the churning lake.

"Got a job for a one-handed painter today?"

"You weren't all that great with two!" she squeaked. "Besides, I've set up an appointment for you with Fran."

"An appointment?" I caught the mischievous gleam. "What's going on, Charlie?"

"Last night Karen and I worked out a plan for your cast. Figured you were too old…" Her lips twitched at my wide-eyed glare. "Or maybe too classy to just have it scribbled on. I checked with Fran when we first got in and she said to send you along in a little while."

"For what?" All I got in reply was a teasing smile. I sipped the coffee, refusing to admit that it was good. I heard the rattling call of a kingfisher, the sound too large for the small bird, and saw one dive from a wire toward the lake. It made me remember and I tried to imitate the bird call I had heard from the cattails two days ago. Charlie looked at me curiously. I repeated my effort, then said, "I kept hearing that when I was jogging. I was planning to ask you what it was but those guys came along and I got interrupted."

Charlie was aghast. "Interrupted! You nearly get killed and you call it interrupted!"

I lowered my head but peeked up from beneath my brows.

She heaved an exasperated sigh. "It was a marsh wren." With that she leaped to the pier in one fluid motion. "Go see Fran when you finish the coffee." She spun around. "And don't you dare think about jogging."

"Aye, aye...mate."

Suddenly she squatted on her haunches, all little girl again. "Meg and me talked after you went to bed last night. She said I could live at her house when I finish with the *Willow*. That it could be a permanent home if I wanted. And Cap says I can have a real job here."

"Is it what you'd like, Charlie?" I wanted to get nearer to her but was afraid it would send her rushing off.

"I want the job here. It's the first place I've ever felt like I belonged." She tried to swallow the catch out of her throat. "And it felt good at Meg's—like I could belong there, too." Her small face was set in granite, and she stared at me unblinkingly. "But it'll be like Big Charley some day."

Now I had to swallow the catch. I said as firmly as I could muster, "Meg's tough. She's got a lot of good years yet. They can be good for both of you."

Charlie blinked, stood up, and tried to regain her aplomb. "She's going to call Roberta about it." She knocked her foot against a piling. "Do you think she'll take that stuff about me as well as you did? I know Roberta told you."

"Young as you are, there's the same flash of seadog in you that I've seen in Meg and Cap. They'll probably think your past is just the thing to prepare you for the rough and unexpected around here." I lifted my cup. "Good coffee."

She rolled her eyes and was off.

Fifteen minutes later I stood on the dock below the office. The large window was shaded sufficiently from the morning sun for me to see Meg at her desk and on the phone. Charlie stood in front of the desk, her rigid stillness communicating all the way out to me how alertly involved she was with Meg's conversation. I was sure it was with Robbie Exline.

"Say all the right things, Robbie," I whispered aloud.

I nodded to greetings as I walked to the *Second Wind*, moving purposefully to avoid questions about my arm. I saw two male figures on the deck of the *Siren Song* and assumed they were more of the returning crew. Tiger meowed a welcome and instinctively stayed out of my way as I boarded the sailboat clumsily.

Fran appeared to assist me. She waited until I was seated before tapping my cast through the sling. "I had to hear about this from Cap, Charlie, and Marilyn Neff! Didn't fuss at Charlie, but we're going to lambaste Meg for not calling us in to help."

I said placatingly, "I was in capable hands. And it was still storming. There wasn't any need to call out anyone else to get drenched."

Donna came on deck. "We know that, Lexy. We just don't like thinking we were dry and snug and so unaware of a friend in trouble."

Fran stomped about the boat, the black tufts of hair quivering with each step, the gold tooth flashing each time she faced into the sun.

"What's being done to take care of all this? That Detective Exline looking into it? Putting a guard an you?"

"Can you imagine me needing more of a guard than Charlie...and Meg, and you and Donna, and Cap? When Charlie left me to finish my coffee, I saw Cap come out on his porch. I knew full well he was keeping an eye on me. And I'm going to be sensible. Going to play weak sister, dumb dyke, scaredy-cat queer. Sorry, Tiger."

That put Fran back in a good humor. "While keeping your eyes and ears wide open, I bet."

I hmmed noncommittally, then aimed the subject a different direction. "How did you hear about it from Marilyn?" Immediately I answered my own question. "Oh, you were going to The Cat last night."

Both women softened. Donna said, "We had an absolutely fine time! It was a quiet night and we weren't the only oldies. Marilyn had dinner with us, introduced us to several people." She looked fondly at Fran. "We danced. And that bartender Melody is a delight! She told us Thursday nights were a good blend of all ages, and that the young crowd pretty much fills the place on the weekends."

Fran broke in. "I want to go some Friday or Saturday night! I want to see those young dykes in action. Maybe pick up something from them." She smirked. "Or maybe teach them a thing or two."

"Fran!" Donna was laughing.

Again I experienced the pall of loneliness. I wanted to be a unit as they were—with Wren. I swallowed and glanced at the *Song* looming near. How could I regret my lapse and, at the same time, clench my teeth over sensual memories?

Fran gripped the top of my head with her broad hand and turned it away from the yacht. "Time to get out of the sun. And I've got a job to do. Charlie's orders."

I clutched my sling with my good hand. "What did those two kids come up with?"

Fran motioned for me to get up. She gave a villainous laugh. "Come with me,my lovely…and find out."

We went below. Tiger jumped up on the small table between the berths and nosed a box of colored pens. Donna scooped him away, and Fran pointed commandingly. "Put that cast there."

I still clutched the sling. "Fran…"

Donna said, "It'll be all right, Lexy. I've seen the list."

Fran withdrew a folded piece of paper from her pocket and propped it against the box. She smacked my good hand as I reached toward it. I growled, which brought Tiger's ears up and forward. Resigned to my fate, whatever it was, I removed my arm from the sling and placed it on the table. I took a last look at the clean whiteness.

As Fran set to work with the colored pens, Donna expanded on their evening at The Cat. I divided my attention between her and the designs being so quickly and skillfully created. First was a paintbrush wearing a baseball cap turned sideways—Charlie. Next came a soccer ball—Karen. There followed an eye with a part of the iris shaded in for Meg, the same jaunty cap as on the marina sign for Cap, and a badge for Robbie. I admired the perfect rendition of the strutting neon cat that marked the entrance to Marilyn's bar—no doubt Fran's suggestion. A sail billowing full was obviously Donna and Fran.

"See, Lexy," Donna said. "Didn't I tell you it would be all right?"

I asked Fran, "How did Charlie know you could do these?"

"She saw my pens when I was sketching out the changes we want down here. Hold still. Got one more to do."

I glanced at the new sketch she was starting, assuming it would develop into a willow tree, began to say something to Donna, then jerked my eyes back, horrified to realize what the design was turning out to be. Fireworks! Slowly my mouth dropped open.

Donna bent over to look. "Fran Stover! That wasn't on the list!"

"No," Fran said calmly. "Charlie whispered this one to me." She spoke over my sputtering. "Quit being a baby. When the time comes, I'll turn this into a willow tree with a few strokes of my magic pen." She grinned like an impudent gremlin. "Also Charlie's idea." She actually rubbed salt in the wound. "I hear *Siren Song* is hoisting anchor soon."

Donna said, "I saw a woman going aboard early this morning. Don't know what they do their weeks ashore, but it certainly shapes them up."

"What do you mean?"

Fran was the one who answered. "Like those inner-city kids I worked with in Toledo that got sent to summer camp for a month. Went away kind of meek and scrawny and came back filled out, walking taller. That kind of thing. Makes me wonder if the Princess works them like galley slaves then sends them off to be fattened up for another voyage in chains."

Donna spoke more mildly. "Fran is being harsh, but there is something strange about it all. We used to try to speak to some of them passing to or from the boat when we were on deck. Never got a response—even when we used the little Spanish we've picked up."

I stroked Tiger who had escaped Donna's arms to come check out my cast, measuring what I had heard. Granted my contact with the lady in question had been limited and of a special nature, but I had sensed no cruelty in her. Something diamond-hard perhaps—a beauty to wound yourself on—but no malicious intent to harm.

Fran lifted her head and stared upward as though seeing through the ceiling. She said, "I feel a wind rising. Want to go out with us, Lexy?"

I jumped up, startling Tiger. "No way, ladies. Not when I'm one-armed." I thanked Fran for her time and expertise and accepted Donna's assistance off the sailboat.

She said, "A little paint will cover those fireworks, Lexy."

I replied, "I'm beginning to trust Charlie's perceptions. I think she's reminding me that truth is truth—and needs to be faced before being filed. I"ll know when to ask Fran to turn it into a willow."

We smiled our good-bye.

Once again standing below the office, I could make out Charlie seated at Meg's desk. Meg herself was approaching from the work dock.

"Ahoy, Lexy. That child in there is something! I gave her a lesson in the computer and she soaked it up like the first spring rain. Left her to play with it awhile." She shook her head slowly. "Somebody somewhere doesn't know what they are missing."

"Our gain, Meg."

She nodded. "A better way to look at it. You take it easy today. Can't be certain you're out of rough water yet with that concussion."

"I plan to read the afternoon away aboard the *Willow*. Wanted to see Cap first if he's still around."

"He may be back in his trailer by now. I was talking to him a little while ago down at the work dock. He and Dougie and I keep our own boats there. He was checking them for storm damage."

And checking for his gun at the same time, I thought, if Doug hasn't yet told him about dropping it in the lake. I was sure there were hiding places that a police search could miss. Aloud I said, "Has he said anything about any more police contact, or detectives?"

"Only that George Treder was questioned. And the lawyer he hired to get the injunction to stop Steve from closing off the road into here." Her eyes were troubled. "They can do a lot with circumstantial evidence, can't they?"

"But they like to have much more than that to charge someone. And Steve apparently trampled on more people than the ones around here, Meg. The police have other places to look as well." I changed the subject. "I saw you on the phone, with Charlie there standing at attention. Robbie?"

"I'll let Charlie tell you about it." The light in her eyes told me it was good news.

I went around the office and crossed over to Cap's trailer. He opened the door before I hit the porch.

"Get in here out of the heat, young woman. Meg didn't keep you below deck very long." He ushered me in and pointed to a small couch. "I've put the word out at the diner and around to let me know if anybody hears any solid scuttlebutt. I haven't been minding things like I should have lately. That's changed."

I fingered my sling. "You couldn't have prevented this, Cap."

"Maybe not. But if I'd stayed out of the bottle Friday night...been with Meg and Doug like I should have been...or stood up to Steve years ago like I should have..." His voice trailed away.

"Mind if I ask a few questions, Cap?"

"Ask away."

"I'm still trying to place people Friday night mainly so that I can be sure who wasn't near Steve at the wrong time. Do you know what time Doug came in?"

"I heard him but have no idea when it was."

"Before or after Meg knocked on the door?"

Cap looked wary. "I never heard her knock. I told you, Lexy, I got too deep in a bottle. She say when?"

"She said she came up on the porch twice after the fireworks. She didn't knock the first time because she heard you talking to someone."

Cap looked perplexed. Then his face cleared and he pointed to a picture on a table to my right. "I would have been talking to Mary. And I don't have to be drunk to do it. It's an old habit. I pour out my worries to her. I told her I was scared it was our last Fourth of July here." His face brightened, the dimple deepening. "I told her good stuff over coffee this morning. Mostly about bringing Charlie in."

I turned other pictures toward me as questions skittered through my mind like marbles on concrete. Was Cap there all night or not? Did Meg really approach his door two times? What time did Doug come in? I tapped one of the pictures. "Who's this? He looks so familiar."

"My older brother—by ten years. Somewhere in his twenties in that picture. I never got to see him as much as I wanted to. He left home when I was only eight. He was a land rover like I was a water bug. Climbed mountains, went caving, that kind of thing. Became a firefighter. Not the city kind. Forest fires. He died fighting one." He cleared the emotion out of this throat. "You can see his dimples in that picture. He would tease me about having only one when he had two. Steve got his nose and chin—but no dimples. A sign, I guess." That last was said morosely. He slapped a hand over his knee. "Too bright a day to have the yaws. We bury Steve Monday. After that, me and Meg and Charlie got a marina to run. And Doug'll do all right with his." The broad pirate grin was back.

I stayed awhile longer, scattering more questions among the chit-chat. But I was either fishing a dry hole or all my bait was being cleverly ignored. When I left, I saw Charlie walking the ledge back to the *Willow*. I followed after her. Jumping down, she saw me and leaned against a piling, waiting as I used the steps in front of the A-house to reach the dock. She kept her eyes on my sling. Trying to act as though it was an imposition, I pulled my arm from the sling and held out the cast for her inspection.

"Oh, wow! That's better than I expected! Ain't...isn't Fran great!"

"All in your point of view," I said grumpily. Her dancing eyes said she wasn't buying it.

We sat down on the bench. I stretched out my legs, she tucked hers under. She said, "Meg called Roberta."

"And?"

"She said living at Meg's and having a steady job would help get that other stuff settled. She's got a doctor lined up for me to see, and a lawyer, so they can make a case for me being seventeen right now. Wants me to pick out a date sometime in the fall for my birthday. Says the lawyer will get it made legal."

"Got one picked out?"

Charlie scuffed her foot along an uneven plank. "Meg let me work with the computer. Told me to check all the marina records—see how they were set up. There was one on her. Her birthday is the fourth of September. I just now asked her if I could use it. She kind of cried, Lexy. I didn't know what to do."

My eyes misted but I laughed at the same time. I pushed at her with my cast. "You already did it, Charlie."

I looked at the designs on the cast, then out over the marina. The mist in my eyes became tears. One slipped down my cheek. Charlie jumped up, then squatted in front of me. "What's wrong! Is it your arm, your head?"

I had to quell her panic. "No. no," I said half angrily. "It's my heart." I couldn't believe I was being so sappy.

She stood up. "What?!"

I tugged her back down beside me. I explained, "This place and its people have become another home to me. Just like at The Cat."

"You can handle two homes, can't you?"

I caught the tear with a finger and tasted its salt. "That's just it. I can. But I've decided I'm ready for a home with Wren now, too. Is she going to understand about me wanting and needing to keep these others?"

Charlie spoke with the same no-nonsense tone I often heard from the Admiral. "It's kind of silly to spoil your time here now with worry about that. Just ask her when she gets here. If she's the right person for you, she probably already knows stuff like that about you anyway. Probably just waiting for you to quit being a knucklehead and see that the two of you are sails an the same boat, but you don't have to be in the same positions all the time."

"Damn, Charlie! You can't be just seventeen. You've got too much sense."

She pushed off from the bench and leaped to the *Willow's* deck. Stretching a hand toward me, she said, "Coming aboard…mate?"

Nineteen

I woke up slowly but kept my eyes closed, glad to be experiencing the gentle sway of the *Willow* again. I felt the weight of the book I had been reading on my stomach and the rough cast against my side. Carefully pointing with my heels to keep my calf muscles from knotting, I slowly stretched my legs. A limbering-up walk was called for.

Removing the book and sitting up, I discovered a note from Charlie pinned to the sling dangling empty from my neck. It notified me that there was a great chicken salad in the fridge from Donna if I woke up hungry. I had, and Charlie was right about the food. Chunks of white meat were combined with mandarin oranges, grapes, pecans, and a light dressing. I spent little time consuming it all.

Outside the boat I found it cooler than expected for a July afternoon. Most of the sky was blotted by blobs and clumps of white clouds, the kind that took on recognizable or fanciful shapes but didn't threaten immediate rain. A walk to the big marina would give my body the exercise it craved.

On the way I mentally reviewed the conversation with Cap which I had transcribed into the notebook now nestling in my sling. I was concerned most about what he didn't say. He had not spoken of the argument with Steve near the houseboat at the start of the fireworks. He hadn't indicated any knowledge of how Doug had disposed of the gun. He hadn't backed up Meg's accounts of coming to the trailer.

At the marina I encountered Joseph outside the office cleaning paint brushes. The ugly green had been covered over with a light tan, flecks of which dotted the young man's black hair, dark arms and chest.

I teased, "Don't think you're any neater a painter than I am, Joseph."

His handsome face brightened in a wide grin as he stood up. Even the indentations near the corners of his mouth contained dabs of paint. "But I got enough on the building to make it look better. Doug wants to brighten up the place." He looked up at the sky, rivulets of sweat flowing down his neck and into the thick hair of his chest. "Tell me it's not going to rain, Lexy."

"It's not going to rain, Joseph. Honestly, I don't think it is. Those clouds look like they are on their way somewhere else."

He put the lid on the paint can, moving it and the brushes to the corner of the building. Next he started pulling up scrawny shrubs from under the window and along the walkway. He said, "My aunt works at a nursery. She's going to drop off some bushes and stuff on her way home from work. Charlie said she would help me plant them early in the morning." He pointed to the dirty sign I was leaning against. "That's going to go, too. Doug's trying to come up with a catchy name."

"Have you and he done any talking about other things?"

He knew what I meant but kept working away in silence for a minute. Then he spoke without looking at me. "That gun business isn't easy to bring up. It would be easier if he would, but he hasn't. Doug's my boss now, Lexy. More than that, he's my friend. Don't want to mess that up—especially when I didn't expect it to happen."

"How's that?"

He revolved on his heels to face me, and slapped dirt from his knees. "When I first started working here, I heard bad stuff about him and Cap from Steve and Ed Pike. I just assumed it was true. Then my motorcycle gave out up the road a piece one day. Doug came by and helped me out. We got to talking. Found out we liked some of the same things—sailing, the Atlanta Braves, Dos Equis beer. We started spending some time together—even double-dated. After a while we found out that our situations were kind of alike, too."

"In what ways?"

"Family stuff. Doug's mother died when he was young and Steve didn't care about him. My mother died about the time I started school and her husband—I'd always known he wasn't my father—tossed me to her sister like I was a bag of trash." He shrugged as though throwing off the memory. "But we both got good second families out of it—good homes to grow up in. We know it's the people who care about us that count, not other things."

"Count yourself lucky. A lot of people die never having learned that."

"Steve did." The young voice was rank with bitterness. "The way he died shouldn't mess up things for Doug now that everything's going his way."

"That's exactly why the police are going to be looking at him." I smacked the sign hard as I pushed away from it. "His inheriting this place is going to make them look even harder. That's why he has to be straight with them."

Joseph began laughing. My indignation dissipated when I saw that the sign had toppled over in the loose dirt and lay on the ground. I laughed, too. "Good thing that didn't happen while I was leaning on it. If I'd broken the other arm, I'd have been..."

Joseph finished for me, "Out in the middle of the lake in a leaking rowboat without a paddle—or arms to paddle with." He picked up the sign and propped it against the wall next to the door.

We sat together on the brick rim of an unused flower box. I retrieved the orange notebook from my sling, balancing it on a knee and unclipping the pen. I said, "I want to run through some facts again. Correct me if I'm wrong...or add what you can." He nodded judiciously and I began cataloguing, "You left the barge; Doug dropped you at the dock out there, and took the motorboat back to Cap's. Did you see Steve or Pike anywhere around?"

"No. The office was dark. In fact it was dark everywhere. All the lights that had been turned off for the fireworks were still out."

I asked, "What about what they normally drove? Here or gone?"

His thick black brows drew together. He pointed to his right. "Pike's truck could have been down there with the ones that belong to the few people living on their boats. But I'm not sure. I wasn't looking for it. I am sure Steve's wasn't here. He drove a flashy white sports car."

"How soon before Doug drove by heading south?"

"Twenty minutes, half an hour...maybe more." He responded to my skeptical expression. "He would have cleaned up the boat good. We had used it a lot that day. Cap doesn't tolerate a boat being put to bed messy. I spent some time standing on the dock watching the fireworks being set off along the shore and from some boats out on the lake."

My thighs jerked at the memory of the pops and whistles interspersed with the cries Damaris and I drew from one another. Quickly I said, "And you left right after Doug went by? That's when you saw Meg coming from the boat dock. Right?"

"I thought it was her car, but it was only in my light a second. I almost went back to check. Then I figured Cap might be with her and they were just cruising up and down to see that everything was shipshape after all the celebrating."

"What made you think that?"

"I don't know. Maybe because Cap's trailer lights were still on." He leaped to his feet. "Tia Elena is here."

A small red pickup with high sides of wooden slats pulled up. The woman who got out was short, plump, and energetic. Her thick dark hair was held back from her face by a bright yellow scarf. She spoke Spanish to Joseph, gesturing to the back of the truck. He towered over her, looking where she pointed and nodding obediently to rapid-fire instructions. Then he said something, glancing my way.

The woman approached me, wiping her hands on faded work jeans. "I am Joseph's Tia Elena. He thinks I should sit while he empties the truck. Who does he think put all that in there?"

I stood up, smiling, and took her hand. "I'm Lexy."

Her hand was rough and scarred from many nicks and scratches. It made me think of my grandparents' hands—farmers' hands.

We sat on the brick border. Elena said, "Joseph has spoken of you and your friendship with Charlie. He has much admiration for her. He says she is like his mamacita and tia must have been—brave and strong." The soft musical voice hardened. "A boy's pretty dream. We were young and alone, frightened and desperate. But I was the lucky one. Hands that reached for me wished only to help. Not so for my poor sister."

I knew that much lay behind those simple statements but would not be shared with me. She shrugged, as I had seen Joseph do, and began asking me polite questions about my life at the marina while keeping her eyes on Joseph removing black plastic containers of shrubs and plants from the truck. When Joseph completed the task, she watched approvingly as he began to water them.

I shifted my position and my notebook fell to the ground, a piece of paper fluttering from it. I picked up the notebook and Elena the paper which was at her toes. About to hand it to me, she suddenly turned her head and spat in the dust. Quickly she apologized, but added defensively, "That is a bad man!"

The paper was from my notetaking at The Billet. She had to be reacting to the name Patrick Nagel, the man who had co-owned the excursion boat with Steve MacKay.

I asked forthrightly, "Oh? I just found out that he did business with Steve MacKay, also a bad man, but that's all I know. What do you know about him?"

Her eyes were black, liquid pools that I couldn't see into, yet I knew she was judging me.

She lowered her voice. "He runs what is called a pipeline from Cuba, and perhaps other countries. Boats pick up people who manage to escape. They are smuggled into this country, promised work and the chance to become citizens. They work hard and the places they are put are terrible. That is not the bad part." She pointed to the paper now in my hand. "That man takes much of their money for helping. He forces some into evil things."

The set of her face warned me off from asking what, but I could imagine. No doubt prostitution, perhaps drug dealing, similar illegal activities. I did ask, "Why don't they report him to the authorities?"

Her tone was mildly reproving. "To be imprisoned or deported? And men such as him have ways to deal with betrayal. The people he 'helps' have no voice."

I considered that the articles now being written by a colleague might give them a voice. Meanwhile I needed to get this information to Robbie in the hope she could get it to those investigating MacKay's death. The people being hustled into those vans right outside this office might have been part of Nagel's pipeline. Steve's death could have been an old-fashioned falling out among thieves.

Joseph came up and Elena gave him an invoice for the greenery. He offered to show her around the marina but her lively face settled into contempt. She said in a flat voice, "No. I have no desire." She struggled to produce a weak smile. Patting his arm, she said, "You are the sailor. I am a woman of the soil." She said good-bye to me and got into the truck, backing and turning expertly.

Joseph watched after her with a still face and a distant look.

I said, "Disappointed that she didn't want to see things, Joseph?"

"No," he said mildly. "I didn't really expect her to. She doesn't like the water. I've thought maybe it goes back to the days floating on a homemade raft—not knowing if she would ever see land again."

A boxy silver Volvo braked to a sudden stop in the road in front of us, stirring small clouds of dust about the wheels. Damaris del Riego exited from the back seat, bending to speak to the driver before closing the door.

The car reversed its direction and left. She walked toward us, cool and erect.

Her strawberry-blonde hair was coiled in the back of her head, strengthening the lines of her face and her air of superiority. She gave me a tight smile and a nod, then greeted Joseph in Spanish. From their gestures I could tell she was complimenting him on the paint job and teasing him about the amount on himself. His shyness and pleasure at her attention were obvious. Reluctantly he excused himself and entered the office.

"A nice young man," Damaris said.

"Very. Do you know him?"

"Only through the Estradas."

"His aunt and uncle? I just met Tia Elena." I wondered what their connection was.

Damaris drew her teeth over her upper lip, then answered my unspoken question. "I often attend Hispanic cultural activities while I am here. There is a growing community. They are struggling to mingle despite their countries of origin, and to become accepted as citizens of the United States. A daunting task."

"For you as well?" That came out more critical than I had intended.

Her colorless eyes flared in defiance. "I am quite secure in who I am." She began to walk away with a look that said she expected me to follow.

Wanting to trip myself, I followed. We walked toward Cap's marina.

We had gone only a few steps when a horn blasted three times and

Ed Pike brushed by us dangerously close. He skidded to a halt between two parked cars. I could tell he was watching us in the rearview mirror.

Damaris exhibited no reaction. I slapped my notebook angrily against my thigh, then tucked it in the sling, being careful not to expose the designs on the cast.

A corner of her mouth lifted as she said, "You are playing secretary again."

"It's a job I do well," I said sarcastically.

She halted and we faced each other. Damaris stated, "You are a reporter for the *Ledger*, Lexy Hyatt. You were a teacher of English before that."

I was annoyed, irritated. "Do you check out everyone you lay!"

The tolerant smile softened her face but only made me more angry. She said matter-of-factly, "I checked on you after you gave me the note. It seemed a prudent thing to do. It proved unnecessary and I apologize."

My anger was ebbing, my curiosity rising. "What's so important about that note? What's the big deal about calling Immigration?"

We began walking again. She said, "It is no longer a...big deal. It was only a minor...glitch. Is that a good American word?"

I smiled in spite of myself. "Yes." I recognized the technique of deflecting one question with another.

She asked another. "And would what happened to your arm and hand be also a glitch? I heard that the little industrious one had to pull those so delicious long limbs from the water."

I said admiringly, "Your spy network must be something." I ended up telling her much of what had happened, though I glossed over the men as probable gaybashers. Mainly I wanted Charlie to get her due.

We had reached the marina and went around to the patio behind Meg's office. Damaris held out her hand. "I leave soon but I owe you a favor. I will repay it if I can. If not this voyage, perhaps another."

We shook hands—and I remembered a line of Amy Lowell poetry: 'The touch of you burns my hands like snow.' I released her hand and fingered the notebook through the sling. I said, "Perhaps you can right now." She raised an eyebrow. I asked, "Do you know of a Patrick Nagel?" Her eyes were like dull ice. I hastened on, "Another reporter is trying to expose the smuggling of Hispanics to provide cheap labor in rough conditions. I wouldn't mind throwing some information his way." Something in her hard stare propelled me to be truthful. "This man may be connected with that…and with Steve MacKay's death."

Her jaw line relaxed and her eyes were no longer so coldly bland. "I will see what there is to pass on to you."

I sat at a patio table and watched as she walked away. Just as she reached the point where the *Second Wind* was tied off, Charlie scrambled off the boat, nearly colliding with her. Damaris put a hand on Charlie's shoulder, and began speaking to her. I couldn't make out Charlie's expression at that distance but I knew the stance. I willed her not to throw off the hand. She didn't. She nodded once to something Damaris said, then walked toward the patio.

I expected a caustic remark about the Piranha Princess. Instead I got a question about Donna's chicken salad, to which I replied, "I liked it so much I ate it all." I waited for her next remark.

Charlie surprised me again. "I'm not going to tell you what she said." She put one foot against the bench. "So quit sitting there like a turkey buzzard waiting for road kill."

Before I could retort, Meg stuck her head out the door and called, "Charlie, Roberta's on the phone for you." She gave me a half wave, half salute.

Charlie was back in a flash. She was grinning but nervous. "I've got appointments with a doctor and a lawyer tomorrow. Meg's going to take me. Roberta wants to talk to you a minute."

The 'talk' turned out to be questions about my health and behavior.

I answered them semi-curtly and told her she was spending too much time with the Admiral. She brushed that off laughingly and gave me details on the doctor and lawyer appointments, concluding with, "We're going to get her off probation, Lexy! Get her record expunged. Get her a first-class chance for a real life. You and Meg Gilstrap are a big part of that. Feels good, doesn't it?"

I replied, "It does. Robbie, I hate to get a compliment and then beg for a favor, but—"

"Ask away."

I fed her my information and theories concerning Patrick Nagel, Steve MacKay, and the vans outside the office on the Fourth.

She said shrewdly, "Sounds worth looking into. I'll channel it to the right ears. Don't suppose you're going to give me your sources?" I grunted and she continued, "Didn't think so. You stay dry. You know what I mean?"

I grunted again. She ended the call with, "Got to go. Got city business to do. That's what I get paid for—but just in money." I could hear the smile along with the residue of pride in what she was accomplishing for Charlie.

Meg was going over some river charts with two men as I punched in the newspaper's number followed by the Iron Maiden's extension.

She picked up on the first ring. "Miss MacFadden here."

"It's Lexy Hyatt. May I request some more research if your schedule allows for it?"

"The subject matter, please." The Iron Maiden as usual.

I gave her Nagel's full name and an abbreviated version of my interest in him. On a hunch I didn't understand, I added the name of Elena Estrada with the little I knew to identify her. I was thanking her in advance and concluding the call when she said, "A moment more, Miss Hyatt. The Señorita?"

"Yes?"

"I have acquired further information. Very limited. Purposefully vague. It is my guarded deduction that she is of the tradition of Zorro and the Scarlet Pimpernel. Call me at The Billet tomorrow evening if you require more than that." She hung up.

I replaced the receiver but kept my hand on it. Zorro I knew. The Scarlet Pimpernel I wasn't so sure of. I moved out of the way as Meg returned to her desk. I said, "Do you know anything about the Scarlet Pimpernel?"

"You've pulled that one from deep water. Old movie—black and white. Leslie Howard—Melanie's husband in "Gone With the Wind." Don't remember it too well but it was something about a gentleman, a dandy, pretending to be silly and ineffective and unconcerned. Then he'd put on a mask and take up a sword and go do good deeds, or help people escape, something like that."

That fit with what I knew about Zorro. Now how did they fit with Damaris Del Riego? Her name even sounded like something out of the

Zorro mystique. I smiled as I visualized her in a mask with those strange eyes of endless depth, a sword in her sure, capable hands. Quickly I extinguished the smile at the sight of Charlie holding the door for Donna and Fran.

Charlie went to the back room and began bringing in card tables and chairs which the others helped set up. I remembered what Fran and Donna had said about the crew coming and going from the *Song*—the before and after look, their reticence. Maybe the yacht and Damaris' apparent superficiality were her mask and sword—a way of moving people in and out of Central America who needed protection and secrecy. I was ace-of-spades certain she was no more a callous aristocrat than her brother had been.

A prickly thought jabbed at me. If information of her activities had come Steve MacKay's way, maybe through Nagel, he might have wanted to contact Immigration and use his cooperation to camouflage his own activities. What would Damaris have been willing to do, or have done, to stop him?

Twenty

Charlie gave me a nervous wave as she got into Meg's car. Up at dawn, she had hurried to help plant the shrubs and flowering ground cover with Joseph. Then she had returned to the *Willow* to clean up for her appointments. Despite witnessing her growing tension, I knew that nothing I could offer would diffuse it.

The best I could do was hug her and say, "Some things just have to be gotten through, Charlie. My technique for something like this is to keep looking at the time when it will be over."

"Like how?"

"Well, I guess a really miserable time I faced was supervising the preparations for the Junior Prom when I was teaching. I spent an inordinate amount of time looking at calendars, specifically the date after the night of the prom, and telling myself, 'Lexy, my friend, you will wake up that morning and it will all be over.' It helped."

Her eyes had remained clouded but she gave me a brave smile. "I'll give that a try ."

Now, watching them drive off, I wished I had a date to look to beyond the problems and worries engendered by Steve MacKay's murder.

Earlier I had reviewed all my notes. Given the span of time during which the murder could have taken place, no one had an alibi the entire time. Not Cap, Doug, or Meg. Not even Charlie or me...or Damaris. Actually the circle could be widened to include Fran, Donna, Gina Lewis, Joseph, and possibly Ed Pike or the unknown Patrick Nagel.

I shoved my fingers through my hair, but I felt more like knocking my cast against a piling. I hissed into the rapidly heating air and headed for the office. I was halfway considering a phone call to the Admiral. I missed her hard banter. It might clear my mind.

I stopped and kicked at a coil of rope. I muttered half aloud, "It's Wren you're missing, goose. But you are not going to call her. You're going to leave her be with Nancy. That relationship has nothing to do with you...or with Wren and you. Let it pass."

Something made me turn toward the *Siren Song*. Damaris was at the railing as I had first seen her, binoculars to her eyes and aimed at me. I stared directly into them hoping she could read my eyes. I willed them to say, "I'm passing on you. I could come aboard now and take you. It would be power sex, meant to release—not renew. I choose not to do that."

She lowered the binoculars. I walked on to the office.

Cap, hanging up the phone, looked out of place at Meg's desk. His bushy white brows jutted out below the deep wrinkles of a worried frown, but his face relaxed into a welcoming smile for me. He said, "Meg's got me doing desk duty again. Be glad when we get Charlie worked in full time. She's gonna know the place from stem to stern. How's that arm?"

"Starting to itch." I shifted it back and forth in the sling.

He flashed a toothy grin that deepened the single dimple and shoved back from the desk. Making a quick trip to the back room, he returned with a wire hanger, bending it in his strong, wide hands. "Work that down in. Should do the trick."

A couple of moves and I was sighing with relief. "Thanks, Cap. How about letting me man the desk for awhile? I'm kind of at loose ends."

"I'll take you up on that, mate. I was planning to shanghai Fran for the job." His worried frown returned. "I just set up an appointment with that detective who was nosing around here for my gun. Doug's going with me. And a lawyer." He slapped a paper clip off the corner of the desk with one hand and caught it with the other. "Over breakfast this morning the boy told me about sending it down into the muck. He said he hadn't fired it—not at Steve, not at anything. I figure the police finding that out ought to count more for us than agin' us."

I hoped he was right. And now that it was a done deal, I hoped I hadn't been wrong in prompting Joseph to talk to Doug about it, as it appeared he had. I knew from experience how murder could complicate friendships.

Cap left and I dealt with three phone calls in rapid succession by simply taking messages for Meg. A delivery man dropped off boxes of snack foods for the machines and I signed for them. Admiringly I watched the skillful maneuvering of boats coming in from a morning out on the lake. I calmed down a couple returning from three weeks in North Carolina and alarmed not to find Meg behind the desk. Regretting not having brought a book with me, I settled for perusing the stack of charts kept on top of the file cabinet.

I hadn't heard the door open but looked up at the sound of a chair being scraped toward the desk. Fran plopped down, jarring the unruly curls. She said in her no-nonsense voice, "I came in here to chit-chat with Meg. Guess I can settle for you."

I countered, "Donna and Tiger throw you out?"

She touched her tongue to the gold tooth. "Hah! Tiger's sleeping and Donna's gone to buy us one more week of supplies. We're going to settle home in Mossville for awhile after that. Let Charlie have at the boat whenever she has the time." She glanced out the front window at Cap, neatly attired with his hair combed back, coming off his small porch. "Something going on?"

I said only that he and Doug had an appointment with a lawyer, but I explained in detail where Meg had gone with Charlie and why. I included Charlie's choice of Meg's birthday for her own.

Fran said eagerly, "That explains it. I can't wait to tell Donna."

"Explains what?"

"I crossed paths with Meg early this morning. She said to mark September fourth on our calendar. That there was going to be a birthday celebration this year." Her voice dropped. "She told us once that she and Cap stopped paying attention to birthdays after they lost their spouses. She said it was too painful. Looks like that wound has finally healed."

She got up grinning. "I'll celebrate that with a good old-fashioned Coke, potato chips, and a candy bar—if you won't tell Donna."

I stood up and fished in my pocket for change. "I'll join you. Charlie was too nervous for breakfast and I didn't bother."

While we were munching away, Fran returned to the subject of birthdays. "You know, Donna and me getting together so late like we did, our birthdays were never a big deal to us." Her dark blue eyes gleamed. "Every day was." I smiled at that. "Of course," Fran added, "her family sends her cards and stuff."

I asked, "Do you have any family, Fran?"

She looked out the window. "Not to speak of. After my parents went, the rest kind of shied away from me…me being like I was. I didn't fight it. And now there's only a few cousins and a couple of nephews I never see." She puffed out her cheeks, then blew out a long breath as though emptying herself of ghosts. "Couldn't understand Steve MacKay shoving a good family away from him. Don't know which would cut deeper. Don't want to make some Supreme Being mad by saying this, but I hope him being gone lets all the cuts he made heal. Especially whatever he did to Meg."

Silently I echoed that hope. Meg deserved to be able to think of her husband without an overlay of hatred toward the man who played a part in his death.

Fran suggested cribbage and I agreed. We played until she saw Donna drive by and went to assist with the supplies. I put up the cribbage board and wiped food crumbs from Meg's desk. Again I toyed with the idea of calling the Admiral, but I knew she would be readying The Cat for a busy Thursday evening. I understood what was going on. I was feeling an unaccustomed loneliness. I snapped loudly, "You've done this to me, Wren Carlyle!"

I was glad when a small number of marina residents came in to set up for card games. It was good to be greeted pleasantly and accepted. But when Meg pulled up out front, I hurried out to hear what they had to say in privacy. Meg winked at me over the top of the car as Charlie got out looking peeved.

Charlie complained, "I was poked and prodded and measured and questioned! Jeez! I felt like I was in one of those movies where aliens are treating a human being like a lab rat." She slowed down. "The lawyer wasn't so bad though. She just talked to me about some stuff. Said she had to wait for a report from the doctor and then she'd get with Roberta and they'd try to get things set up right for me." Her quick eyes darted from Meg to me. "Don't know how I'm gonna make it up to you, with all of you helping me."

Before I could speak, Meg said, "You've been doing that since you got here, Charlie." Then she headed into the office in response to a call for a fourth needed at a pinochle table.

I said, "I've been gorging on junk food, Charlie. Do you want any?"

"Nope. We got chicken boxes in between the doctor and the lawyer. Lexy…" I knew better than to push her through the hesitation. "…There's something going on at Doug's marina. Cop cars are there."

"Did you see Cap or Doug?"

"No, but I saw their trucks. I don't know if Meg noticed. I wasn't sure if I should to tell you." She cut her eyes at my sling. "Didn't want you to have any more trouble. But I don't want Doug and Cap to be in trouble either." She shifted awkwardly from one foot to the other.

I jerked my head down the road. "Walk with me to my car. It needs to be cranked up. You hold the fort at the *Willow* while I give it a little run up and down the road." I saw the objections rising in her eyes. "That's just the right distance for a one-armed drive. And I can't get in any trouble with the police right there. Let's move."

She stood stiffly, radiating dogged resistance. I repeated sternly, "March."

At my car, Charlie said, "The Princess told me that as long as she was still in port, if I thought you were flirting with danger, to let her know." Her lips compressed into a hard, straight line. "I might." I nodded acceptance. Her lips softened. "She sure got a lot out of the word 'flirting.' Made it sound…sound…"

"Suggestive?"

"Yeah."

"You'll be hearing your share of that kind of thing someday, Charlie. When you do, relax and enjoy it."

I left her looking unsure if not perplexed.

I wasn't sure what prompted me to drive rather than walk. An assertion of independence, perhaps. The two cop cars Charlie had spotted were actually a patrol car and a van parked with the trucks between the office and the diner. I found only Joseph in the office, pacing in front of the dockside windows.

"What's happening, Joseph?"

"They're diving for the gun." Concern and tension made him look older. "Doug and Cap are out there trying to show them where—at least Doug is."

"How specific can he be? Since you're the one who really tossed it overboard."

He let out an explosion of breath and slapped a dead insect off the low sill. "When they came through here, Doug was talking like he dropped it in. He gave me a squinty-eyed look. Figured that meant not to say anything. Should I have said something, Lexy?"

"It probably doesn't matter that much. Will they be able to find it?"

He shook his head slowly. "I don't know. I'm not any more sure of the location than Doug can be. We had to zigzag in and out of boats, change speed, wait for a clear space. That chunk of concrete could have hit deep muck and been swallowed up. Or it could be sitting on a hard place just waiting to be found." One corner of his mouth lifted. "I don't know if I'd rather be out there or in here."

"I vote for the air conditioning. And for sitting down."

Gallantly Joseph waved me to the desk chair while he pulled a scarred stool from behind a rack of booklets.

I glanced around. "Hope you're going to paint in here, too. Brighten the room. After you sweep out the dust and dirt," I added pointedly.

He grinned. "Right after Doug sweeps out Ed Pike. And he wants me to stay on. Make it a real job. Help him run the place."

"Going to?"

"I'm thinking about it. It's scary how easy it is to wipe Steve MacKay out of a place. It changes everything. Doug says I could live aboard one of the boats. I'd like that. It's time to be on my own."

"I remember the feeling. I didn't realize all the baggage that came with being on my own, though." Guiltily I thought of what it must have meant for his mother and aunt to strike out on their own. His solemn face told me he was thinking the same. I looked away in time to see Ed Pike pull up in front. Gall rose in my throat but I forced myself to appear at ease.

"Damn him!" Joseph spoke bitterly. "Doug told him this morning to stop parking like that."

I watched Pike lumber a few feet out into the road where a pickup waited. It was light blue, old and dirty. Pike spoke to the two men inside. I scraped my teeth back and forth. I was certain they were the guys Charlie had dumped Coke on outside the diner. I fingered my sling and tried to visualize them with nylon stockings blurring their features. They could have been the ones.

As Pike headed for the office, the truck wheeled and screeched off the way it had come. I wondered if the police presence had anything to do with that.

Pike's florid face colored more when he saw me at the desk. He snarled, "Think you work here, bitch?"

Joseph came off the stool. Pike's chest swelled. "Come on, boy. Have at me. I'll black your eyes and move that nose to the other side of your pretty face."

I stood up. "Have a thing for noses, do you, Mr. Pike?"

The belligerence faded to wariness. "Just expect people to know their place. And that desk is mine. Especially if the cops are here to haul off what's left of the MacKay family." He sneered at Joseph. "You better crank up that tin-can cycle and go job hunting. Diner could use a bus boy. You're the right color."

Joseph's eyes smoldered but he didn't rise further to the insults. Pike's attention was diverted by the entrance of Gina Lewis, her figure overflowing a lime green bikini. Pike ogled her lewdly. He said, "Got to go flush out some pipes. Wanna come watch?"

She smiled, but drawled meaningfully, "You got nothin' I want to see." I expected aggressive retaliation, but Pike brushed by her, reaching to push through the glass door.

I called, "Mr. Pike."

He turned, hand on the door.

Keeping my tone fakely polite, I said, "About that job hunting. Maybe you should consider it. Patrick Nagel might have more jobs available."

He went so deadly still I thought I could hear his heartbeat. Unless it was mine. I knew foolhardy when I heard it—when I did it. But I also knew a lexicon of adages—like 'Give a man enough rope…' I knew I had just handed a dangerous man some extra lengths. Now I had to make certain I didn't get wound up in them.

Gina Lewis raised an eyebrow at me as the door swooshed shut. "Don't think you made a friend there. Better protect that other arm."

I lifted my arm in the sling away from my body. "You know anything about this one?"

She puckered her lips and shook her head. "Unreliable scuttlebutt." She turned to Joseph who was glaring after Pike. "Hear you might be settling in here permanent, Joe. Interested in a houseboat? I'm thinking about trying the Gulf Coast for awhile."

He struggled to relax but anger put an edge on his words. "I've got my eye on something different. The *Maria*."

Gina raised both her eyebrows at that, but said nothing. Joseph asked me if I would hang around for a bit longer. He wanted to go to the end of the pier and see if he could tell how it was going with the divers. I motioned him on his way and sat down again at the desk. I toyed with a sharp-pointed spindle, empty of notes, thinking I could jab it into Pike's belly overhang if need be.

Gina leaned against the stool. "Doug and me had a little talk—turned out friendly. He's going to keep an eye on the houseboat. Rent it out to weekenders if possible till I decide for sure about a change of residence." She tilted her head. "If I nosed around, would I find out you had anything to do with smoothing the boy's ruffled feathers?"

I leaned back and stretched out my legs. "I imagine you'd just be rooting up more unreliable scuttlebutt."

Her laugh was hearty. She changed the subject. "I didn't really think Joe would be interested in my place. But I'm kind of surprised he'd want the *Maria*."

"Why?"

"It's one of Steve's boats. Pretty little sloop. In good condition for her age." She looked down at herself. "Like me, I hope. Steve never took her out much. No one else ever touched her. I thought she was named for his wife until I found out she had been a Janet, Janice, something like that. Not his mother's name either."

I said, "Maybe the name came with the boat. I heard it was bad luck to change a boat's name."

"Only to a real sailor. Steve wasn't one of those. Cap is. So's that Charlie. Saw her sail in here one day with Doug before things got so heated—the barricade and all that. He was teaching her. She handled that skiff like she was part of it—or it was part of her."

I smiled. "I've seen that. She makes me feel all elbows over knees." I spun the spindle across the desk.

Gina tugged at her bikini as she moved away from the stool. "I haven't heard that phrase in a long time. Makes me think of the womanfriend I'm going to visit over on the other coast. I was godmother to her first daughter. Haven't seen either of them in years." She started for the door, then stopped and looked back at me. "She had hair the color of yours. Must be what made me think of getting in touch with her." She reached the door and looked back again. "Don't let the kid get to you. You've got your own style of handling things. "

She left me smiling and feeling good—until I thought of the divers and the gun they were seeking—and the chilling animosity of Ed Pike.

Twenty-one

After a lengthy wait for my call to be transferred, I caught Robbie at her desk completing paperwork on her day's activities. The haggard tone fled her voice as she told me that the preliminary report from the doctor who had examined Charlie was very positive. The detailed report would be in her hands tomorrow, and she and the staff psychologist had an appointment with the judge at one o'clock.

I hated dampening her enthusiasm with news of the police presence out on the lake and Charlie's concern. I explained about their diving for the gun Doug claimed had never been fired. Quickly she agreed to find out what she could in the morning. When she asked about encounters with Ed Pike, I hesitated a fraction too long and she jumped down my throat.

"Lexy Hyatt! The man is dangerous! Keep your distance! I had a sheet run on him. He has a string of arrests for assault—but no convictions. They were all on Hispanics who either disappeared or refused to press charges. And there are unproven rumors that he has run prostitutes out to grove and truck farm camps. And maybe in the backs of some fancy Americanized bodegas. He'd be fronting for someone, of course. Leave things to the police. We do have some training, you know."

"I know, Detective Exline, but I'm here. I see and hear things. I'm involved."

Her tone was a combination of frustration and resignation. "No, you are not involved. People you care about are. I know from a few months ago what that means. And how far I'll get trying to drop an anchor on you to hold you still." She had laughed at that. "See—I can talk like a sailor, too. Seriously, Lexy, be careful."

I agreed to that, then directed the conversation away from me and toward The Cat. I learned that Hal had received a boost from a change in medication, that Melody and her partner, Victoria, were going to do the riverboat cruise up and down the Mississippi and hit all the jazz clubs, and that Marilyn was going to sponsor a four-woman racing scull in the Labor Day races. I told her about Meg's pleasure at sharing her birthday with Charlie.

The call concluded, I cradled the receiver but kept my hand on it. I tapped it with my middle finger while trying to purge my mind of the desire to call Wren. I reminded myself sternly that I had decided not to do that anymore, to permit her the ease of giving Nancy Marshall her undivided attention. But I wanted her voice. I wanted...

Startled, I yanked my hand away as the phone rang. I barked my shin against the inner side of the desk at the same time. Irritated by the stinging pain and the disturbance of my drift toward Wren, I snapped a "Yes?" following the second ring.

Mildly Meg drawled in my ear, "Are there problems there, Lexy?"

I said contritely, "No. My shinbone just lost an argument with the desk."

She said, "Charlie told me you were there. Barbara MacFadden called. Said she would be leaving some information you wanted with Schooner at The Billet when she left work for the day. Said it was just bits and pieces...additions...perhaps of no value, perhaps meaningful when juxtaposed with other minutiae." Meg added with a chuckle, "Her phrasing. Want me to run you in?"

"Thanks, Meg, but no. It can wait until tomorrow. Or Saturday morning. Is Charlie still mad at me for cranking up the car?"

"You've seen that strong streak of worrywart in her. But Fran and Donna have sidetracked her. Roped her into learning pinochle. Told her she needed some sit-down skills to appease us old ladies." She added with great emphasis, "When we get old."

"That's never going to happen, Meg. I'm going to hang around here for a while yet. I'll check with you all later."

I was glad she didn't ask any questions. I knew what I intended to do. Getting up from the desk, I walked to the window. Joseph was approaching. Dejection robbed his features of their strength, making him look more a boy than a young man.

The moment he entered he said, "They haven't found anything yet. I don't know how long they'll keep at it." He gave me a weak smile. "Thanks for covering here."

"My pleasure, Joseph. I'm going to head out now. I don't want you to tell any fibs, but you don't have to volunteer that you saw me head out toward Orlando." I waggled my arm in the sling. "I don't use this arm much in driving anyway but I've got a bunch of nursemaids who think it handicaps me."

His wide grin was good to see. "I understand. Tia Elena stomped around and fussed for weeks when I got my first cycle. Wanted me to stick to the driveway and parking lots. I liked her wanting to protect me but..."

I finished for him "...but you can't live behind the defenses somebody else thinks you need. I got old enough, though, to understand what it costs those people to let us try our wings. Don't think I'm tough enough to be a mother. Or an aunt."

On the road I lowered both front windows a third and enjoyed the rush of air, warm though it was. Although clouds were massing overhead, a reddish-amber sun was beginning its slide down a clear western sky. If I didn't dawdle at The Billet, I would be able to get there and back before total dark and, hopefully, before rain.

I fudged on the speed limit until I hit Orange County but continued to make good time since the heavier traffic was leaving the city. As I was passing the Kumquat Mall, I had to hit my brakes hard to avoid a car zipping out in front of me. A horn blasted behind me. I frowned in my mirror at a truck jacked up on large wheels. Even though I signaled a turn into the small strip containing The Billet, I got another horn blast. There were a lot of vehicles in the front so I swung around to the side.

Inside I took a chair at the bar and watched Schooner arranging money in the drawers of the scarred wooden cash register. She turned and winked as she skillfully topped off glasses of draft beer. "You're getting to be a regular, Lexy. Going to have to run you through a boot camp somewhere."

I countered archly, "What's with you overactive types? A police detective thinks I should work out, someone else used to tell me to take up karate, and now you want me to play soldier."

Schooner put both hands on the bar and leaned toward me. "Maybe you should listen to us. Seems to me I heard about a black eye a few months ago. Now you're sporting a cast. What's next?"

I huffed, "Not going to be a what's next." As she backed away and lifted an empty glass, I said, "Not tonight. I"ll take a cup of coffee though. Has Barbara been in?"

She snagged a mug from a stack emblazoned with a variety of military insignia. The coffee smelled fresh and strong. Before she moved down bar to take an order, she reached under and slid a folder toward me.

'Bits and pieces' was an accurate tag for the contents—copies of portions of newspaper columns. The Iron Maiden had highlighted in yellow the Nagel and Estrada names. I shuffled through the pieces, skimming the Nagel references.

They dated back to the 1970s. The earliest reference was to his presence aboard or part ownership of boats rescuing Cuban nationals escaping to the United States.

Later clippings linked his name with a group of people buying large tracts of damaged or failed citrus groves and converting the land to truck farms. Also, there were acquisitions of real estate in and around Orlando, and a boat construction business in Sanford. I read an article carefully on grand jury hearings relating to crime by illegal immigrants, hardcore criminals having been included in the release of political prisoners from Castro's jails, and gang activity increasing in the Central Florida Hispanic community. Nagel's name was listed among those being deposed.

Suddenly the horrendous boom of a nearby lightning strike made the glassware rattle and everyone duck. Schooner's "Here it comes!" was muted by rumbling thunder and the downpour assaulting the roof. I closed the folder and scooted back from the bar.

Schooner said, "Hold on there, Lexy. You're not going out in that. It'll lighten up fast."

As though heeding her words, the next roll of thunder was a low mumble and the rapid drumming on the roof began to soften and slow. Within five minutes I was sure I could make it to my car without risking a lightning strike or extensive rain damage. Schooner refused my money for the coffee, and I tucked the folder under my shirt.

Hugging the building, I dashed to my car. Because of the rain, it was darker than I expected. I hoped it wasn't raining at the marina or that I hadn't been missed yet. I tugged the folder from beneath my shirt and tossed it on the seat. Two pieces of paper fluttered to the floor. I retrieved them just as a rush of hard rain beat a hollow tattoo on the roof of the car. I postponed starting up.

The spotlight on the corner of the building penetrated the rivulets of water cascading down the windshield enough to permit me to read if I angled the slips of paper toward it. Elena Estrada's name was highlighted in yellow. It was a birth announcement for Luis Estrada.

I spotted the Quintana name a couple of lines further, assuming it was Joseph's mother being listed as godmother.

I nearly crumpled the paper as a webwork of lightning brightened the entire sky. At least there was no booming explosion, and the rain again decreased to a light patter. I started the car. As I waited to pull out on the street, I hit my light switch. They were set on high beam and before I could lower them, they bounced off a silver Volvo across the street. It looked very like the one I had seen Damaris get out of at the marina. I filed the thought.

At a five-points traffic light that I knew would mean a long wait, I picked up the other piece of paper that had escaped the folder. The column dealt with an awards ceremony sponsored by the Catholic Diocese. Three of the five honorees were highlighted—Patrick Nagel, Manuel and Elena Estrada, and Damaris Del Riego. The Estradas were honored for their work in helping establish a health clinic, Nagel for his donation of a building for a youth center, and Damaris for financial support of art and music classes. I returned the papers to the folder feeling an unease. I remembered Elena Estrada's bitter contempt for Nagel. Damaris had not indicated personal knowledge of the man when I requested information on him.

The light flashed green and my wheels spun on the wet pavement. Due to the rain and the semi-darkness, I drove extra cautiously. Feeling foolish, I occasionally glanced in my rearview mirror to see if the silver Volvo had pulled out to follow me. I chastised myself for that, realizing there had to be more than one such car in Central Florida. And what possible reason could Damaris have now for checking on me? She had already done so.

As the road turned to skirt Lake Monroe, another downpour cascaded water over my windshield faster than the wipers could eliminate it. I slowed and considered pulling over, but there were few safe places between the pavement and the lake itself and too many palm trees and cement picnic tables. A large delivery truck passed me going the other way and I had to fight to keep the car on the road.

I thought of the Volvo again when headlights appeared behind me and drew closer, but they were too high. A jacked-up truck I was sure. I didn't dare let go of the steering wheel to wave my arm requesting that the driver dim his high beams and drop back. I was breathing deeper and my mouth was uncomfortably dry.

I ducked my head to avoid the painful glare from the rearview mirror, and leaned forward trying to increase my vision. Neither movement helped much. Fearful of hydroplaning, I wanted to slow even more but couldn't risk touching my brakes with the other vehicle so close. Just as I muttered, "Damn you!" I was jolted by a nudge from behind. I jerked my left arm from the sling and tried to grip the wheel with the part of my fingers not trapped in the cast. The muscles in my free arm strained to hold the car steady.

The loud metallic thump of a harder blow unnerved me and my stomach dropped as my right wheels left the pavement. I lost my side mirror to the trunk of a palm tree before I could safely bring the car back up on the road.

I bit hard into my lower lip and increased my speed, fighting desperately to keep the car from fishtailing. I must have surprised the other driver because I gained some distance on him. I hoped for the safety of a lighted restaurant or convenience store parking lot. But none materialized.

Then there were headlights in my left side mirror. Someone was passing the truck. Crazy under these conditions! Somehow the car slid in between me and my pursuer.

Ahead on the left the soft glow of a neon gas sign blossomed in the fluid darkness. I swung off the road too abruptly and slid sideways in loose gravel, almost striking the tall, thick pole supporting the sign.

A silver Volvo pulled up next to me. I twisted in my seat in time to see tail lights, dimmed by the rain, soon disappearing entirely. I took a deep breath and whistled through gritted teeth.

A short, slim man got out of the Volvo and walked around to me. I lowered my window. He wore dark pants and jacket and a billed cap. He stood erect, oblivious to the rain, his face calm and composed. Raindrops beaded on the slick bill of the cap and on his small mustache. Politely, in carefully enunciated English, he said, "Are you all right, Miss Hyatt?"

I blinked my eyes against the invasion of the rain and was very conscious of the zigzag of droplets down my cheeks. One trickled into my mouth as I said, "Yes. Who are you?"

His answer was oblique. "I chauffeur Señorita Del Riego when she wishes."

"You were outside The Billet. Why?" I knew my antagonism was misdirected

"I was requested to assure your safety."

Reminded that he had most likely just saved me from a crash or a second dunking in a lake, either situation potentially deadly, I stammered out belated appreciation.

The mustache twitched but his placid face exhibited no emotion. "I was happy to be of service. Permit me to examine your car." He walked around it slowly, then returned to my open window. "The bumper and trunk lid are dented. A mirror broken off and the trim scraped. None of the damage should affect performance. If you will allow me time to place a call, I will follow you to Captain MacKay's Marina. I believe you reside aboard the *Willow*." He touched fingers to the bill of his cap.

I rolled up the window as he reentered the Volvo. I wiped my face with the sling, but it only rearranged the wetness instead of drying it. Through the rain-streaked windows of both cars, I could see the outline of a cellular phone in his hand. Calling the police or his mysterious boss? He had made points by not asking if I felt competent to continue driving.

He started up his car and I did the same. I blamed the slight tremble of my fingers on the tension of gripping the steering wheel so fiercely for so long. But I knew better. The rain had declined to a drizzle and, except for the Volvo following at a respectful distance, I actually enjoyed the isolation of the dark road winding through Mossville, along Lake Arrow, and soon approaching the marinas.

I had time to consider what had happened. Only a few hours ago I had again challenged Ed Pike. I was sure the jacked-up truck was his answer. I didn't require a third event to make me cautious. I would leave the vengeful man to the police from now on. But Damaris? Had her concern for my safety been prompted by my recital of the events leading to my broken bones or by my reference to Patrick Nagel? That I intended to pursue.

I pulled up along the ledge above the *Willow*. I would move the car in the morning. The chauffeur-of-no-name helped me in my drop to the bench first, then to the slippery planking of the dock. I towered over him but recognized his wiry strength. He handed me aboard the *Willow*, touched the bill of his cap again, then withdrew with the silence of a night animal.

The rain had become a light mist. I widened my stance for balance, and steeled myself for confrontation as I heard the hatchway door slide open. I turned and faced Charlie.

She glanced above me. "Want me to put your car under the trees?"

Her calmness bothered me more than a tirade would have.

Not wanting her to see the damage to the car, I said, "Can't it wait till morning?"

We went below and she tossed me a towel. Vigorously I began drying my hair, still waiting for her attack. Suddenly I knew why none was forthcoming.

I snatched the towel from my head. "You called in Damaris," I asserted.

Her smile was tight and smug. "I warned you. Donna wanted us for what you call supper. Meg, too. When you were nowhere to be found, Meg said she bet you snuck off to The Billet by yourself." Her chin jutted out defiantly. "When the storm came up, I went to the *Song* and told the Princess." She added less adamantly, "She came by a little while ago and said you were all right and would be aboard soon." After a pause, "Do I get to know what happened?"

I told her.

Later, from the darkness of her berth, Charlie asked tentatively, "Long Legs...are you mad at me?"

I answered, "No. You saved me a second time. If I promise not to need it a third, will you forgive me for sneaking off?"

"Deal," she replied, relief in her voice.

I turned on my side and snuggled into the smooth softness of my sleeping bag.

Twenty-two

Charlie plopped another case of soft drinks at my feet. Filling the machines one-handed was slow work, but I was in the mood for doing mindless activities. Actually I was continuing the pattern of the morning. I had helped Charlie finish the interior of the *Willow*, mostly by handing her items or holding something in place. She had completed the last of the wood trim, installed a handrail in the shower, and replaced worn handles and knobs.

We had talked little. Both of us needed the space. She was still uncomfortable about having gone to Damaris when I was missing. I was ticked off at myself for having so foolishly provoked Ed Pike and so thoughtlessly put myself at risk while worrying others. I had emptied my mind of Steve MacKay's death and my fears concerning the suspects as well. I wanted my mind calm as Lake Arrow at the moment. Wanted to let all that I had heard and observed, all that the Iron Maiden had collected, churn away in deep water below my awareness. Maybe the truth would eventually rise to the surface where my rested mind would recognize it.

Charlie collected the money containers from each machine. She was gnawing her lips. Her glances at the wall clock told me the source of her agitation. Robbie Exline and the psychologist would be meeting with the judge about now. There was nothing I could say to ease the waiting. I was waiting with her—and the outcome mattered as much to me. I wanted Charlie unshackled from the past. I sensed a stirring just below my conscious mind. I wanted her free from the present, too.

When I finished with the machines and had carried the empty cases into the storage room one at a time, I joined Charlie at a card table. She was separating and counting coins. I emptied one of the containers into a pile, and dribbled the nickels through my fingers.

"You gonna play or work?"

"Both," I replied. "And if you turn your head, I just might snitch some chips before you close up."

She pushed back from the table. "Oh, all right."

"Hold on, Charlie," Meg called from her desk. "I see Donna heading this way with a cooler. Might be better pickings." She moved to hold the door open.

It was definitely better pickings. Large, flat bowls were placed in front of Charlie and me filled with chilled macaroni salad containing green peas, onions, bright strips of peppers, almonds, and flakes of seasonings.

Each bowl was rimmed with deviled-egg halves. I looked askance as none was placed before Meg.

Donna smiled. "Meg's is waiting on the *Second Wind.*"

Meg explained, "One of the gals I met at The Billet is going to be joining us. We're going to sail the lake and let her see the sights." She put one hand on my shoulder and plucked at Charlie's ear with the other.

"That is if anyone I know is going to give me the afternoon off."

Charlie eagerly agreed and I seconded.

Meg added, "Why don't you see if you can set up a file in the computer on the food and drink machines that would let us track sales better."

A car pulled up out front, and both Meg and Donna went to greet their guest. A medium-sized, roundish woman got out and saluted. She had the whitest, short frizz of hair I had ever seen and a pleasant ruddy face. She was ushered around the building, down the steps, and along the pier to the *Second Wind.*

Charlie and I cleaned our plates in a hurry. I could tell she was anxious to get at the computer, so I volunteered to keep at the coin count and shooed her to the desk. We worked in companionable silence until interrupted by Cap. When I commented on the sweat trickling down his neck and dampening his bright red and white striped shirt, he owned up to having walked from Doug's marina to the boat dock and back here.

"Needed to sweat out some temper," he admitted. "Guess you know about the divers." I nodded. "They never found the gun. That bulldog of a cop came barking at us a little while ago! Questioned Doug and me separately. Implied we were each protecting the other. Wanted to know where we really dumped the gun. Stuff like that." He swept his hand through a pile of coins, knocking some on the floor. One went rolling toward the door and Cap went after it. He scooped it up and glared defiantly. "He made a rough wake. Ordered Doug and me to make sure we stayed put around here. Like we're the kind who'd jump ship!"

Charlie stayed intent on the computer but I knew she was listening carefully. I said, "You or Doug would be down at the station if he had anything solid, Cap."

"That's what I told the boy. But I'm worried, Lexy. Law enforcement is like everything else nowadays. The number crunchers want the paperwork to look like everybody's getting the job done. Even if they have to force numbers where they don't really go."

"They still have to have proof. There is proof out there somewhere pointing to who did it."

"Aye." He gave his shaggy head a shake, tossed me the coin, and went to look over Charlie's shoulder. Before she could explain what she was doing, the phone rang. At her hesitation, Cap said teasingly, "You're manning the desk, mate."

Quickly following her greeting, Charlie said, "He's right here," and held the receiver to Cap. She ducked around him and joined me at the card table. In a low voice she said, "It's Doug."

Mostly Cap listened, the lines of his tanned face shifting from surprised interest to wily pleasure. I gleaned nothing from his single word responses. His final remarks were, "Is Joseph there? The two of you should be able to run the place easy. Aye." He sat down with a loud sigh.

I asked bluntly, "Good or bad news, Cap?"

The swaggering old pirate was back, broad grin and deep dimple. "Good! State troopers showed up with a warrant for Pike's arrest. Took him off in handcuffs!"

Charlie was excited. "For Steve's murder?"

Cap's good humor faded some. "No. Doug said the charge was something like transportation of illegal aliens over a four-county area. That's why the State Police, I guess. And some guy in a suit who watched everything like a hawk." He looked at me alertly. "But one thing might lead to another. If Pike killed Steve, this might be the start of them finding it out. Anyway, Doug's glad to have him out of there. Joseph is moving aboard the *Maria* tomorrow and the two of them will be able to manage the marina just fine." He headed for the door. "I feel like doing some honest work!"

He left with much more exuberance in his step than when he had entered. But something was prickling my mind, making me uneasy.

Charlie went back to the computer, and I finished counting coins. I stood up stretching, then went to the window. I could see Damaris at the railing of the *Song*, her hair loose and free. She wore a white, one-piece garment that made me think of the playsuits of my childhood. Her bare arms and legs flashed in the sun.

I was startled by three figures walking past the window toward the steps to the dock. They walked close together and made their way to the yacht speaking to no one. More of the returning crew, I thought. I was reminded that Damaris intended to sail before long. If I were to get any information from her, it would have to be soon.

My mind was rested enough now. It was time to get on the horse again. I laughed sarcastically at such an inappropriate metaphor for the surroundings.

"What's the joke, Long Legs?"

I turned my head. Charlie's back was to me, her fingers now flying, now stumbling at the computer keyboard. She turned, but looked past me through the window at Damaris greeting the new arrivals. Her face reflected the innate maturity that centered her. Or was it a maturity hard wrung from a difficult childhood?

She mused, "The princess isn't what I thought. She's not a piranha. Not a parasite either. I heard Steve say that when he was calling everybody here names." Her eyes came to mine, edgy with a trace of embarrassment. "When I went to her about you, I could tell she knew how to get things done. She's not just playing around, is she, Lexy? She's...she's..."

I found the words for her. "She has an agenda. A good one, I think."

Charlie made a single, brisk nod. Then as though to break the seriousness of the moment, grumbled, "Just as long as it doesn't include sailing off into the sunrise with you in tow. Some people around here might miss you." She returned to emphatically punching keys. Amused but pleased, I began replacing the empty coin containers in the machines, and closed the doors.

I stood with my hand on the last door. The prickling sensation was disturbing my mind again. Something was trying to get my attention. I jumped as Charlie appeared at my elbow.

"Problem with the door?"

"No. With my brain. There's something that wants to be remembered." I hissed. Now used to my ways, Charlie simply rolled her eyes. I said, "I'm going to get my notebook and a folder out of the car."

Charlie touched my arm. "Let me." She glanced at the clock. "If I leave, it might make the phone ring. Doesn't look like it's going to while I'm here."

I gave her the keys, and she headed for my car as though unaware of the weight of the mid-afternoon heat. I laughed aloud as the phone rang before she was halfway there. I nearly laughed again when it turned out to be Robbie Exline. She asked if I could get Charlie to the phone.

"She's running an errand. She'll be back in just a minute. What's the news, Robbie?"

"She gets to hear it first, Lexy. I do have something for you, though. I can't give you much in the way of details, mostly because I don't have them, but something big is going down. Just about everybody and his brother is involved—FBI, DEA, ATF, Immigration, state and local. They're starting today with little fish. Stay out of the way. My source says your Ed Pike may be scooped up in the net today."

I didn't interrupt her to say that it had already happened.

"When they move up the food chain, Patrick Nagel is expected to be among the catch. A lot going on there, Lexy. For twenty-five years or more he's been on the edge of all kinds of corruption. But he always kept his hands clean enough to avoid prosecution. Even managed to get himself accepted as a good guy here and there."

I thought about the clipping placing him among the Estradas, Damaris, and others as a benefactor of the Central Florida Hispanic community. I asked, "What about connections with Steve MacKay?"

Robbie responded, "I've rooted up just a little on that. MacKay was a few years younger than Nagel. They appear to have linked up in the

Keys a good twenty to twenty-five years ago. There's a paper trail of business partnerships the last ten or so years. Maybe enough of a connection to lift MacKay's death out of the personal realm there at the marina."

Her voice contained more hope than I felt. I hadn't yet learned anything that backed the falling-out-of-thieves theory. About to say so, I stopped as Charlie breezed in, my notebook and folder in her hands. She rushed to the desk, her eyes glued to the phone in my hand. I said, "Friend of yours just came in, Robbie."

I exchanged the receiver for my material. Though I would have preferred to listen, I went out to a patio table and forced myself to sit with my back to the window.

I flipped through the pages of my notebook. Nothing there stilled the prickling that continued to disrupt my mental calm. Before I could open the folder I'd picked up last night at The Billet, the rich, fluid voice of Damaris took my attention.

"May I join you?"

"Please." I shifted the folder under my cast.

"Shouldn't you have that in a sling?"

"I've been working with Charlie. It was easier using this," I tapped the cast, "to prop, hold, push. It isn't easy keeping up with her even if all your parts work."

Damaris touched her tongue to her lovely lips. I shivered with remembering. She said, "You are fortunate that she was ahead of you last night."

I frowned but admitted, "I know. And I owe you."

"No. I was returning the favor I owed you."

I narrowed my eyes and spoke sharply. "And the information on Nagel you implied you would gather for me?"

Her pale eyes revealed no reaction to my rudeness. She said calmly, "The urchin..." Her playful tone made the term acceptable. "...is pacing back and forth at the window."

I motioned Charlie to come outside. I could read the joy in her eyes. "Out with it, Charlie! Now!"

"Roberta got it done." Her voice was tense with the effort to control her feelings. "The judge accepted the report on my age. And I didn't know it, but Marilyn had sent one on how good I've worked, and Cap did one on me having a permanent job here." She drew a quivering breath. "I'm off probation. And Roberta says my arrest record will get wiped out." The excitement escaped. "I'm just like other people now!"

I put my good arm around her waist and hugged her to me. "You'll never just be like other people, Charlie. You're even better."

Damaris held out her hand. "May I be the first to congratulate you?"

"Thank you, ma'am." Embarrassed, Charlie stepped out of my grasp. "I need to get back inside." She started, then turned back. "Lexy, Marilyn is going to pick me up early Monday morning. We have some things to go do." She rushed into the office.

I considered how that would be my third and last Monday here. And nothing yet solved—not Steve MacKay's murder, not my relationship with Wren…Damaris brought me back.

"The *Song* sails tomorrow." She swept my body with those intriguing eyes. "This has been a more…rewarding stay than usual." She had changed—softened about the edges, melted inward. Then she was the cool goddess again, all fragility gone. "I do have some information on Patrick Nagel for you. And a small amount on MacKay. I am not certain any of it will help." I made no comment and she continued speaking, "My country, and others nearby, suffer conditions that need changing. I am part of a loose network trying to produce change. It is much like a long battle. Advancement and retreat…gains and losses…even death."

For the first time I saw something stir behind her eyes. I knew she was thinking of her brother. She went on. "I help with planning and funds, with getting some people to safety and returning others to the battlefield. Occasionally we have used Nagel and his greed-based network without his knowing he was being used. Not the best of operations but, as is said, it's not a perfect world. The note you unwittingly passed on to me indicated he was having suspicions. I am assuming he meant for MacKay to contact Immigration about me. That would not have suited me."

"And you stopped him?" Too late I realized how that sounded.

"Obviously his death stopped it for the moment. To ensure my safety, I—I believe you Americans say—started a ball rolling. Mr. Nagel will not continue to be a threat."

I realized what a different world she inhabited from mine. I felt young and inadequate, naive and pampered. More than ever I wanted to solve Steve MacKay's murder. And it was more than wanting to be a hero—Sheena ruling the jungle, Seven-of-Nine saving the *Voyager*. I needed to accomplish something that counted.

Damaris was staring at me as though she saw the conflict, recognized my need. But her smile was enigmatic. She gazed out over the boats, docile in their slips, as she gave me more data.

"When I started mooring here, I had Captain MacKay checked out very thoroughly. That turned out to include information on his son. As good and righteous as the father was, the son was an inferior and impure vessel. As a very young man, he spent summers in the Keys. He was involved in small-time smuggling of Cuban cigars. It wasn't long before he was recruited by Nagel for other activities. When he stepped into control of that marina," she nodded toward the south, "it was a ready-made situation for some of those activities. That's all I can give you, Lexy."

I thought of something I wanted to know. "Is Elena Estrada one of your people?"

Immediately I felt a protective shield of coldness settle about her. "Let us leave it at your having asked."

I knew that was as close to an affirmative as I was going to get. I said, "I think she hates Nagel."

Damaris thawed a fraction. "She has cause. She was part of a group of refugees fished from the sea and smuggled into this area on the pretext that the government here would send them back if they weren't hidden and protected. She was separated from her younger sister, rented out to a nursery, most of her wages confiscated. But things soon changed for her. The owners of the nursery were good people, struggling to get started. They eventually stood up to Nagel's front man, and pulled their workers free of him. Paid them better, helped them learn English and find affordable housing. When Elena could, she tried to find her sister. Not easy since there weren't many Hispanics in this area yet, so no well-functioning grapevine. But she accomplished it. She is not a woman who accepts defeat."

"I only met her recently, but I saw that. Her hatred of Nagel?" I asked.

"Before her sister was placed in a grove camp, Nagel apparently kept her for some time…used her. He or one of his minions."

Now I went cold. No wonder Elena Estrada spat in the dust at the mention of Nagel's name.

Damaris added angrily, "It was impossible for the girl to make a good marriage after that!"

I remembered Joseph telling me how the man married to his mother had never wanted him and had given him to the Estradas when his mother died. Not for the first time I felt guilt at my safe, loving upbringing. I watched an eagle in gliding flight. "You're not coming back here, are you?"

"With the events I have set in motion, it would not be wise. There will be other marinas suitable to my needs." She touched one of the designs on my cast. "But none will offer such remarkable fireworks."

I watched her walk all the way to the deck of the *Song*.

Twenty-three

I had the Sunday morning lazies. I could hear the bump and rattle of boat trailers being towed to Cap's public ramp. Much earlier I had heard Charlie on deck. I knew she was making everything shine bright clean before Marilyn showed up tomorrow. I hadn't heard any sounds from above in quite awhile—only bird calls and shouted commands as boats put out for a day on the lake. I thought about stirring—but didn't. I lay in my berth, hands behind my head, eyes closed, enjoying the tranquil rocking. I heard, or felt, Charlie drop lightly onto the deck. The hatch slid open.

"You awake, Long Legs?"

"You bet. Not dressed though."

"You might want to check the window above my berth."

I knelt on Charlie's berth, but still had to slouch to look out the small window. Sleek and imposing, its eye-shaped windows staring boldly, the *Siren Song* was leaving the harbor for the wide waters of the lake and eventually the river that would take her to the Atlantic.

"Safe passage, Damaris," I whispered. "Safe life."

Charlie gave me plenty of time before she came below. When she did, she found me dressed, sitting cross-legged on my berth sorting clippings and copy. She chattered as she dusted and polished. "I just got back from touring the *Maria* with Joseph. He went aboard this morning. I met his cousins Luis and Carlos. Luis is the oldest. Him and Joseph kind of square off with that macho stuff. Dumb. Carlos was kind of shy. You could tell he really looked up to Joseph. They brought his things in a truck."

"Did his aunt or uncle come?" I stayed with my sorting.

"No. Just the cousins. And they're gone now. Oh, Doug is moving, too. Going to bed down in a room off his office until he gets a trailer like Cap. Joseph is going to help him get his things out of Cap's trailer and then Cap wants us all there for fried egg sandwiches. Called it a getting-on-your-way breakfast."

Charlie suddenly got so still and quiet that I looked up to see what was wrong. Her eyes were wide but her mouth was pinched tight. "You're gonna get on your way too, aren't you? I saw in the computer yesterday that you only paid for A-house use for two weeks. They're up today."

"But my vacation isn't. I've got a week to go and Wren isn't back yet. Think you can put up with me for a few days more?"

Her pleasure warred with her desire to appear nonchalant. "I guess." She went back to polishing with a vengeance.

"Charlie..." I waited till she stopped and looked at me. "Sit down," I commanded.

She sat gingerly on the edge of her berth as though ready to up and dash off at the first wrong word.

I said, "My parents moved here to Florida when I was too young to know, but I grew up hearing them talk about missing the change of seasons. I would hear the excitement in their voices describing the first sign of spring as a yellow jonquil coming up through the glaze of a late snow. During our drab September heat, they'd pine for the nippy coolness of a midwestern fall and the brilliant colors of autumn leaves. People would ask them why they stayed here. They'd give the old answer that many do. 'We got sand in our shoes.' Don't know how many times I heard them say that."

Charlie tilted her head waiting for me to make my point.

I did. "The other day I got Lake Arrow in my lungs. That...or the friends I've made here...will keep me coming back. Okay?"

Her taut form relaxed, but she maintained her own macho posturing. "Okay by me." She leaped up and snapped her cleaning rag.

A small loose piece of copy in my open folder lifted into the air, then dropped toward the floor. Charlie's nimble fingers snatched it up. She gave it a quick glance. "It's a birth announcement." She fingered the piece of paper. "I wonder if I ever had one of those?"

I held my breath—then realized that she had not spoken with the raw bewildered anger or pained sadness I would have heard in such a pronouncement two weeks ago. I felt like cheering, but instead, reached my hand to accept the paper. "It came with a bunch of notes from a friend on anything I could find about the marinas and this area.

"Luis Estrada's birth announcement. You are digging, aren't you?" Charlie handed it to me, pointing to a line. "Look, Lexy. Hmm." She turned away to start polishing galley fixtures.

I stared at the line Charlie had pointed to. Scenes and comments drifted in front of my mental eyes—none pausing long enough for me to examine them. I felt like I needed to vomit.

"Lexy? Lexy!"

I blinked and focused on Charlie.

"Are you all right?"

"The boat's started rocking too much. And my stomach's empty. Guess I need those egg sandwiches Cap promised. I'm going to wander that way." I raced from the *Willow* without a backward glance.

I took the steps to the A-house two at a time, then stood panting. I heaved a great sigh, wishing I could expel my anxieties with it. I walked to the edge of the building and watched Joseph jump into the back of Doug's truck and spread his arms to steady some boxes as Doug drove off. Slowly I walked to the trailer.

The door was ajar but I rapped anyway. Cap called out, "Come aboard—but only if you're hungry."

I didn't expect it, but the smell of eggs frying in bacon grease was more than I could resist. Cap withdrew a foil-wrapped tray of sandwiches from the oven. The eggs were fried hard and the toast was the limp buttered kind I loved. I took two.

Cap pointed to a platter of crisp bacon. "There's coffee, milk, or orange juice. Or do those long timbers of yours need all three?"

Through a mouthful of sandwich I mumbled, "Milk, please. This was one of my favorite suppers when I was a kid."

"Doug's, too. But he's no kid anymore. Even heard Meg call him Doug instead of Dougie for the first time. Things, they be a changin', Lexy."

I had a hard time swallowing the bite in my mouth. There was going to be more change than he knew. I hated being part of it but I couldn't walk away. The wrench I had experienced walking away from teaching had taught me that I must never let it become a pattern.

Meg and Charlie arrived together, exclaiming about the smells and declaring their hunger. I settled on the couch next to the table of pictures while Meg took a chair across from me. Charlie perched on a stool from which she could reach to turn the bacon as Cap cracked eggs into another skillet.

Soon we were joined by Doug and Joseph who scooped up sandwiches and bacon. They settled on the floor. The conversation ebbed and flowed, subjects were raised and dropped. Mostly I listened—and watched. Meg's wrinkles were less deep, Joseph's dimples were more so, Doug seemed taller. Charlie's bright eyes darted everywhere, then she slid from the stool to help out. Boldly she made Cap lash his flying hair beneath a bandanna; she replenished my plate and glass; she refilled Meg's coffee cup; she tossed a stack of napkins to the young men.

The only cloud to pass over the cheerful gathering was Cap's solemn announcement that he and Doug would be attending a private graveside service for Steve Monday morning.

Meg said, "I'd like to stand with you, Andrew."

Cap could only nod.

I opened my mouth to offer to cover the office, but Meg said, "Fran will stand a watch. Says you young folks have been having all the fun. I think she wants some time with the snack machines."

We all laughed and the cloud passed.

When Doug and Joseph proclaimed full stomachs and pleaded the necessity of getting back to work, Meg said to Doug, "Not until you come over and pick out a cribbage board. A piece of the old life to go with the new."

I was glad to see him scramble to his feet and hug her where she sat. He said warmly, "We'll do it right now."

Cap followed them out and stood on his small porch as they crossed to the office. Charlie began scooping up dishes. Joseph joined her. I leaned forward to rise from the low couch, but he touched my shoulder as he passed, saying, "Kitchen's too little for three."

Charlie was running water in the sink. She sneezed from breathing in tiny soap bubbles, then said, "Wouldn't want you to get that cast wet and make all those pretty designs run."

Joseph turned to grin at me, but froze, the grin only half formed. He was staring over my head out the window. I jerked around and smacked my knee on the table, sending picture frames toppling. A police car had pulled up out front and the detective and a uniformed officer were getting out. I heard Cap stomp down the steps, and saw him approach the two men. I could hear their voices but not the words.

Joseph was on his knees picking up the pictures. Fortunately no glass had shattered. Charlie came to his side and glared at the scene outside the window. I watched Joseph gazing intently at the picture in his hands.

I said, "Do you know who that is?" I took the picture from his hands and replaced it on the table. "It's Cap's older brother. He was a firefighter. He died young. You have his dimples and the shape of his face."

I heard a gasp from Charlie. Joseph made no sound. I kept talking. "Friday night…and this morning…I saw your mother's name listed as godmother to one of your cousins. Maria Quintana. I already knew you were going to move aboard Steve's sloop, the *Maria*, but I didn't make a connection. It's a common Hispanic name. But it's been jabbing at my brain—asking to be recognized. There is a connection, isn't there?"

He nodded. His dark eyes were like cave openings, nothing inside revealed. His voice had a blank quality. "I went after a job at the marina because I'd found out Steve MacKay was my father." Charlie made a sound like a wounded animal. "Luis and me were interested in the same girl and fighting about it. He told me I wasn't fit for a good Latina because of my rotten father. He told me who that was and how Mackay had 'owned' my mother. He'd heard my aunt and uncle talking about it a long time ago." He kept speaking tonelessly. "I came here to see for myself what kind of man MacKay was. At first I thought he was a strong man. When I saw the name of the sloop I told myself he must have cared for her." He clenched his teeth. "I found out way different."

I heard more voices and looked out the window again. Meg and Doug had joined Cap. The veins in Doug's neck were bulging. Meg was agitated.

Joseph was still on his knees. When I asked, "What happened, Joseph?" his body shuddered with a silent cry.

Charlie put a hand on his shoulder, her face fraught with pain and disbelief. Joseph slumped back on his heels, his broad shoulders drooping.

"I knew about the movement of illegals through the marina. I had been able to talk to some of them when Steve used me to give orders to them in Spanish. When I saw all those vans that night, I knew there was going to be a lot of them coming through." He lifted his head and looked at me. "I had been trying to decide what to do. I had thought about telling Tia Elena but I was afraid for her…and worried about letting her know I'd found out about my father. When Doug handed me the gun to ditch on the way to the barge, I hid it under my shirt. Just threw the block of concrete overboard." He made a sweeping gesture.

"What did you plan?" It was hard for me to read murder into his intent. There was the same gentleness in him that I had seen in Cap, just as I had seen, but not connected until now, their way of gesturing or slapping at something with a broad movement.

"I wasn't really clear on it. I thought I could threaten him into stopping what he was doing. He showed up right after Doug let me off at the dock. I pulled the gun on him and told him what I wanted. He laughed at me! Said if I was smart I'd take a raise and come into the business with him. Said he could use a smart spic. I couldn't stop myself. I said I was one son who was through working for his father. It just spilled out. I told him who my mother was…"

Joseph was gripping his thighs so hard I thought he would draw blood. Charlie's face was beseeching me to stop all this. I wished I could. I said, "Let it all go, Joseph."

He drew a deep breath that quivered. "Steve laughed again! And lifted his head to watch some rockets that had been shot from boats…like that meant more than what I had said. Then he said something like 'Damn, boy, you came from good times. Every time I take out the *Maria*, I'm riding your mother all over again. She was one sweet piece of brown meat.'" Joseph lifted a stricken face to me. "I didn't know I squeezed the trigger, Lexy. But I did. At the same time a bunch of rockets went off, so I guess no one heard it. He just crumpled up on the dock. I went into the water with him and towed him out into the lake…and let go. I had dry clothes in my cycle bags. I was putting on my helmet when Doug went by heading for Mossville. I went home."

The inability to speak spread through all three of us—until Charlie squeaked, "They're hurting Doug!"

I whirled and saw Doug forced against the police car, handcuffs being placed about his wrists. "You can't let that go on, Joseph."

"I know." His voice came from a hollow shell. He lifted himself erect, towering over Charlie, and over me as I stayed seated. He left the trailer.

I lowered my head and clasped my hands between my knees. It seemed an eternity before I heard the sound of car doors closing and the spin of wheels. I was grateful when Charlie stepped closer and I could lean my head against her hip. She touched my hair.

Twenty-four

Monday began badly.

I was rudely dumped from my berth by a roll so severe I was afraid the *Willow*'s mooring lines had snapped. The movement didn't stop and I had a hard time climbing back in my berth. I didn't dare lie down again. My stomach felt like it was full of rocks scraping my insides.

Charlie was nowhere to be seen but I saw a crack in the sliding hatchway door. I was thrust side to side before I got it open, only to be blasted by stinging rain. Through the muted gray of a stormy morning, I saw Charlie buffeted by wind and rain, struggling to lash the *Willow* tighter to the dock. Her hair and sleeping shirt were flattened to her body, making her spare frame appear even slighter, but she was equal to the task.

I backed out of her way as she dropped through the opening and padded toward the head. She said, "Just a squall, Long Legs. It'll pass soon."

I began mopping up her wet tracks to keep my mind off the pitch and lurch of my stomach. I hoped the storm would wash away the pall that had settled over the marina after word of Joseph's confession and arrest had spread through the floating community yesterday. The rest of Sunday had been a day of fits and starts as those of us most involved began to cope.

Cap and Doug had gone to the Estradas. I learned later that Joseph's family had fought through their bewilderment, anger and grief to come together as a family to provide support for Joseph and secure good legal representation.

Meg and Charlie had covered at Doug's marina while Fran and I manned the office at Cap's. Offers of assistance had come from many of the boat residents. I had no idea how things would eventually turn out, but no one was functioning in a vacuum—unless it was me and Charlie.

I was living with the awareness of my role in Joseph's fate even if I did believe that he would have stepped forward to save Doug without my prodding. Charlie was again having her world wrenched and skewed by forces beyond her control. I believed us both to be as sturdy as the *Willow* and as well cared for, but for the moment we all three had squalls to weather.

Charlie was right. Within twenty minutes the squall had passed. We had lost the dawn, for the sun was already above the horizon brightening the blues of sky and lake. I watched Charlie dress and groom carefully. She was ready at least a half hour early for Marilyn's arrival, and pacing.

Finally I calmed her down by asking as casually as possible, "Something you want to talk about, Charlie?"

"No." The reply was sudden and emphatic. "I mean...I'm...I'm just not sure how much you want me to tell Marilyn about Joseph...and everything."

"Just that. Everything. She'll understand."

Charlie sat down across from me. "Everybody's hurting about Joseph. And about what he did and why he did it. Cap has to be hurting the most—finding out he was his grandson and all." Her eyes narrowed. "And maybe you for different reasons. How long will we all hurt, Lexy?"

I was a classroom teacher again passing out phrases that I hoped would someday make the bitterness of living go down easier. I said, "There's a poem by Emily Dickinson that says it better than I can. 'Time is a Test of Trouble—But not a Remedy—If such it prove, it prove too—There was no Malady.'" I recited it a second time more slowly.

I could see Charlie chewing on the words in her mind—head down, biting into her upper lip. Then the face she lifted to me was clear with understanding. "She's saying how long it hurts tells how much it matters to you!" She was sure, and pleased with her comprehension. More seriously she said, "The hurt of losing Big Charlie is the only one I still have from before I came here." She sought the safer ground of cockiness. "I don't even get mad about being named Charity anymore. That ain't me!" She stood up, her familiar glare defying me to correct her English.

I stood as well. "No…it ain't."

We heard car doors. Charlie zipped up and out the hatchway. I followed only a tad more slowly. We both needed a dose of the Admiral.

I bumped into Charlie who was staring at the two figures standing above us on the ledge.

Marilyn boomed in a laughing voice, "I thought I'd exchange Wren for Charlie. Anybody down there object to that?"

It took a dig in my ribs from Charlie for me to find my voice. "No objections, Admiral." I didn't take my eyes off Wren.

Charlie leaped to the dock, and stretched a hand back for me. Wren settled gracefully on the ledge, already dried by the strong breezes tagging after the squall, her legs dangling toward the bench. She reached a hand toward Charlie.

"I'm Wren, Charlie. I've heard a lot about you on the ride here. You and I are going to need a long talk later about how to keep this awkward redhead out of trouble."

Charlie swallowed hard. Marilyn cut across her discomfort. "Later is right! Let's go, First Mate. We've got places to be." Over the roof of her car, she said meaningfully, "We won't be back until late afternoon." Charlie grinned and ducked into the car.

Wren smiled with her eyes, the green glimmering in the rays of the morning sun. "Well, sailor, do you have a girl in this port?"

My stomach trembled a little, but Damaris Del Riego was a rocket whose streamers had faded to disintegrating ash. "I do now."

I stepped up on the bench and managed to hoist myself up next to her, close enough to catch the fresh-bathed scent of her. I felt tension, but not strain.

We sat silently side by side enjoying each other's presence. Wren gazed at the marina, the harbor and the lake measuring everything with her artist's eye. I asked, "Approve?"

"Very much so. After the hospital room this is very…releasing." She spoke without looking at me, her voice tremulous and low. "She went Friday night. I spent Saturday tending to things she wanted done…arranging for cremation." Now she looked at me. "In two or three weeks I'll claim her ashes and scatter them where she wished. Will you go with me?"

"Yes." I gripped my sling with my good hand to keep from touching Wren's hair as the wind lifted and stirred it about her face.

Her brow furrowed. "I got in late last night. Called Marilyn this morning. Accepted her offer of a ride here. I heard some on Charlie, a little about a murder. I was warned that you had an arm in a cast but to get the details from you. I would like them now."

I gave them. I shaved some corners and rushed along some short cuts believing that someday I would fill in the gaps for her. Now and then she slowed me with a question or a comment. Concern and delight flashed across her face at some of my descriptions. Giving her the events of the two weeks made me realize fully the scope and depth of all that had happened. I needed her for this just as she needed me for her final service to Nancy Marshall.

We sat in silence again. I saw Fran and Donna going up the steps toward the office. Meg joined them on the patio. I knew glances were being directed our way. Then Meg went around the building toward Cap's trailer and I remembered that they were going to a graveside service for Steve MacKay.

I scooted from the ledge to the dock. I said, "Time to give you a tour of the *Willow*." I vaulted smoothly to the deck, checking Wren's footwear—fortunately she was wearing sneakers—before assisting her aboard. I didn't want to let go of her hand and was glad to find the hatchway door still open. I led her below.

Before Wren could assess the surroundings, I took her in my arms and hungrily sought her mouth with mine. She came tight into me, and we muttered and nibbled and probed. Her mouth tasted faintly of coffee, her throat of vanilla. I put my hands in her hair, she dug hers into my hips. At last we stood breathing heavily against each other, our legs spread for balance as the *Willow* welcomed us with a gentle sway.

Wren's lashes fluttered against my cheek. I drew back just enough to kiss her eyelids.Then I moved us toward the V point where the berths came together in an area wide enough for two. I removed my arm from the sling which I tossed on my berth. I hissed in frustration at my efforts to remove her shirt one-handed.

Teasingly she got up and stepped away from me. Keeping her face still and calm, her lips invitingly parted, she removed her clothes.

Mesmerized I followed her movements—smiled at the emergence of her breasts, groaned as she stroked her dark gold triangle provocatively. Then she straddled my legs and sat on my thighs. I smoothed my cheeks against her breasts, touched my tongue to each hardened nipple, thrilling to her responsive shudder. I murmured against her skin, "I've missed you so, Wren."

Her voice crackled with desire. "Show me."

I braced her back with my cast and spread my legs. I worked my hand into the opening that created. "Oh, so sweetly wet!"

"I began to get wet on the way here...thinking about you. I could hardly sit still. I was afraid the Admiral would notice. Oh, yes..."

I had begun to tease at the opening. She strained against my arm, her head back, exposing the long line of her neck. Her moan lengthened and deepened as I entered the hot, moist cavity. I uttered my own moan as I felt her thick fluid ease my way.

Then I held my hand still, enjoying her efforts to work my finger deeper, enjoying her pleadings. I began rotating in the narrow passage. She began lifting and pushing, her fingernails digging into the thin flesh of my back. I increased my motion, slowed to a stop, sped up again. I sucked at the hollow of her throat. When I felt her cry of climax begin as a low rumble, I muted the rising cry with my mouth. She collapsed against me. I kept my hand where it was, kneading the soft lips with my palm.

Wren put her hands on my shoulders and pushed back enough to see my face. She tightened on my finger. "I may never let you go."

"Who says you'll get the chance to?" I pushed her to my side, then down on her back, my finger still embedded. I pulled up my legs to stretch beside her. I read the excitement in her eyes, felt the yielding of her. I feasted on her breasts, tongued her navel, licked the soft, fine hair. I felt the throb and jerk of her as I withdrew my hand.

"No, Lexy! I want you in me."

"I will be." I waved my hand under her nose. "Smell yourself on me." She opened her mouth and lifted her head.

"No," I said. "It's for me to taste." I put my finger in my mouth and drew it out slowly. Wren's eyes widened and her chest heaved with rapid breaths. I whispered huskily, "Now I'll put it back in. Maybe two. Can you take three, my greedy friend?"

I took her hard. I had never been so aggressive. Her body writhed beneath mine, inviting more. This time there was no muting her rising orgasmic cry. I didn't care if anyone heard. Finally she cuddled against me...feeling smaller...more mine.

After awhile, Wren lifted on one elbow and propped her head on a hand. "Lexy. On the way back down here, I did a lot of thinking. I figured out how wrong I was to ask you to move into my house. I know that made you uneasy." She touched a finger to my lips to stop whatever I might have started to say. "And I can't move into your apartment. Neither would work. I want you to think about our finding a place together. Ours...fresh and new to us." I tried to speak but she increased the pressure of her finger. "Don't say anything now. Just think about it. I won't rush you." She smiled impishly. "What I want right now...is your flesh!"

Wren began removing my clothes, commanding me to lift and turn, remarking on my leaner, harder body. "Turn toward me a little. It's my turn to feed on you." Anticipation rippled through me like the waters stroking the *Willow*. She placed her head on my thigh and I drew up the other leg. She brushed the tight muscles with the tips of her fingers. "I want you relaxed." My leg fell back slowly and I was completely open to her. I felt the tickling of her hair and then she was breathing into me.

I was suspended, floating on nothing...conscious only of the ebb and flow of her tidal breaths. When I felt the slide of her tongue, I could only hum a sound. I wanted to clamp on it as she had my finger, but I was robbed of all control. Colors danced across my eyelids as I succumbed to the thrust, the laps, the curl. I was melting, dissolving, dissipating into pure sensation. All of a sudden Wren wrapped me in her legs and arms as I went rigid with the explosion centered between my legs and racing into every channel of my body. Weakly I breathed her name. I felt her smile against my pulsating skin.

We lay entwined—touching, kissing, expressing our pleasure at being together. Wren fell into a light sleep. After two weeks in a hospital room and her long drive back home, she had to be exhausted. I closed my eyes and trusted my body clock to warn me at the approach of mid-afternoon.

But it was Wren's clear voice that retrieved me from my drifting. "Tell me what those represent." She was trailing a finger across the designs on my cast.

I explained each one in terms of the person it represented.

"And this one?" The rocket becoming stars and green tendrils.

"The Fourth of July celebration."

Wren's eyes were shrewd, but I saw no challenge or discomfort. She knew but she didn't know. When would I tell her? Would I tell her?

She prodded us from our makeshift bed. "We had better straighten up and air out—the boat and us. I don't want to offend or embarrass Charlie. I liked what I heard about her. I liked what I saw."

An hour later we leaned against the pilings near the *Willow*. I pointed out the osprey and the kingfisher doing their late afternoon fishing. I explained the gathering of card players. At that point I saw Marilyn's car pulling in next to the office. She went in the building and Charlie proceeded slowly toward us along the ledge.

At the A-house Charlie came down the steps to the dock. She carried a large brown envelope, turning it around and around in her hands. She smiled shyly at Wren's warm greeting, her eyes darting to and away from me.

Finally she thrust the envelope at me. "Here, look at this. You said I could pick any name I thought would go well with Charlie. I tried out a bunch. I like how this works."

I pinched open the metal clasp and withdrew a document. I swept through the official language identifying it as the designation of a legal name with all the attendant rights and privileges of such. As I reached the bottom, my eyes misted. The large, dark, block letters blurred and squirmed.

I blinked furiously and the letters cleared and settled—CHARLIE ROBERTA HYATT.

I slanted the paper toward Wren. She put an arm around my waist and her cheek brushed my shoulder as she leaned forward to read. She exhaled a long, soft "Oh..."

I looked down into Charlie's now unwavering gaze. I knew I needed to be careful, not load her choice with more than she intended, but simply take the honor in stride. I worked to keep my voice from being thick with emotion. "Wren and I are going house hunting soon. She's a design artist and I'm a bookworm of a reporter. There are a lot of things we won't know how to check out or evaluate. Would Miss Hyatt be available to help us out?"

Wren's fingers dug into my waist.

Charlie's face glowed.

It was a good day.

Other Mysteries from New Victoria

ALSO BY CARLENE MILLER **KILLING AT THE CAT $10.95**

Lexy Hyatt gets a chance to prove herself as an investigative reporter when a woman is found dead at The Cat, her favorite lesbian bar. But it's a struggle to maintain her objectivity when her own ex-lover appears to be the prime suspect.

"Killing at the Cat *is a brisk, sexy read with a large cast of characters."*

—ForeWord

"Steeped in the details of lesbian culture and romance." —Publishers Weekly

SHAMAN'S MOON by SARAH DREHER $12.95

The seventh Stoner McTavish Mystery

"A beguiling blend of fantasy, mystery and humor. (The series) works because she draws her characters so freshly and convincingly."

—San Francisco Chronicle

In the sleepy little New Age town of Shelburne Falls, dark forces are afoot, hungry ghosts with Aunt Hermione as their prey. Stoner McTavish, lesbian travel agent and reluctant detective, along with her lover, Gwen, and her business partner, Marylou, must stop them before it is too late. But how can you stop an enemy you can't find?

DEAD AND BLONDE A Meg Darcy Mystery by JEAN MARCY $10.95

A blonde woman in your bed can be a disaster. PI Meg Darcy rushes to police detective Sarah Lindstrom's side after Sarah finds her ex-lover beaten to death. Tension lasts until the final page with mystery, murder, love, and revenge.

About the first in the series, Cemetery Murders...

"A rousing good read, one of those mysteries spiced with tension and flavored with colorful characters that make it perfect leisure time reading."

—Midwest Book Review

NO DAUGHTER OF THE SOUTH by CYNTHIA WEBB $10.95

Laurie Coldwater returns to her hometown and the white southern roots she has rejected to look into the mysterious death of her black lover's father. Things turn ugly when she finds herself confronting the KKK.

Send for a free catalog or order from

NEW VICTORIA, PO Box 27, Norwich, VT 05055

Phone 1 802-649-5297 or 1 800-326-5297 EMAIL: newvic@aol.com

OR—buy our books from your neighborhood feminist bookstore

More New Victoria Mysteries

STALKING THE GODDESS SHIP by MARSHA MILDON $10.95

Underwater archeologist Marguerite Delaney has been using a sunken model of a Minoan Goddess Ship as a teaching tool. When the charming Lily Barton is found dead, tied to the wreck, Marguerite becomes the prime suspect–after all, her lover Stephanie was having an affair with the victim.
While searching for motives in Lily's past, PI Cal Meredith uncovers a sordid web of exploitation. Suspects and villains abound against a background of fishing boats and cold water scuba diving.

MURDER IN THE CASTRO by ELAINE BEALE $10.95

Manager of an agency which advocates for victims of gay bashings, Lou Spencer finds one of the project's counsellors stabbed to death in his office. As the Castro community reacts in outrage, Lou is left trying to hold the besieged agency together while looking for evidence to counter the homophobic assumptions of the San Francisco Police Department and falling in love with a lesbian cop.
"...a mystery that's absorbing and refreshing, and with a cast of characters, headed by the breezy and determined Lou Spencer, whose lives are charmingly engaging." –Richard Labonte, A Different Light Bookstore

JUST A LITTLE LIE An Alison Kaine Mystery by KATE ALLEN $12.95

This fourth Alison Kaine mystery features cool characters and kinky sex. Girlfriend Stacy is putting on a leather event which is more work than she ever imagined–with tantruming tops, badly behaving ex's, and picketing separatists. And Alison cannot ignore the undercurrent of malice and deception beneath the bantering and blatant sexuality of the Wildfire conference.

Kate Allen's works are *"...more intricate, powerfully written and realistic than most lesbian mysteries."* –Women's Library Workers Journal

"Kate Allen presents issues facing the lesbian community with a humor and a humanity seldom seen in books today." – Bad Attitude

Kate Allen's Web Page http://www.users.uswest.net/~kateallen/">Kate Allen

NEW VICTORIA, PO Box 27, Norwich, VT 05055

LOOK FOR US ON THE WEB AT: **http://www.opendoor.com/NewVic/**